Dancing With You

A Palm Harbor Novel

Book 4

Kimberley O'Malley

Published by Carolina Blue Publishing, LLC

Copyright 2022, Carolina Blue Publishing, LLC

ISBN: 978-1-946682-34-5

For my son, Lucas Alexander, as he graduates from high school. Off into the world you go! I am so ridiculously proud of you and all you have accomplished.

"You have brains in your head. You have feet in your shoes. You can steer yourself in any direction you choose. You're on your own, and you know what you know. And you are the guy who'll decide where to go."
-Dr. Seuss

Other Books by Kimberley O'Malley

Contemporary Romance - Windsor Falls Series
Coming Home
Taking Chances
Second Chances
Saving Quinn
Finding Kat
Coming Back

Contemporary Romance – Palm Harbor Series
The One That (Almost) Got Away
Leaving the Friend Zone
Letting Go

Cozy Mystery-Addie Foster Series
Death Comes in Threes
Dyeing for Change
Murder by Numbers
Angel of Death
Death by Chocolate
'Twas the Mystery Before Christmas
A Dress to Die For

Praise for Kimberley O'Malley

The One that (Almost) Got Away - Palm Harbor Series, Book 1

"I love that the Author has such a versatile platform. She hit another story out of the park with a slow burn. The end result is awe inspiring and what stories are made to be."

-Cookcrs 1, Verified Amazon customer

"This was such a fun and cute book, so light and refreshing!! I absolutely loved it !! :) On top of that, this is a great first book of more to come, and I am absolutely looking forward to the next book !!"

-C. Pippins, Verified Amazon customer

"Amazing Read!!! In true O'Malley fashion this is another great!!! Loved the characters and storyline...i absolutely fell in love with Jaime and Griff and cannot wait to see what happens with Sam & Jack...so excited to hear there will be more too come!!!

-A. Williams, Verified Amazon Customer

Leaving the Friend Zone - Palm Harbor Series, Book 2

"I absolutely loved the storyline and characters! At some point, I think everyone can relate to this book. A lot of laughs, heartbreak, drama and love shine through! Highly recommend!!"

- S. Barowski, Verified Amazon Customer

"Loved the second installment of this series almost as much as the first!!!! A definite must read for everyone!!!!"

-K. Swift, Verified Amazon Customer

"This was a very emotional read. I laughed and cried and literally screamed a few times. I wanted to smack the two of them. And then we meet Sam's mom and I wanted to throat punch her. I truly love this sweet series. I love the characters and how relatable and real they are. I'm looking forward to the next book."

-KittyMoon, Verified Amazon Customer

Letting Go-Palm Harbor Series, Book 3

"This story has all of the feelings you love and hate all tied into a town of awesome people."

-L. Rea, Goodreads Customer

Prologue

"I think heartbreak is something that you learn to live with as opposed to learn to forget."
-Kate Winslet

Luca Rinaldi blew on his hands before dashing inside Mama's Cucina, his family's Italian restaurant. Christmas Eve had brought rare, freezing temperatures with it to Palm Harbor, South Carolina. Normally, he preferred the heat and sunshine, but something about a nip in the air said Christmas to him. He grinned at the thought. He'd been grinning for days already, and it had nothing to do with the weather.

She was coming home today.

"Luca, is that you?" his mother called from the kitchen. She bustled through the swinging doors to frown at him. "What took you so long and why the dawdling? You know everyone is due here very soon!" she chided.

"As if I could forget," he joked. He glanced at his phone. "Mama, we have hours yet before they arrive. Chill already."

"I'll give you chill," she threatened before swatting him with the towel in her hands. "It's Christmas, Tesoro, is it too much to ask everything be perfect?"

Luca sighed, knowing he'd never win this battle. "Of course not, Mama. But the other three hundred and sixty-four days of the year? What's your reason for perfection then?" he sassed, stepping from reach of her deadly aim.

"Don't make me get the spoon, Luca, you're not too old

for a good rapping across the knuckles," she threatened. "Besides, with Riley finally coming home, I would have thought you'd want everything perfect."

Her sly smile told him everything he needed to know.

"Oh, is Riley going to be here tonight? I didn't know," he said, trying to appear calm over the thundering of his heart.

Mama cornered him against the host stand and pinched his cheek. Suddenly, he was seven again and caught raiding the cookie jar.

"When will you two get your timing right, Luca? Life is short, you know. No guarantees," she proclaimed with a slight tremor in her voice.

No one knew better than them. Angelo, Luca's father, and his mother's one true love as she liked to say, died when Luca was in high school. The hole he'd left in their lives, and in their hearts, would never be filled.

"Enough," Mama commanded with a sniff. "Tonight is vigilia di Natale. We will eat, drink, and be merry. And you will see your beloved Riley again after so much time."

She bustled away before he could say anything. He shook his head. What could he possibly say anyway? He followed her into the kitchen to prepare for the onslaught of to-go orders. On Christmas Eve, they closed the dining room at one and remained open for takeout only through six. Then, his extended family and friends gathered for a hardy, traditional meal. It remained one of his favorite nights of the year.

Having Riley here for the first time in longer than he cared to remember became the cherry on top. Donning an apron, he set about tackling the mountain of orders already waiting.

Later that evening, when the last order had been whisked out the door, Nico, his cousin, flipped the 'open' sign to 'closed' and everyone sighed in relief.

"Let the party begin," Nico cried.

Other family members milled about, rearranging, and setting tables. Luca smiled at the thought of the merriment to come. His friends, Jack and Griff, would be bringing their respective other halves, Sam and Jamie, for the first time ever. Although the two women were loyal customers, and the official restaurant accountants, they'd never been to the Christmas Eve festivities before. He grinned at the thought and couldn't wait to see their expression when they saw the mountain of food served.

Then he pictured Riley's bright, hazel eyes and freckle-spattered nose. She hated her freckles and always tried to cover them, which he never understood. He thought they were cute, but apparently 'cute' wasn't a word women wanted to be associated with. He shook his head. Sam had once told him men knew enough about women to fill a thimble. On a good day.

"Quit the daydreaming, everyone will be here soon," Matteo jibed and elbowed him as he passed. "And by everyone, I mean you-know-who," he threw over his shoulder.

Great!

Even his older brother was giving him crap about her. Did everyone in Palm Harbor know? He shook his head. Probably. The blessings and curses of a small town were often one and the same as his mother liked to remind him.

A blast of chilled air wafted over him as the front door opened.

"Merry Christmas!" Griff called as he entered. He helped his pregnant wife, Jamie, off with her coat before striding toward Luca. "Hey man, great to see you."

Luca gave him a one-armed hug. "Merry Christmas to you also." He stepped up to Jamie and hugged her, careful to not squash her growing stomach. "You look amazing," he said.

Her cheeks grew pink. "Oh, Luca, you charmer! I look eighty weeks pregnant already," she demurred.

"Nonsense, Bella," cried Mama, coming out of the kitchen. She kissed both of Jamie's cheeks and then Griff's. "Ah, so lovely to see you again. I feared you might have moved away, it's been so long,"

Luca rolled his eyes. "Mama, they were here last week," he reminded her.

"Like I said, so long." She jabbed a finger in his chest.

"Smart aleck this one, then he wonders why no wife."

"Oh, I don't wonder. Jamie married *him* instead," Luca joked, pointing to Griff.

"And here I thought I was the one you wanted," Sam declared as she approached them with Jack at her side.

Everyone laughed, and another round of hugs and greetings started.

"My Luca is such a flirt," Mama pronounced. "Came into the world that way. Nothing to be done about it, I fear." She laid a hand over her ample bosom. "No grandbabies for me," she lamented.

"It's not like I'm the oldest," Luca challenged, laughing and pointing to his *older* brother, who suddenly had something he had to see to in the kitchen.

"I hear you," Griff said, laying a hand on his wife's belly. "My mom wasn't exactly subtle about it either. Jamie saved me from a lifetime of reminders."

"Come, everyone, enough of this silliness. Come, sit, and prepare for the feast," Mama commanded, eyes sparkling. "Jamie, Sam, I hope you've brought your appetites. I'm so very touched you could join us tonight. Luca will show you to your table."

"Your wish is my command," Luca joked. "This way folks." He led them to a booth for four near the buffet table, chatting as they went.

After seating them and taking their drink orders, which he handed off to Nico, he went back to making sure everything was ready in the kitchen. From the time he was old enough to do so, he loved coming to the restaurant with his parents. The heat and bustle of the kitchen thrilled him. The scented air comforted him. But cooking called to him. The first time he created food for another human being, he'd been hooked.

Now, in the chaos of prep for such a huge meal, Luca grinned. This was fun. And maybe, just maybe, if he hid in the kitchen for a little bit, he wouldn't risk whiplash every time the front door opened.

Where was she already?

He hid as long as he could before risking the wrath of Mama Rinaldi. When he couldn't hide any longer, Luca removed his apron and walked back into the dining room. Without even looking, he knew she'd arrived. A tingling at the base of his neck told him.

His Riley was here somewhere in the throng of people. It's how he'd always thought of her. As his.

The tapping of a fork against crystal caught his attention. He turned to see his mother holding court at the buffet table.

"Now that my younger son has deigned to leave the kitchen, we can begin," she started to laugh. "Thank you all for coming and sharing this meal with us. It has been a very good year for the Rinaldis, made better by your company and continued support. We couldn't do this without each and every one of you." She raised a glass of red. "To family and to love. What else is there?"

"Great food!" came a male voice Luca suspected belonged to his friend, Jack.

"Of course, my friend, there is always great food, but that is where the love comes in," she corrected. "Salute!"

"Salute!" echoed in many voices throughout the restaurant.

"And now we eat," Mama said, inviting everyone to do so.

Bedlam reigned as more than fifty people made their way to the buffet. But the sound faded around him as she came into view. Finally. Riley.

He stared at the back of her head. Less than six feet away from him, she stood. Her auburn hair was longer than last time he'd seen her, maybe five years ago now.

Well, four years, nine months, one week, and a few days, but who was counting?

Of course, he'd seen her at Griff's wedding in October, but they'd barely said hello to each other, so it didn't count in his book. Busy with her medical training clear across the country, Riley had only managed to fly in for the weekend. He'd only seen her at the wedding itself, and since his family had catered the event, Luca had been more than a little busy.

Not to mention she'd gone out of her way to avoid him.

Maybe because four years, nine months, one week, and a few days ago, he'd broken her heart...

"Honey, what do you recommend?" a man asked her as he got in line behind Riley, placing his hands on her shoulders.

She smiled up into his eyes. "Loosening your belt," she joked. "Seriously, Thomas, prepare to be blown away. There are no wrong choices here tonight," she assured him. "Mama makes the best Italian food this side of Sicily."

Luca watched the man glance at the buffet table that practically groaned under the weight of the dinner before shaking his head.

"I don't suppose there's anything other than carbs available," he said to Riley.

"Thomas!" she shushed him before Luca's mother approached the couple.

"My topolina has returned to me!" she exclaimed, coming up to join the couple in line. She pulled Riley into her arms.

Luca watched as Riley's cheeks reddened. He couldn't help but smile. She always hated being the center of attention.

"Mama, it's so good to see you again," she murmured when his mother finally released her. She turned to the blond man with her. "Thomas, this is Mama Rinaldi, whom I've told you so much about. Mama, this is Thomas Lyons, my boyfriend."

Luca clenched his hands at his sides hearing the words. Acid churned in his gut.

Did you think she'd stay single forever?

Mama looked Riley's date up and down. Luca bit back a laugh. He could tell from his mother's posture she found him wanting.

The man held out a hand to Luca's mother. "Dr. Thomas Lyons. Nice to meet you, ma'am."

"So, you're the one who has kept our Riley from us, then?" Mama demanded.

"Oh, uh, well, not really. We're both involved in our residency programs in Arizona," he explained, glancing at Riley for help if the pained expression on his face meant anything.

Riley threw her head back and laughed. The sound of a hundred tinkling bells danced over his skin. Riley laughed with her whole body; unlike any woman he'd ever met. She gave one hundred and fifty percent to everything she did. He missed that.

He missed her.

Mama reached out and pinched the man's cheek. Luca winced. She wasn't known for soft pinches. It would leave a mark.

"Oh, my dear boy, I was joking. No one has ever made my topolina do anything she didn't want to," she explained.

"Oh, I see. Sorry, I didn't get the joke. I heard you say so earlier, topolina. What does it mean? Is it a nickname for Riley?" he asked.

Mama clapped her hands. "It means 'little mouse' in Italian. It is a term of endearment rather than a nickname. When Riley was a child, she was always the quietest of the pack. Quiet as a mouse, our Riley was. You could always find her somewhere curled up with a book. Of course, this paid off. She's a big doctor now. Very impressive!"

"Oh, Mama, please," Riley implored. "No bragging. Come on, it's Christmas, and the smells in here are making me ravenous," she added. "Let's go before they don't save us any, Thomas."

"Very nice to meet you, Mrs. Rinaldi," the man said before allowing Riley to drag him up to the buffet line.

Luca chuckled to himself. His mother always told everyone to call her Mama upon meeting them. Everyone except Dr. Thomas Lyons, apparently.

Luca went into the kitchen to start grabbing desserts. Okay, really he needed a moment to gather himself. He had managed to avoid speaking to Riley so far. Cowardly, yes, but necessary. Seeing her with this man— really any man would have been a nightmare— had proven too difficult. He glanced at the stainless-steel counter, tempted to bang his head against it a few times.

If only that would help.

Her life was in Arizona. He simply had to get through dessert. Even in a town this small, he could probably avoid her over the holidays. Surely, she had to return to the west coast soon. And take her boyfriend with her.

Feeling the tiniest bit calmer, he reached for a tray of espresso cannoli to take out to the buffet table. He paused at the door when he heard a man's voice. A voice he'd just heard for the first time tonight.

"Excuse me, everyone. If I could have your attention for a moment, please," Riley's boyfriend asked.

Luca slipped through the door, pan of desserts forgotten in his hands. As he feared, Thomas stood in the middle of the room, Riley at his side. He wore a huge grin while she stared into middle space.

"Sorry to interrupt the festivities. Thank you so much, first of all, to the Rinaldi family for including me tonight," he began in his oh so smooth tone.

Like we had a choice, Luca thought as his gut knotted.

Thomas beamed down at Riley.

"Riley and I met about five years ago. I didn't have the pleasure of growing up with her like some of you in this room had. I'm going to need those stories later," he joked. A ripple of laughter filtered across the room. "We had the same pediatrics rotation in medical school. She loved it. I hated it. But I met her, so it was worth it."

Luca set the pan down on the bar next to him. His skin grew cold as he realized what was coming. No, this couldn't be happening. Not here, in *his* restaurant. Not with *his* girl. He glanced at the front door and fleetingly wondered if anyone would notice if he made a break for it. He realized he didn't care. He couldn't watch this.

Then he saw her face. Riley's face was completely blank.

No blush. No tears of joy. No smile. She stared at the floor while Thomas droned on about fate and good fortune. Didn't he know her well enough to know she hated to be the center of anything? And in that moment, as his heart shattered into a thousand pieces within his chest, Luca knew he couldn't leave with Riley standing there like that.

And then that stupid man, who didn't seem to notice his about-to-be fiancée had turned to stone, dropped to one knee in front of her. He clutched a small, white bear in his hands, holding it out to her as an offering. The crowd gasped. What little color she still had drained from Riley's face.

The stuffed bear closely resembled one he'd given her about a million years ago. Luca shook his head, wondering how much worse this could get. He didn't have to wonder long.

"Riley Jane Layne, I know this isn't your original bear from childhood, but I thought I'd try to get you a new one to replace the one you lost. Will you do me the honor of becoming my wife?" he asked. He held up the bear, and the overhead lights caught the glint of the diamond tied with a ribbon around its neck.

Time stood still. Luca's heart stopped beating. He forgot to breathe altogether when Riley stared into his eyes over the other man's shoulders.

"Yes," she whispered.

Luca turned and fled into the dark and freezing night.

Chapter One

"Beginnings are always messy."
-John Galsworthy

Seven months later, Mid-July

Riley Layne stood in the darkness, just outside the bright, red and white sign proclaiming Palm Harbor General Hospital's emergency department, not hiding really. She preferred to think of it as gathering herself. She didn't even start until tomorrow, but something had drawn her here tonight. Unable to sleep, she'd gone for a run along the ocean, filling her lungs with humid, salt-laden air.

The scent of home.

After more than a decade away, she'd finally made it home for good. She'd come quietly, without fanfare, as she wanted. The exact opposite of how she'd left. She grimaced remembering what a big deal her family had made of her leaving for college, then an even bigger one for medical school.

If they knew she was home, the fatted calf would be on a spit somewhere, roasting for sure. It wasn't what she wanted. She never had. As the youngest, and by far the quietest, of her siblings, Riley like to do things her own way, something they never quite seemed to grasp.

But he did...

She shook her head, refusing to think about Luca or

remember the pain in his brown eyes the last time she'd seen him. The pain she'd caused. Better not to go there. Too much time had passed. Too many hurtful words between them also. The past could not be erased. Better to look forward than back, she figured.

The squealing of tires and frantic screams dragged her from her musing. Riley whipped her head around to see a late model sedan jerk to a halt mere feet from her.

"Help us!" a man in his twenties screamed.

And just like that, years of training kicked into action. Riley sprinted to him.

"Sir, what's the matter?" she asked, peering into the car.

"My son, help my son!" the man continued to scream.

He ripped open the back door, and she saw a woman holding a young boy. Both were covered in what looked like way too much blood. Dimly, she registered other voices behind her. Knowing they raced against the clock, Riley reached into the car and grabbed the limp little boy.

The mother stared at her, eyes wide, and resisted letting go.

"My name is Dr. Riley Layne. You have to let me help your little boy. Right now. What is his name?"

She glanced down to see bright red blood oozing from a wound in his upper arm. Knowing she didn't have time, Riley tore the boy from his mother's grasp, turned, and sprinted. She clamped one hand over the wound, praying she could squelch the bleeding for now.

"I need some help!" she yelled to a woman in navy-blue scrubs who met her with a stretcher. "No time for that. Where's your trauma bay?"

They locked eyes for a nanosecond before the other woman turned and ran. Riley followed, hoping the little boy had enough time, and blood, left.

The next few minutes passed in a blur as a whole team enveloped her. Bright lights flooded the treatment room. She lay her patient down in the middle of the stretcher, keeping her hand clamped where it was, literally holding his life in her hands. His too pale face broke her heart.

A man with salt and pepper hair rushed in. "I'm Dr. Matthews, what do we have?" he barked.

"Not sure but most likely an injury to his brachial," she replied. "I happened to be in the ambulance bay when his parents pulled up.

"His parents drove him here?" he said, brows meeting his hairline. "Lovely," he muttered under his breath. "Let's take a look."

"Caleb!" a woman's hysterical voice screamed from behind Riley. She turned her head enough to see the little boy's mother standing in the doorway. A large man in maroon-colored scrubs held her back.

"Let her come in," Riley said.

She felt all eyes on her but couldn't think about it now. Within seconds, the woman popped up at her side.

"I know this looks awful, and I'm not going to lie to you. Caleb is very sick right now. But Dr. Matthews here is doing everything he can to help Caleb." She glanced up at the attending. "Aren't you, Dr. Matthews?" she asked in a calm tone she did not feel.

"I certainly am," the other doctor answered.

"Pediatric patients do better when their parents are with them. Research has proven that time and again. Mom, I need you to hold it together for a little while longer. Can you do that?"

The woman nodded, one hand pressed against her mouth.

"Okay then. And where is Caleb's dad?" Riley asked.

"I'm right here," the man who she'd seen in the dark lot answered from the doorway.

"Dad, you can stand at the bottom of the stretcher. I'm afraid it's a bit crowded right here at the moment. I need you both to talk to Caleb. He can hear you, even if he can't respond right now. Everyone here has a job to do, and that one job is to help Caleb. So talk to your son and stay out of everyone's way. Understood?"

"Yes," the little boy's father answered in a shaky voice.

"I need you tell us what happened, please," she asked him.

"We thought he was asleep," the man began before dragging in a ragged breath.

Riley glanced at his blood-soaked pajamas. Paw Patrol, just like her nephew liked to wear. She swallowed the lump in her throat and shoved the thought away.

"Keep going," she said. Around her, the medical team worked on Caleb.

"He snuck back out to the yard to play with Duke. He's our dog. My wife and I were watching TV. We never heard him leave the house. We heard glass shattering and ran outside. We found him lying on the ground. The glass from the patio table was shattered all around him."

The mother sobbed next to her. Riley snuck a glance. Both parents had tears running down their faces.

"I have a nephew this age. He's a ninja. I joke Patrick should wear a bell around his neck so we can keep track of him. Does Caleb have any allergies to medication?"

"No," the mother answered in a shaky voice.

"Is he treated for any chronic conditions? Maybe asthma or diabetes? Anything like that? Anything at all?" Riley asked.

"No, nothing," she sobbed. "We've been so lucky with him. It took so many years to have him. He's our m-m-miracle," she said, sobbing.

"Hey now, you need to pull it together for Caleb, understand?" Riley gently chided.

"O-okay," the mother agreed, sniffling.

Within minutes, arrangements were made to fly Caleb to a regional medical center where he would go straight to the OR. Only when they stabilized him and took him to the landing zone did Riley feel like she could breathe again.

Then she looked down at her blood-soaked running clothes. The little boy's blood covered her hands, arms, really everywhere she looked. She walked to the corner of the room and started to wash away all traces of what had just happened.

She glanced up into the large mirror hanging over the industrial sink and caught a glimpse of herself. Large, hazel eyes stood out in a too-pale face. Her freckles seemed to glow. Tendrils of sweat-dampened hair had escaped from her hairband, stuck to her face.

That's when she started to laugh. She couldn't stop once she started and laughed until tears ran down her face and her stomach hurt. She bent over the sink as Caleb's blood swirled down the drain, and still she laughed until her tears mingled with his blood.

"Are you okay in here?" asked the woman she'd first seen at the entrance to the hospital.

"Well, depends on who you ask," she joked.

The other's woman's eyes widened before she laughed also.

"I have a problem when I get stressed. I get this uncontrollable laughter," Riley said by way of explanation. She grabbed some paper towels to dry her hands. "I've tried everything, but I'm afraid I'm hopeless."

"Well, considering you may have just helped saved the little boy's life, I'd say it's a tradeoff." She stepped closer, holding out her hand. "I'm Harper Monroe, by the way. Nice to meet you."

She finished drying her hands and tossed the paper towel before shaking Harper's hand.

"Nice to meet you, Harper, I'm Riley Layne."

"Layne as in Griff Layne's younger sister?" Harper asked. "Wait, even better. You're *Dr.* Riley Layne, our new attending."

Riley's face heated but she held Harper's gaze. Something she'd worked on for years.

"Guilty on both counts, I'm afraid," she acknowledged.

"Oh my gosh, does Griff know you're back? He's going to be so excited. You're all he's talked about for weeks. Well, you and Amelia Grace, of course," she added with a huge smile.

"You know my brother and niece? Of course you do. Everyone knows Griff. He is by far the most outgoing in my family. I am, by far, not. And no, he doesn't know I'm back yet. I told them all I'm coming home next week to give myself some breathing room." She groaned. "I know it sounds terrible. I love my family, but they're a lot. How do you know him?"

"My boyfriend is Owen Daniels, whom I'm sure you know. I met your brother through him. I was actually working here the night Amelia Grace made her grand entrance," she explained.

"Oh my gosh!" Riley exclaimed. "Harper, of course. I've heard such wonderful things about you." She waved a hand down her bloodied clothing. "I would hug you, but I'm a bit of a mess. Thank you so much for being here for them that night. Griff says you were really terrific."

The other woman's cheeks pinked. "Just doing my job," she demurred. "Not gonna lie. Seeing Owen in the back of the ambulance, all bloody, really shook me. Then along comes Jamie and Sam in full spinal precautions. Well, it's not a night I'd like to repeat anytime soon."

"Can't even imagine," Riley said. "Up until now, I've only practiced in places I didn't know people." She blew out a big breath. "Tomorrow, that changes."

"Well, welcome home and welcome to the ER. I've only been here for a few months but love it already. Let me grab you a scrub top to change into before you leave," she offered.

"Thanks, I would appreciate it."

After Harper left the room, Riley stared at herself in the mirror again. This time she grinned. The wild hair, too pale skin and hated freckles be damned. She was home!

"Yes!" she shouted to her reflection.

"Harper tells me you and I are colleagues," a male voice sounded from behind her.

"Gah!" she yelped, whirling to face Dr. Matthews. She clutched her chest as her heart pounded like a herd of wild horses within it. "Sorry," she muttered, face flaming. "Don't usually talk to myself until the second week on the job."

To her vast relief, the older man threw back his head and laughed.

"Oh, you're going to liven this place up," he commented before stepping further into the room. "Brody Matthews, nice to meet you. I'm guessing you're Riley Layne then."

She shook his hand. "I am indeed. So nice to meet you, sir. Your paper last year on the use of Glucagon in the treatment of patients taking a beta blocker and suffering from Anaphylaxis was brilliant."

"Ah, you're the one who read it," he joked.

"I read a lot," she said. "I'm a bit of a nerd that way."

"Nothing wrong with that," he said. "I hear you're a local girl, too. Welcome home, Riley. Your family must be thrilled to have you back. Weren't you most recently in Arizona?"

"Yes, I just finished at the end of last month. Took a few weeks off for a little time to myself while I made my way back home," she explained with a grin. "Wanted a break before I hit the ground running."

"Well, we're excited to have you. We've been down one full-timer since June. And we don't have anyone who shares quite your level of your enthusiasm for Peds. Not gonna lie about that. What you did tonight, jumping in like that. Amazing!"

She ducked her head at the unexpected praise.

"I was just doing my job. Well, about to be my job. I mean tomorrow, it'll be my job." She twisted her hands. "Sorry, I tend to babble. Now, you see why I like kids so much. Way less pressure," she joked.

As if sensing her discomfort, Dr. Matthews took a few steps back. "Well, I just wanted to formally introduce myself. And to let you know how happy I am you're joining us. If there's anything you ever need, please don't hesitate. I've been here for over two years, so I know my way around pretty well."

"I appreciate that," she said. "Have a good rest of your shift."

"Thank you," he said before turning to leave.

When she was alone in the room again, Riley blew out a long breath. *Get ahold of yourself!* Some days, she wondered why she hadn't gone into research and avoided people altogether. Then she straightened her spine. Although still introverted, she'd fought hard to shed the crippling shyness which plagued her since childhood. Growing up the youngest of five had its advantages and disadvantages.

"I see you met Brody," Harper said, walking back into the room.

"I did. He seems really nice." Riley pointed to the open treatment room door. "Do you mind closing that? I need to change."

"Of course," Harper responded, pushing the door shut with her hip. She handed Riley a plastic bag normally used for patient's belongings. "Here, not sure if your shirt can be saved or not."

"Oh, thanks. My mom is a whiz at stain removal. Comes from having five kids. If anyone can do it, she can."

She whipped off her shirt and tossed it in the open bag Harper held. Then she glanced in the mirror and spotted more of Caleb's blood on her torso.

"Guess I'm not done scrubbing yet," she muttered. "Tell me about my niece. I can't wait to get my hands on her."

Harper laughed. "That's what I say every time I visit her. She's the cutest little munchkin ever. And her personality is really starting to shine through. Let me just say, she's giving your brother a run for his money," Harper said with a laugh.

"Good! About time someone did. Don't get me wrong, I love him, but he's long overdue," Riley commented.

"Well, I don't know how well you've gotten to know Jamie, but that woman is no pushover. She's a great match for him."

Satisfied, she'd managed to remove most of the blood, Riley grabbed a towel to dry her skin before pulling on the scrub top.

"Thanks for this, by the way. And I don't really know her at all, sad to say. We only met for the first time at their wedding, and even then I was only in for the weekend because of my residency." She laughed. "I was lucky to get that. The program was no joke. And then of course I was here for Christmas briefly."

She closed her eyes for a moment on the memory of that debacle. Christmas had not gone the way she'd planned at all.

"Oh my gosh, that's right!" Harper exclaimed. "I didn't even get a chance to ask you about your wedding plans yet. Now that you're back in Palm Harbor, does that mean you'll be getting married here? Your family must be so excited. The last one to tie the knot and all."

"Uh, about that..."

"Harper, we need you," a woman said, barreling through the door. She stopped when she saw Riley. "Oh, sorry."

"No, that's fine. Didn't mean to take her away from the floor," Riley apologized. She turned to Harper. "Thanks again for lending me something to wear. It was nice meeting you, and I look forward to working with you."

"You, too," Harper said, before following the other woman out of the room.

Riley glanced at her empty ring finger, glad she had another day before having to explain.

Chapter Two

"As much as you try to organize your life, life will surprise you."
-Bryce Dessner

Luca drank deeply from his ice-cold beer, savoring the chill against his parched throat. He leaned back against the booth, half listening to his friends rag on each other. The restaurant had been crazy busy with tourist season still underway. Even though local schools started next week, folks from neighboring states and beyond would trek to Palm Harbor to enjoy a few days of hot, sandy beaches and boardwalk fun. Mama's Cucina, his family's restaurant, had been crazy busy this past week.

"I think he might be sleeping with his eyes open," Jack commented, catching Luca's attention. "He has that same look Griff wore for most of the summer."

"At least I had a new baby to blame," Griff said in his own defense. "What's your excuse, man?"

"I don't know, maybe the fifty thousand tourists I've fed this week," he offered up. He pointed to each of them with his bottle. "On the other hand, I've been trying to arrange this night for weeks. Who's the only one not whipped into submission?" he asked with a grin.

"Hey, I resemble that remark," Owen joked. "And very happily. Not gonna lie to you, my friend, I'd take Harper over your ugly mug any day of the week. Luckily for you, she's working tonight."

"I rest my case," Luca said. He took another swallow and chose to ignore the funny little pain in his chest.

"He's just jealous," Jack joked. "Not our fault he's lonely." He took a swallow of his draft beer. "Hey, I know. Maybe one of our women could set him up with someone."

"Great idea," Owen seconded. "I'm sure Harper knows some desperate single nurses from work." He grinned at Luca. "Want me to ask?"

"You could always ask Miss Harriet," Stella, their waitress, suggested as she brought another round. She placed their empties on her tray then turned to look Luca over. "You know she knows everyone. Surely she has some hairdresser's second cousin's granddaughter for you. But then, you're not exactly hard on the eyes, you don't really need Miss Harriett."

Luca ducked his head when the guys gave a round of catcalls and whistles. Stella, as always unfazed by their behavior, winked and sashayed away.

"High praise coming from Stella," Griff commented. "Hey, speaking of hospital people, maybe Riley can hook you up with one of her new doctor friends."

Luca went completely still. Breath froze in his lungs. He forced himself to meet his friend's gaze.

"Oh?" he asked, hoping he sounded more indifferent to them than he did to his own ears.

"Yeah, she's so happy with her new job, she's actually making friends and fitting in. Well, as much as Riley ever can anyway," his friend added.

Luca curled both hands into fists under the table. He knew Griff didn't mean anything by his words, but words hurt, nonetheless. He slowly unfurled his fists and flexed his hands. His days as Riley's champion were long gone. He'd thrown away that right.

"Thanks, but I'm fine," he said. "Just because y'all have drunk the Kool-Aid doesn't mean I have to." He lifted his beer and saluted them. "This is fine for me." He took a long drink to wash down the bitter taste of his lies.

"So that's a no to Miss Harriett's niece's neighbor's dog

walker also?" Jack asked, grinning. "You know she asks about you all the time. 'Oh, that handsome Luca, all those brooding good looks, wasted!' Really, dude, put her out of her misery. You know the woman lives for matchmaking."

"I'm good. Promise," he said, trying to not squirm.

Riley had been back in Palm Harbor for one week and four days now. He could probably count the hours, too, but admitting it would make him pathetic. He hadn't seen her yet. Knew it was inevitable in a place this small but had lucked out thus far.

Like you haven't been looking…

Truth was he'd missed her since she left for college more than a decade ago. Growing up, Riley had been his best friend. Then they'd become something more. Almost. Something undefined. Something that ended up ruining the closeness they once shared.

They were an odd pair, mismatched really. Luca had two years on her, but because of her 'big brain' as he like to tease, Riley skipped kindergarten and then fourth grade. The Laynes and Rinaldis were close friends, so the children knew each other well growing up. But Luca's older brother, Matteo, and all of her older siblings had at least several years on them, often leaving the two of them in the dust, so to speak.

He'd hated it, wanting to play all the sports with the older kids. Riley loved it, content to just spend time with him. He had never gotten it until he understood the depth of her shyness. She simply preferred one on one friendships, and from an early age, Luca was it.

Now, she barely spoke to him. Funny how life changed like that, he mused.

"Hey, Griff, I meant to ask how your sister was holding up. Broken engagements can be rough," Stella sympathized. She squeezed his shoulder as she passed him. "Please tell her I was asking for her and expect to see her in here one night soon."

Luca was sure Griff answered Stella, but for the life of him he had no idea what he might have said. All he could hear was the sound of his own blood rushing in his ears.

Broken engagement?

He had no idea how long he sat there, probably staring into space, when Griff waved a hand in front of his face.

"You really do look worse than I did. What's going on with you?" Griff asked, not joking.

"What? Oh, nothing, just tired. The restaurant has been crazy busy. You know how this time of the year is. We lose some of our summer help back to college." He took another drink of his beer, hoping his answer got them off his trail.

However, it did nothing for the million questions bouncing around his brain like ping pong balls on crack.

"Yeah, Griff, Harper mentioned the women all had lunch a few days ago. Sounds like Riley has officially been inducted into the coven," Owen joked. "She mentioned Riley seemed okay with the breakup."

Luca stopped himself from leaning in. He didn't want to miss a second of this conversation. But he also couldn't look like he cared too much. That would be blood in the water. Hard to balance when he could barely string together two coherent thoughts at the moment. The whole time she'd been back in Palm Harbor, he'd steeled himself for seeing the happy couple around town.

He didn't know what to do with this new information.

"To be honest, all she's done is work since she got home. Heck, she came home a whole week before she told us she was, moved into a house she bought sight unseen. Didn't bother mentioning it to anyone. Sprung the other news on us." Griff shook his head. "The part about no longer having a fiancé. I'm not sure what to think."

Luca barked out a laugh, drawing the attention of everyone at the table.

"What?" he asked. "You can't actually be surprised."

Griff just stared at him. "Something you want to share with the class?"

Luca rolled his eyes.

"Her entire life, your family treated Riley like she was a baby," he started to explain.

"Well, she was," Griff bit out.

Luca shook his head. "She was the baby of the family. There's a huge difference."

"But she was always so different than the rest of us. So..." he threw up his hands.

"So quiet? So scary smart?" Luca suggested. "Should I keep going?"

Jack and Owen both sat back, folding their arms over their chests as though watching a sporting event. Griff's mouth tightened.

"What are you not saying, Luca?" he asked in a very controlled tone.

Luca sighed. This was neither the time nor place. But apparently it was.

"Because Riley was so much younger than the rest of you and so quiet and so ridiculously brilliant, y'all treated her differently. She hated it. It made her feel, well, odd. And she already felt odd every day of her life."

"How come I'm just learning this now?" Griff asked.

"Because while you may be her brother, I was her best friend."

*****

"And this is why blocks are for building and not putting up your nose, right, Grant?" Riley asked the little boy in front of her. She held up the snot-coated plastic bit with forceps for him to inspect.

But being a boy, he reached out for it, yelling, "Cool!"

Riley laughed, scooting back on her wheeled stool far enough to be out of reach.

"Not cool, Grant," his frazzled mother claimed. "I'm so sorry, Dr. Layne."

"No worries. Little boys have been sticking things up their noses as long as little boys have had noses." She dropped the offending item on the tray before scooting back to her patient. "Now, I just need to take a quick look to make sure you didn't hurt yourself kiddo."

She talked to the little boy as she shone her light inside his nose, ensuring herself, and mom, everything looked fine. When she finished, she patted the child on his head.

"As cute as you are, I'd prefer to not see you in here again. Do we have a deal?" she asked, taking off her glove and holding out her hand to him.

"Deal Doc," he said, shaking her hand and whole body with his enthusiasm. A sly grin stole across his face. He glanced at his mother. "Didn't she say I could get a prize if I did good?" he asked, all big eyes and innocence.

Both adults laughed.

"Good memory, Grant," Riley praised him. "My nurse will be right in to send you guys home. Make sure you remind her, okay?"

"Okay, Doc."

"What do you say, Grant?" his mother asked, nudging his shoulder.

"Thank you, ma'am."

"You're so welcome," She turned to his mother, who looked much happier than when they'd arrived. "Lexi will be right in. He'll be fine, but don't hesitate to come back or follow up with your pediatrician with any concerns. Nice meeting you."

"Thanks again," his mother said.

Riley stepped out of the curtained area, stopping to sanitize her hands, and headed behind the desk. She sank into a chair at the front near the trauma bays where the providers sat. A bank of computers in this area with dictation capabilities allowed for quick and efficient charting. Gathering her thoughts, she signed into one of the terminals.

"Now that right there is reason enough to be glad you're working with us," Brody Matthews joked as he dropped into the chair next to hers. "If your being here saves me from small child foreign object extraction, then I'm all for it."

"Careful what you wish for. If I take all the small child ones, that leaves you with all the adult ones." She turned and grinned at him. "And we all know those are much worse."

Riley turned back to her computer, heart pounding. *She'd made a joke!* She dictated Grant's notes then checked for accuracy before signing off on them.

"How are you liking it so far?" he asked. "How's being back home?"

Riley thought about it for a moment. Well, the second part. First part was easy.

"Great and different are the best words I can come up with," she admitted. She pushed hair behind her ears. After wearing her hair long for so much of her life, the mid-length bob still took some getting used to.

"Everyone's treating you well here, I hope," he said, leaning into her a little. "Because I'm happy to have a little chat if they're not," he said with a grin.

She darted a glance at him then laughed, relieved when she saw his expression.

"Oh, you were joking," she mumbled. "I have a bad habit of taking people too seriously sometimes."

A rich, deep laugh burst from him.

"And I have the exact opposite problem," he wheezed out between chuckles. "Sorry, my wife used to 'gently remind' me all the time I might not be as funny as I thought I was."

Riley froze at his mention of his late wife. She'd already heard, of course, about his losing her to ovarian cancer. She'd been here a week already after all. She would be surprised if everyone on staff didn't know her shoe size yet.

"I, uh, was sorry to hear about your wife," she mumbled, dreading the heat she felt in her cheeks.

"Thank you, Riley, but it's been almost four years. I should have known the gossip mill would have filled you in. Then let me add how sorry I am to hear about your broken engagement," he added.

"Oh, but that's not the same thing at all," she exclaimed, face now feeling like the Arizona desert she'd left behind.

He cocked his head, seemingly studying her for a moment. "Maybe not, but loss is still loss."

She grabbed a pen from the desktop, twirling it in her hands to give them something to do while she tried to think of what to say to that.

"Dr. Layne, there's a new kiddo in room four for you. Possible ankle fracture," Holly, one of the ER nurses, called from across the desk.

Riley jerked her head up, relief coursing through her.

"Coming," she called and bolted from her chair. She caught up with the nurse in a few strides and smiled at her. "Please, call me Riley. I've never been a fan of all the titles."

Holly shot her a look before grinning.

"Okay, then, Riley, let's go meet the would-be skateboarder."

Riley looked back over her shoulder to find Brody staring at her. She wondered if it meant anything. She'd never been any good at reading cues between men and women.

Especially between one man and herself...

Chapter Three

"Gossip is the Devil's Radio."
-George Harrison

Sweat dripped into Luca's eyes, burning them, but he finished his set before collapsing on the bench. After replacing the weights, he reached for a towel and swiped his face. The skin on the back of his neck grew tight. He turned to find Miss Harriet standing there clad in the brightest sweatsuit he'd ever had the misfortune of seeing.

"Good morning, Luca," she all but purred.

"Good morning, ma'am," he said, grinning. The spry octogenarian, also Palm Harbor's most reliable source of information, was dressed for battle. He didn't envy his friend Griff, whose senior class she took. "Ready for your workout, I see."

Her heavily made-up cheeks pinked up. "Why yes, I am. Have to keep the old ticker in shape," she joked. "I wanted to check in with you. See how you were handling everything."

His stomach took a dive.

"Uh, handling what exactly?" he asked, knowing full well what she meant but not caring to acknowledge it.

That was mistake number one. She pounced.

"Why Riley being back, of course, you silly man," she explained, stroking his sweaty arm. "Everyone knows how close you two always were. Why when Riley left for school, you were just devastated."

"Riley and I were friends, Miss Harriet. To be honest, we haven't really kept in touch all these years," he admitted.

One heavily penciled brow arched. "Really?" she drawled, drawing the one word out to at least four syllables.

And that would be mistake number two.

"Well, not sure if you've heard, but she is single again." She winked at him then. Winked! "Just saying. And now I have to get to class." She waggled the fingers of one hand. "Have a great day, dear."

Luca let out a groan and sank back onto the bench. He buried his head in his hands.

"I see you've been on the receiving end of a Miss Harriett special. Don't worry, we've all been there, man," Jack said, laughing.

Luca lifted his head. "She's something. Not sure what but something."

Jack roared with laughter. "She certainly is. Can you imagine if she ever used her power for evil?" He faked a shudder. "She has a good heart and likes to see people happy. And besides, everyone knows about you and Riley."

Luca's gaze snapped to his.

"Well, maybe everyone but Griff," Jack amended.

"There's nothing to know," Luca ground out.

"Maybe not yet, but she is single again. And you're perpetually single." Jack tapped his chin with one finger. "Wonder why that is?" He lightly punched Luca's shoulder. "Just something to think about. See you later, dude."

"See you," Luca answered, already lost in his own thoughts.

"Luca, wait up!" Riley called.

He closed his locker and turned to wait for her. He watched her walk toward him, all crazy hair and bright eyes. His heart did a weird flip in his chest. He had no idea what it meant, but things had gotten weird around her lately.

She stopped in front of him. "Ready for lunch?" she asked, holding up hers. "We aren't all as lucky as you. Who knows what I have today," she griped. "I know Mom tries, but nothing will ever be as good as lunch by Mama," she joked. She grabbed at his, missing as he pulled it out of reach.

He held his own lunch above her head, not hard since he already had at least six inches on her.

"Nice try, squirt! And I'll have you know, I made this myself."

Her eyes rounded. "Oooh, another experiment from the kitchen of Luca Rinaldi? Can I get a bite?"

He stared at her perfect, pink lips, completely forgetting whatever her question may have been. Then her small hand waved in front of his face.

"Luca? Are you in there?"

"Oh, sorry," he mumbled. "Just thinking about something else. What, he wouldn't tell her of course. "Yes, if you ask nicely, you may have a bite. Come on before all the tables are gone."

The pulsing music and sounds of Getting it Done dragged him back to present times. He smiled, remembering freshman year. He couldn't wait to start high school, psyched to play baseball, even if he didn't make varsity right away. Riley had more of a love/hate relationship with it. She loved the notion of all those science classes waiting for her inner nerd, as she called it, but hated the idea of more people to deal with. Because Palm Harbor was so tiny, especially back then, they'd been bussed to a county high school. Great for people like her brother who thrived on meeting new people. Not so much for her.

Luca shook his head, sweat flicking in all directions. High school had not been Riley's friend, in more ways than one. He still wondered if he had made it better or worse for her.

*****

Riley sat in Brody's truck, still not quite sure how this had happened. One minute they'd been joking around at work yesterday, the next, she'd agreed to dinner with him. Tonight. As friends? Maybe. Was this a date? She had no idea. She fiddled with her purse strap and stared out the window.

"Hope you like Italian," he said.

No, no, no, no… okay, no reason to panic. There were tons of Italian restaurants in Palm Harbor these days.

Riley tried to slow her breathing without looking obvious. As in it was obvious she was on the verge of a panic attack.

"Italian?" she croaked.

He shot her an odd look before returning his attention to the road.

"Yes, I know this great place that serves the most amazing, authentic Italian food," he said.

Please, don't say Mama's Cucina she willed him in her mind. Anywhere but there.

"Maybe you've heard of it? Mama's Cucina?" he asked, stealing a glance at her.

She only managed a high-pitched squeak.

"Riley, are you okay?" he asked.

"Yep, sorry," she responded, not sure what else to say. He turned into the parking lot, saving her from answering further.

"You're going to love this," he promised.

Wouldn't be so sure…

"Oh, wonderful," she said, wondering why the universe hated her so.

She stared straight ahead as he parked and got out and decided to give herself a pep talk. *You've got this. This is not a date. Luca will not be working. Surely, he gets some nights off. And it's a Wednesday, so that's a good night to have off. Right? Not like it's a weekend.*

Her door opened, startling her.

"Oh! Sorry, didn't see you there."

"Where did you think I was?" he joked.

"Somewhere else?" she joked in return, wishing she were literally anywhere else but here.

He grinned before helping her down. Riley walked across the parking lot, each step harder than the one before. *You can do this.* Worst-case scenario, Luca was working. Okay, she would handle it.

Riley had found worst-case scenarios helped her through life. By imagining the very worst, then surviving it, life became more manageable. And as she did, the worst cases had grown easier. Worst never really was as bad as expected. She could do this.

She felt Brody's hand at the small of her back. This was feeling more like a date. She didn't even know how she felt about that. Maybe she could think about that later… He opened the door. Her breathing hitched. Her palms grew damp. This always took it out of her. Just step inside.

"Bella!" Mama Rinaldi all but screamed from just inside the door. The rotund woman rushed forward, grabbing Riley's face in her hands before kissing both cheeks. "It's true, my Riley is back. I would not know this, as I have not yet seen you, my topolina," she scolded.

Riley's face heated, but she hugged the woman who was nearly a second mom to her hard.

"I'm so sorry, Mama. I'm only just back and threw myself right into work." She pulled herself from the embrace to look at her. "I've missed you," she said. "It's so good to be back."

Mama's eyes brightened with unshed tears. "Ah, to have all my children back now." She clapped her hands. "This is a miracle. Our little Riley is now a big, fancy doctor no less." Then she glanced around Riley, eyes narrowing at Brody. "And who is your *friend*, Riley? He looks familiar."

Didn't figure a Mama inquisition in your worst-case scenario, did you…

Riley gulped. "This is Dr. Brody Matthews. He's a friend and coworker at the hospital. Brody, this is Mama Rinaldi, owner of this amazing place and chef extraordinaire."

"It's very nice to finally meet you, Mrs. Rinaldi," Brody said, extending a hand. "I'm already a huge fan. Since I am a terrible cook, your meals have kept me alive since I moved here. Although I usually get them to go."

She eyed his hand for a moment before shaking it briefly.

"Thank you, Dr. Matthews. You obviously have good

taste," she allowed. Then she turned to Riley. "For a moment, I thought he was the other one," Mama hissed.

Getting worse by the heartbeat.

"Uh, no, not even close," Riley replied.

"All good then. This way," she commanded, grabbing menus and leading them to a corner booth. "I will be right back with some of my world-famous garlic bread."

Riley sank into the booth, thankful for the relative dimness of the corner. Surely, Brody would be able to read the menu by the light of her face. She smiled at him weakly. He grinned back.

"I get the feeling you've been here before," he guessed.

"I pretty much grew up here," she said. "Our families are very close friends."

He burst out laughing before opening the menu. She stared at him.

"Something funny about that?"

"Not at all. But here I thought I would impress you with my restaurant choice." He reached out to stroked one finger across her knuckles. "Obviously, I'll have to work a little harder."

Okay, so maybe a date after all.

She opened her menu more to have something to do with her hands than anything. Riley had no idea what to say to Brody. Commenting on the fact she felt nothing when he touched her might not be a great place to start, she guessed.

Brody closed his menu and looked at her. "Even though I've eaten here hundreds of times, no exaggeration, what do you recommend? I tend to pick the same four or five things each time."

"I can assure you everything on the menu is fantastic," Luca said, answering Brody's question without taking his eyes off her. "Hello, Riley. Welcome home."

So much for small favors from the universe...

She raised her gaze to his, forcing herself to not look away.

"Hello, Luca, and thank you. The place looks great," she

said with a smile she didn't feel. "Smells even better."

"You always did appreciate Mama's cooking," he murmured. He placed a basket of warmed bread on the table. "May I take your drink orders first? Perhaps an appetizer?"

"I'll have ice water with lemon, please," she requested.

"Same for me," Brody said.

"Great. I'll grab those and give you and your date a moment to decide then, Riley. Excuse me," Luca said before leaving them.

Riley sat there, watching him walk away, back straight and stiff. Why did it seem like all she ever did was watch Luca Rinaldi walk away from her?

Chapter Four

"In the madness, you have to find calm."
-Lupita Nyong'o

Luca walked into the kitchen, through it and straight out the back door and into the sultry night. He took a deep breath, and even though it felt like trying to breathe underwater, it was easier than trying to breathe around *her*. He shook his head and began to pace. Back and forth along the lot he went, clenching and unclenching his hands. Although never a violent man, he had the urge to punch the red brick wall of the restaurant.

The thought dragged a harsh laugh from him. Breaking his hand would get her attention. Riley had always been a sucker for anything injured, and now she was a doctor. He could picture her placing a bag of ice on his hand, maybe blowing on his knuckles like she did the time he punched Tom Dennison in the nose for picking on her in fifth grade. Little turd deserved it.

"Who are you considering punching, and can I watch?" Nico drawled from the doorway, humor evident in his tone.

"No one and mind your own business," Luca growled. He kept up his pacing despite the sweat trickling down his spine. South Carolina in August was no joke.

"Come on, you're no fun," his cousin complained. "At least let me help bury the body. Does it have anything to do with Riley's date? He's actually a nice guy." He held up his hand. "Stitched me up last year when I had that little mishap in the kitchen."

"Great! He's a nice guy. Just what I wanted to hear," he grumbled under his breath. "They're not on a date, jackass. She's been back in town for about a minute."

"I don't know, looks like a date to me. He's hanging on her every word," Nico added. "Riley looks really good, too. Grew up nice. What happened to the idiot from Christmas?" He shook his dark head. "How could he not know she would hate that?"

"That's what I thought!" Luca exclaimed. "If you're going to ask someone to marry you, you should at least know them well enough to know a when the person would hate a public proposal." He made a sound of pure disgust. "Amateur."

"So, why are you hiding out here?" he asked, a look of pure innocence on his face.

Luca didn't buy it for a second. His feelings for Riley might be the worst kept secret in his family. Possibly in all of Palm Harbor.

"Do me a favor and take their orders, please," he said instead of answering. Safer that way.

"Sure thing. I always thought Riley was adorable. Those freckles! And you know I love older women."

Smart man, Nico ran before Luca could catch him. He made his way back into the kitchen hoping to keep busy and keep his mind off her 'date' if that's what it even was. It didn't work but time passed. He ignored Nico's pointed looks and his mother's less subtle gestures, kept his head down, and cooked. It's what he did best anyway. Eventually, the last customers left, and silence reigned.

When cleanup was finished, and everything was ready for tomorrow, he thanked his staff and sent them on their way. His mother had long since gone home. Lately, the family ensured she left by eight each night to enjoy a well-earned break.

Truthfully, he loved this time of night. The kitchen was his and his alone. He often stayed until the early hours, experimenting with new recipes or tweaking tried and true ones. He loved to cook but didn't limit himself to 'the old ways' like his mom insisted and his dad before her. Not wanting to head home just yet, he thought about messing around with a recipe that had been tickling his brain for the past few weeks.

He walked out into the darkened restaurant to grab something to drink from the bar.

"Hey, Luca," Riley greeted him in her soft voice.

He froze in his tracks just outside the kitchen door and stared at her, not quite believing she was real. She'd changed into shorts and a plain cotton T-shirt. On her feet were a pair of flip-flops. She looked eighteen again. His breath caught in his throat.

"How'd you get in?" he asked, then immediately wished the words back when he heard their gruff tone.

"I, uh, passed Nico on his way out." She glanced at the ground, jiggling her keys in one hand. "Hope you don't mind."

Mind? He wasn't sure how he felt, but he certainly didn't mind.

"Why would I mind?" he asked, not making a move any closer to her. He knew he was being an ass but couldn't seem to stop himself.

She pushed some hair behind one ear. It was shorter than he ever remembered seeing it. He liked it this way. What he didn't like was how nervous he seemed to be making her, but he wasn't sure what to do about it. He couldn't think of a single thing to say to the person he used to be closer to than any other on the planet.

The thought caused a funny little pain in his chest.

"I don't know. You never came back to the table earlier, so I wasn't sure..." She stopped talking, raised her head and looked right into his eyes. "The thing is, Luca, I'm back. To stay. I wanted to see you in person, to tell you, so it wouldn't be awkward between us."

He barked out a laugh. "How's that working out for you?"

Even in the dim light, he could see the color leech from

her face.

"Never mind," she stammered and whirled toward the door.

He caught up to her in four steps, reaching out to grab her arm.

"Don't go. I'm sorry." Luca dragged a hand through his hair, not sure what else to say to this woman. He dropped his hand from her arm, silently willing her to stay.

"Why are you acting like this?" she asked without turning to face him.

"I don't know," he admitted. Without another word, he walked over to the bar, flicking on the lights around it and grabbed a bottled water from the fridge under the bar. "Can I buy you a drink?"

She didn't say a word but turned and approached him slowly, eyes never leaving his, seemingly searching his face for something. She took a seat at the bar, keeping it between them.

"I'll take a Ginger Ale," she said. "Thanks," she added when he slid one toward her.

"How's the new job?" Luca asked, trying everything in his power to not ask about the guy she brought with her earlier.

Her face brightened, and for a moment, the old Riley, *his* Riley, reappeared. A huge grin appeared on her face.

"Oh my gosh, it's everything I thought it would be, Luca!" she exclaimed. She reached out to touch his arm but pulled her hands back at the last moment, wrapping them around her glass instead.

The small act gutted him. She would have never done that before. Before he'd broken her heart.

"That's great. I'm so happy for you. You deserve it." He fiddled with his water bottle lid. *When did talking with Riley become this difficult?* "Tougher question for you. How's it being back home?"

"Hmmm, that is the tougher question." She tapped her finger on her chin for a moment. "Can I say depends?" She laughed, and he felt it to his soul. "Honestly, I'm thrilled to be home. I missed Palm Harbor more than I even realized I had.

Don't get me wrong, I loved living other places and am so glad I did, but nothing beats home."

He dropped his hands below the level of the bar, tightening them into fists while she spoke. Her leaving had always been the biggest, only really, source of contention between them. To hear how much she loved it ate at his heart. But he put a smile on his face.

"Which place did you like the most?"

"Well, not Vermont." She rubbed her hands up and down her arms for effect. "Too cold for this Southern girl. They used to make so much fun of me. You should have seen the one and only time I tried skiing. Luca, there's a reason snow is a four-letter word!" she exclaimed, outrage clear in her voice.

He threw his head back and roared with laughter.

"You don't have to laugh that hard," she said with disgust in her voice.

"Sorry, but seriously, unless something has changed, you've never been exactly athletic," he said by way of explanation.

"No, that has not changed. Thank you very much for reminding me of one of my many shortcomings," she pouted. "As if my own family ever let me forget."

"Now, calm yourself. I'm only joking. You know I've always had your back," he reminded her.

"You used to," she corrected him. "There was also a time when a day didn't pass without us talking, when we told each other everything." She held up her hands then dropped them on the bar. "Now, I'm not sure what we are, Luca."

He didn't have a clue...

"It's been a long time, Riley," he said, knowing he wasn't answering her unspoken question.

She crossed her arms over her chest. "It's about more than time, don't you think?" Before he could answer, she stood up. "Thanks for the soda. I have an early shift. Nice seeing you again, Luca."

She left the restaurant before he could even think to follow her. Left him standing there, staring after her, wondering what had just happened. And made him think about all the things that had happened since they were kids.

*****

Riley refused to think about anything that had just happened until she got home. Medical school had taught her how to compartmentalize very well. Seeing what she saw on a daily basis, she'd learned to push aside her emotions to a later date when she could take them out and examine them at a better, safer time. Tonight, she was more than thankful for this skill set.

By the time she pulled into the small cottage near the beach, her hands shook. She ignored them and went inside. Only then, in the safety of the darkness, did she allow the first tears to fall. After locking the door, she slid down it to land on the floor and collapse in a pool of her own tears.

She knew coming home wouldn't be easy and seeing Luca would be at the top of the 'most difficult part' list. But she hadn't let it stop her. She'd always planned to come back here. To practice medicine here. And now, she did. But seeing him had been like a blow to the gut. She'd seen him, of course, over the years on her trips back home. But those had been whirlwind visits at best, filled with family gatherings and avoiding him as much as humanly possible.

He'd really grown into quite the specimen. Just over six feet and filled out in a way he hadn't yet back in high school. She smiled remembering how Mama always lamented over her 'skinny boy,' pushing plates of pasta at Luca. His dark brown eyes remained as deep and alluring as ever. How many hours had she spent as a teen drowning in them? Thousands? She shuddered to think. And his thick, black hair still looked like he'd just raked his fingers through it, making her want to do the same.

She sniffed and wiped her eyes, telling herself those were her last tears over one Luca Rinaldi. In the next breath, she called herself a liar. If nothing else, she was brutally honest.

Getting up, she went into her tiny kitchen. Peering into the freezer, she went for the hard stuff. She grabbed a spoon and settled on her couch with a pint of Ben & Jerry's Triple Caramel Chunk. Her roommate in medical school used to joke Riley should buy stock in the company. She joked in return it was cheaper than therapy. Some jokes were painfully close to the truth.

She ate a few heaping spoonsful of the caramel deliciousness, enough for an instant brain freeze headache, then stopped to think about Luca. She closed her eyes, remembering his heavy five o'clock shadow that she'd wanted to rub her hands against. His full lips she'd wanted to taste with her own. Would there ever be a day when he wouldn't affect her so much?

She shoveled more ice cream in her mouth, knowing the answer to the question already. For thirteen years, and across three different states, she'd pursued her medical education. She'd trained with hundreds of people, many of them handsome men. Some of whom had shown interest in her. A fraction of them she'd had an interest in. She'd dated. Heck, she'd even gotten, briefly, engaged.

Riley blamed the sudden pain in her head on the ice cream.

None of those men had come close to making her feel what she'd felt for Luca tonight. And he'd placed his hands on her for a whopping five seconds!

She thought about Brody, desperate to get images of Luca from her head. Brody Matthews was a nice guy. Riley winced, knowing if 'nice' was the first adjective that sprang to mind, he was already dead in the water. She pushed on anyway. Brody was attractive, educated, a doctor like her; they'd have things to talk about. Of course, she never dated coworkers. It was a longstanding rule of hers. Too messy.

But none of that mattered because Brody, through no fault of his own, wasn't Luca. Which was why she'd told him earlier, when he'd dropped her off, that they were going to be great friends. He'd been honest enough to agree they lacked any real chemistry. He also admitted she was the first person he'd asked out since his wife had passed away. This touched Riley's heart. She shared with him that making friends had never been her strong suit and she was happy to count him as one. All in all, not a bad night.

Except she still had no idea what to do about one brooding, sexy Italian…

Chapter Five

"My family is my strength and my weakness."
-Aishwarya Rai Bachchan

Several days later, Riley left her cottage in the early hours for a run. Slipping in her earphones, she hit her 'happy music' playlist on her phone and stepped off her front porch. Justin Timberlake's "Can't Stop the Feeling" got her blood pumping. It always reminded her of one of her favorite patients who had loved the movie, *Trolls*.

She wasn't running away, she told herself, she was running for exercise. In truth, it was a bit of both. The sun had barely painted the horizon in streaks of pink and orange. She breathed in lungs full of salty air, grinning as the sound of her running shoes slapping the road broke the otherwise silent streets. She ran toward the ocean then onto the packed sand, picking up speed as she did.

Riley grinned from ear to ear as a gull screeched overhead. This was home! She'd loved the desert. Loved the mountains. But the ocean and beach were etched into her soul. She ran to the water's edge, then made a right and continued along the beach, dodging the tide as it danced at her feet. Watching the predictable joy of the tide almost made her forget about her family.

Almost…

They were a hard bunch to forget. Other than work, and her aborted date, she'd barely escaped them so far. She winced at the turn her thoughts had taken. Riley loved and appreciated her family. She just needed a little breathing room from them already. Not a day had passed without someone stopping by to 'help' with her new home or give her advice on everything from which dry cleaners to use to where to get an oil change.

She ran faster thinking about it. She loved them and had missed them all so much. And being back home, getting to watch her herd of nieces and nephews grow up would be amazing. She no longer had to rely on Zoom and Facetime. But when were they all going to realize she was an adult? She ran faster.

Her mother was the worst of the bunch. One minute, she bemoaned the end of Riley's engagement, the next, she was already lining up suitable bachelors. And she'd barely been in town…

"Umph!" she cried, as she tripped over something and flew forward, landing face first in the wet sand. Before she could react, hands grabbed her from behind.

"Hey!" she screamed, whirling on her would-be attacker. She lashed out with her sneaker-clad feet, connecting with something solid, as she felt herself lifted off the sand.

"Ouch, stop it already. I'm just trying to help you," a male voice called out.

Her whole body froze. Because it wasn't enough to face plant in wet sand and then try to attack her would-be rescuer. Oh no, the universe wasn't that kind to her. Ever. She turned slowly to face him.

"Morning, Luca," she muttered. "Nice morning for a run, huh?"

"It was," he joked, bending to rub his shin.

She glanced down at it, gasping at the red welt she'd caused.

"In my defense, I thought you were attacking me," she said as she got to her feet.

"You're welcome, by the way," he muttered after straightening.

He stood with the rising sun behind him. Of course, he

did. Because Luca wasn't gorgeous enough already. He needed the sun glinting off his sweat-dampened skin. And of course, he hadn't bothered with a shirt this morning. It took everything in her to not step forward and lick him like a popsicle.

She glared at him instead.

"Excuse me?" she hollered, not caring that her face heated as she spoke. "What exactly am I thanking you for? Scaring the life out of me? Or maybe providing a witness for yet another memorable feat of clumsiness in the life of Riley Layne?" She poked one finger into his rock-hard chest for good measure.

Which, of course, made her want to lick it even more once she felt the muscle underneath his damp, smooth skin.

Damn him.

"Are you finished?" he asked, cool as the proverbial cucumber.

She stood there, staring at him for a moment, and thought about it before nodding. "Yes," she gritted out between clenched teeth.

And how did he respond? The man threw his head back and laughed long and hard. His whole, magnificent torso shook with the effort.

"Seriously?" she asked. "You're going to laugh at me after all that?"

It took a few moments, and a few false starts, but he finally got himself under control. His dark eyes still danced with merriment and more than a dash of shenanigans.

"Oh, Riley, how I've missed you," he exclaimed, shocking her. "Not sure anyone has managed to tell me off quite as well since you've been gone."

"Oh," she whispered, unsure what else to say.

He pointed to an outcropping of rock. "Come sit with me for a minute," he said before turning and heading toward the rocks, leaving her no choice but to follow. He waited until she sat before speaking again. "Who's got you so annoyed already this morning? Well, other than me."

Her mouth gaped open. "What? How did you know?"

"Because I know you, Riley. I was already on the beach when you showed up. I saw you up ahead, running faster and faster. Something, or someone more likely, ticked you off. Who was it? Family would be my first guess." He smirked at her. "Unless it was that guy from the other night."

She pushed her shades to the top of her head. "His name is Brody, and you gave up the right to ask anything about him years ago."

She got up and walked away, refusing to cry in front of him.

Big jerk.

*****

Luca gave her a ten second head start, but only because he couldn't believe she'd walked away from him. Again. Then he jumped off the rock and went after her.

"Wait a minute," he called, unwilling to get kicked again. His shin still smarted.

She didn't slow. She didn't turn. She broke out into a jog.

He grinned and did the same. Having over half a foot of height on her had its advantages. He caught her within a few strides, running in front of her and blocking her path in order to get her attention.

"Stop. Please, Riley. Give me a minute," he requested.

She drew up short, stopping quickly as if not wanting to touch him. He wondered for a moment if she'd felt what he had. The quick burst of electricity. The scorched feeling where they'd touched.

"What?" she asked, fisting her hands on her hips. "More shots you care to take? Go ahead."

"You came into my restaurant with another man, Riley. What am I supposed to do, huh? The last two times I've seen you, you've been with someone else. I had to watch someone ask you to marry him." He reached forward, grabbing one of her hands in his. "I stood there and watched you say yes to him, Riley." By the last word, his voice was so raw, Luca almost didn't recognize it.

Riley stared him down, unshed tears threatening to spill from her eyes.

"Trust me, your restaurant was the very last place I wanted to be. I had no idea he planned that. He had no idea it would be, well, awkward," she finished in almost a whisper.

Her words stung him.

"Is that what we've become, Riley? Awkward? I thought we were friends."

Is that all you want...

"A long time ago, we were friends. Now?" She shook her head then put her shades back on, but not before he saw one tear slide down her face. "I have no idea what we are."

This time, he let her walk away. He stood there watching her first walk then run further from him, until he couldn't see her anymore.

*****

Riley felt his gaze on her back as she walked away from him. Within seconds, she couldn't stand it and took off running wildly back down the beach. Tears mingled with sweat, blinding her, but still she ran. She whipped by the first beach goers claiming spots as the sun fully rose in the sky. She passed them and ran until she could barely breathe. Only when she reached the safety of her home did she stop. Hands on knees, bent over gasping, Riley stood in her small backyard and sobbed as she struggled for air.

How had it come to this? This man, her Luca, who had once meant everything to her, now seemed a cold stranger. She dropped into the hammock and closed her eyes as memories assaulted her.

"But I don't want to learn how to dance," twelve-year-old Riley protested to her mother. She really didn't. "I'm going to be a doctor. Doctors don't need to know how to dance."

Mom met her eyes in the rearview mirror. Her face held that pinched look she wore a lot.

"Riley Jane, there's more to life than being a doctor, and all young ladies need to know how to dance. One day you'll thank me."

Mom's tone told Riley the 'discussion' was over, so she opened her book back up and hoped this wouldn't be as painful as she feared. Too soon, they'd arrived at Miss Amy's School of Dance, the scene of just one of many of her humiliations in life (tap truly hadn't been her calling). And now she was back for another. She sighed and placed her bookmark in her book, knowing she didn't have a choice.

Walking on leaden feet behind her mother, Riley followed her inside, already wishing this were finished. Just inside the door, she waited for her eyes to adjust from the bright sunshine outside.

"They got you, too, huh?" Luca whispered from a chair to her left.

She turned and beamed at him. "Oh, thank goodness! They're making you do this, too?" She rushed to grab the seat next to him before someone else did. "I tried to tell Mom doctors don't need to know anything about dancing." She rolled her eyes. "You can imagine how well that went over."

He shrugged. "I didn't even try." He placed one hand on his lean hip and pointed at her with his other. "Luca, all men must know how to dance," he said in a heavily exaggerated Italian accent. "How do you ever expect to find a wife?"

The two collapsed into giggles until the sudden clapping of hands broke them apart.

"This is not how young ladies and gentlemen act in my class," Miss Amy herself intoned, looking down her nose at the two.

Riley bit the inside of her cheek to keep from laughing.

"Since you two find this so funny, you can be partners and demonstrate a Waltz for the class," the instructor advised.

She turned away before Riley could say a word. Not that she'd be able to say anything since her mouth had dried up like the Sahara, and her heart thundered in her ears. She shook her hands as Luca pulled her from the chair.

"Come on, Riley, it's the only way out of this mess," he whispered to her and led her onto the dance floor.

She allowed him to pull her out to the center of the floor, as dread pooled in her stomach. She clutched onto his hands like a life *raft, sure she would faint without him to hold her up. Miss Amy came back, murmuring some words to them, none of which Riley could understand over the roaring in her ears. Dimly aware of the others in the room watching, which only made things worse, she stared straight ahead at a button on Luca's shirt.*

"I can't do this," she whispered to him as tears burned her eyes. "I think I might puke."

He took both of her clammy hands in his and squeezed. "You're not going to puke. We'd just have to be here longer," he joked. "Look at me," he commanded.

She slowly dragged her gaze from his button up to meet his eyes. All joking had vanished. She swallowed hard. There was something, a burning intensity in his eyes, she'd never seen before.

"I've got you, Riley. We've got this. I promise," he whispered to her.

And in that moment, she believed him. Her heart still pounded. Sweat still trickled down her back. Her stomach still threatened to revolt. But she believed him. Music floated through the air, something light and airy without words.

Miss Amy stepped to the middle of the room with a man Riley had never seen before.

"Watch and learn," she said before taking off in a series of steps.

Riley knew the dance teacher was still talking, talking to them most likely, but she didn't hear a word of it. The taste of metal washed through her mouth.

"I can't do that," she cried to Luca.

"Well, maybe not quite like that, but we'll be okay," he tried to assure her.

And then Miss Amy signaled it was their turn. Twenty pairs of eyes or more turned to stare at them. At her really, because that's all she could think. At that moment, Riley hoped she would faint. At least she wouldn't have to feel the weight of others staring at her.

And then the most amazing thing happened. Luca started to Waltz. It wasn't smooth. It was far from perfect. But they were waltzing. She stared at him and then their feet, determined to not trip. Before she knew it, all the other kids partnered up and attempted to

Waltz around them. No one stared at her any longer.

She'd survived.

"Thank you," she gushed, staring into his dark eyes as if for the very first time. Her heart pounded still but now for a different reason altogether.

"It's no big deal, Riley," he said. "I'll always dance with you."

She brushed the tears from her face and sat up in the hammock. That was the day she'd fallen in love with Luca Rinaldi.

Chapter Six

"When you finally accept that it's OK not to have answers and it's OK not to be perfect, you realize that feeling confused is a normal part of what it is to be a human being."
-Winona Ryder

Riley collapsed in a chair, stretching her lower back, before signing into a computer to chart on her latest patient. She glanced at the corner of the screen. Four in the morning already. She smothered a yawn and pulled up her patient's chart.

The past week had flown. With each passing day she felt more comfortable at work. She loved the work itself. That was never her issue. Fitting in and making friends, well that was another story. It would come, maybe a bit more slowly, but it would come. She kept telling herself that.

"Hey, Doc, was I right? Does she have pneumonia?" Harper, one of Riley's favorite nurses, asked from the other side of the desk.

"Uh, uh, you know the rules," Riley joked, typing away and not looking up. A small smile played about her lips.

"Fine! *Riley,* was I right about the pneumonia? Poor thing. Her lungs sounded so wet to me," Harper empathized.

"I'm sure you were, but let's see." She hit a few keys, pulling up her patient's chest X-ray then motioned for Harper to come around next to her. When she did, they both looked at the screen. "Yep, nailed it."

"Poor woman has two little kids at home. No wonder

she's tired," Harper said.

"Let's give her some fluids and start her on antibiotics. She can have a little rest before we send her home," Riley advised. "She'll need it."

"You got it," Harper said, turning away. The she turned around again. "Oh, almost forgot. There's a meeting of The Coven tonight at my house. Seven o'clock. Just bring yourself." She turned and waked away again.

Next to her, Brody burst out laughing. "Did she say 'coven?' Should I be concerned?"

Riley grinned at him. "Yes, she did, and no, you shouldn't. My brother, Griff, jokingly gave that name to his wife and her best friend, Sam, when they became friends with Harper. Apparently, they've added me to the club."

She smiled at the thought. She didn't know the other women well, at least not yet, but liked what she did know of them. Her sister-in-law, Jamie, seemed sweet and was a good match for Griff. She didn't take any of his crap. And Sam, well there really weren't words for her. She wanted to be Sam when she grew up. The fiery redhead lacked a filter and didn't seem to fear anything.

Wouldn't that be a great way to live?

The next night, Riley showed up at the gorgeous old Victorian home Harper shared with her boyfriend, Owen. Walking up the driveway, she heard laughter coming from the backyard, so she skipped the front porch and headed in that direction.

"Am I late?" she asked, rounding the corner of the house, and letting herself through the back gate.

"Arooooo," a large, fluffy dog sang, rushing to greet her.

"Don't mind Scout," Harper advised. "He's singing you the song of his people. He's very friendly."

Riley let the dog smell her hand before dropping to her knees in the grass to hug him.

"I need a dog," she cried to the gathered women. "If only my schedule allowed for it." She rubbed Scout's furry belly when he flopped over offering it to her. "Maybe Owen will let me borrow this one from time to time."

"You could borrow my two as well," Sam offered. "They're a handful but lovable."

"I've always preferred dogs, but I'm seriously considering a cat only because they're so much easier with my odd hours," she confided.

"Come on up, join the crowd," Harper invited. "Food will be here soon."

She walked onto the patio, dropping into a chair next to Jamie.

"Where is my newest niece?" she asked, eager to hold the little munchkin.

"Believe it or not, the guys have her tonight," Jamie said, laughing. "Your big, tough guy brother strapped his tiny daughter to his chest and off they went."

Riley burst out laughing. "When you say 'the guys,' who all is involved in these shenanigans?"

Basically, the other half of everyone seated here," Sam answered. "Apparently, 'Uncle Owen' isn't getting his fair share of Amelia Grace time and planned to snatch her tonight all by himself."

Harper shook her head, laughing. "My man is a mess," she admitted, laughing even harder. "These guys are so competitive. Owen thinks just because Griff has a baby…"

"It might be my fault," Sam said, a definite twinkle in her eye.

"What?" Jamie asked, her nose scrunched up.

"Wait, why would it be your fault?" Harper asked at the same time.

The two women looked at each other then at Sam who sat there grinning. Riley waited for the pieces to fall into place in their minds. In three, two, one…

"Sam!" Jamie cried, throwing her arms around her best friend, "What are you saying?"

"OMG, are you pregnant?" Harper shrieked loud enough for all of Palm Harbor to hear.

"Took you long enough to notice I haven't been drinking anything harder than tea," Sam teased. She flicked a tear from under her eye with the back of her hands. "Damn pregnancy hormones," she muttered.

"And you without a wedding ring! Won't your mother be shocked?" Jamie declared, laughing.

"The only thing that has shocked her so far is Jack's 'lack of pedigree' as she so nicely put it." Her beautiful face twisted like she'd bitten into a lemon. "Riley and Harper, you'll enjoy this, since y'all haven't had the pleasure, using the term loosely of course, of meeting my mother. She encouraged me to 'have my fun' with him before settling down with someone 'far more suitable.'" She tossed her braid over one shoulder. "I told her, quite clearly, where she could put her advice."

"Wow!" Riley exclaimed. "Suddenly, my family seems so much better."

She squirmed in her seat when all eyes turned to her.

"Uh, don't get me wrong. I love my family and am so glad to finally be back with them," she started, searching for the right words. After hearing Sam, she felt a little ill complaining about hers. "It's just, well, they're a bit..." She threw up her hands.

"Much? Perfect? Intrusive?" Jamie supplied, before slapping a hand over her mouth. "Ugh, I can't even blame pregnancy brain for my lack of filter anymore. Can I blame post-partum hormones?" She smiled at Riley. "Trust me, I get it. I love your family and could not have asked for a better one to marry into. But they are a bit much," she ended on a giggle. "I had to draw the line at who went to OB appointments with us."

Riley's mouth dropped open. "Then you get it. Not one day I've been back has passed without someone from my family stopping by or calling to tell me how to do this or where to go for that." Riley threw up her hands. "I'm a grown-ass woman with a medical degree. I've lived in three states all by myself. But the second I come home, I'm right back to being little Riley Jane, baby of the family," she complained.

Scout, as if sensing her distress, walked over and ran his snout under her hand, forcing her to pet him. She laughed and loved on him.

"I really need a pet," she sighed. "Do you know my dad asked me who was going to live in my house with me," she told the astonished group. "Yep, he did. Can't make up that crap."

"What did you tell him?" Harper asked, trying to hold back a giggle but failing.

"In his defense," Jamie began, holding up a hand. "And I'm not defending so much as maybe explaining their behavior. You did blow back into town, sort of unannounced and living in a house you bought sight unseen," she offered with a weak smile.

Riley blew out a long breath. The observation took all the wind from her sails. Her shoulders sagged.

"You're not wrong, but I had no choice. If I didn't come back with a place to live already, I'd be sleeping in my old room right now." She shook her head. "Have you seen it? There are still Harry Potter and Jonas Brothers posters on the wall, not to mention science fair awards on shelves." She shuddered. "It's like a museum."

"You bought a house without seeing it first?" Harper asked, gaping. "That's either incredibly brave or foolish. Not sure which."

"And people say I lack a filter," Sam said, laughing. "Though she has a point."

"My cottage is adorable. Okay, it needs a little work," Riley admitted. "But it's all mine. I think I'll get a cat, a black one because those don't get adopted as quickly from the shelters." She glanced around and saw the expressions on the other women's face. "It's true. I researched it."

"Of course, you did," Jamie said. "Griff is always going on about how smart you are. How you were always reading as a child."

"He's not wrong. I never quite fit," she said on a sigh. "But Lucifer won't care."

"Lucifer?" Sam questioned. She grinned at Jamie.

"That's what your evil spawn of a feline should be called." She turned back to Riley. "So, you'll name your cat Lucifer because he or she is black, I guess?"

"Well, I suppose that fits also, but I meant after the character Tom Ellis plays. Have you seen the show? I mean, that man is smoking!" she exclaimed, fanning her face.

"Evening, ladies, food's here," Luca called, stepping onto the patio. "Harper, hope you don't mind, but I did ring the doorbell."

Riley stared at him for a nanosecond before turning away. *Please don't let him have heard that last part...*

"Mama sends her regards," he said as he set down enough food for a small army. "What are you ladies up to on this gorgeous evening?"

"Riley's getting a roommate," Jamie said, laughing. "A very hot, studly one named Lucifer."

The women all burst out laughing, leaving him standing there with a confused look on his face. Well, not Riley. She wanted to bolt for the nearest dark corner to ride out the waves of embarrassment flooding her face.

"It's a long story," she muttered, flicking a hand as if that explained everything.

But because Luca had apparently decided to become the biggest pain in her butt in recent memory, he merely crossed his arms over his chest.

"I've got time," he said in a voice that made her think of smooth sheets and long, sultry nights.

Not that she had much experience with those things.

"I want a cat, so my dad doesn't worry about me living alone. See, not interesting at all," she blurted out. Why did she always do that when nervous? "Oh, and I want a black one because they don't get adopted as easily. And I'm going to name him Lucifer. And now, I'm going to shut up."

Right after the earth hopefully opened up and swallowed her whole. If it was feeling particularly kind tonight, that was. She tapped her foot, waiting for her face to stop burning. Nope, no kindness coming her way.

"Luca, have you eaten?" Harper asked, much to Riley's horror.

"I'm sure there's more than enough food for another," Sam offered, wicked glance slanted in Riley's direction.

"Isn't the restaurant busy tonight?" Riley managed, hating the squeaky tone that erupted from her mouth.

"No worries, Riley, I wouldn't dream of interrupting a meeting of The Coven," he joked. "Bye, everyone," he called before turning to Riley. She felt his gaze on her, forcing her to meet his eyes. "See you around, Riley."

Then he loped off the patio and disappeared around the corner of the house. She stood there, watching him leave, afraid to turn around, knowing what awaited her. She'd rather face down a three-hundred-pound angry drunk patient than the inquisition that was seconds away. Pasting on a grin, she turned back to the other women.

"Who's hungry? Something smells amazing!" she exclaimed.

All three shook their heads, grinning.

"Nope," Jamie said.

"Nice try," Sam smirked.

"Start talking," Harper advised. "Oh, and I have more wine for you if that helps."

Riley raised her glass. "Hope you have more than one bottle," she joked.

Chapter Seven

"I take 'signs' in my life as seriously as advice from family and friends or proven facts. The universe speaks through events, y'all!"
-Dove Cameron

Luca reminded himself about not believing in signs, for the millionth time, as he sat in his truck in front of Riley's cottage. He glanced at the ridiculous amount of stuff crammed on the floor of the passenger side and sighed. Then he eyed the small cat carrier belted into the passenger seat. A soft yet distinct hissing noise sounded from it.

Riley would have his head...

He glanced at his watch. Seven fifteen in the morning. Her car wasn't in the driveway, which he figured meant she was either on her way to or from work. Or a billion other places but he hoped for on her way home.

"Meow," cried the kitten.

"Guess you agree, huh?" He shook his head. "Now I'm talking to a cat."

Yesterday, just two days after delivering their dinner, Luca had found this little monster foraging for food near the garbage bins behind the restaurant. Inky black and pathetically thin, he'd taken it as a sign from the universe. The kind he didn't believe in.

Riley pulling in next to him cut his musings short. He glanced over and winced. Her eyes narrowed when she saw him. That didn't bode well. He got out of his truck. She got out of her SUV and met him in the middle.

Something in his chest tightened. Even tired and wearing rumpled scrubs, she got to him.

"You cut your hair," he said, instantly wanting to bite his tongue.

Her eyebrows bunched.

"Are you only noticing now? You've already seen me how many times since I've been back?" Then she sighed and rolled her shoulders. "Sorry. Long night. I'm really tired, Luca. Is there something I can help you with?"

His stomach knotted. That tone was all on him. He had wrecked everything between them. It was up to him to fix it. Maybe someday...but he stopped that thought in its tracks. He'd thrown away his chance. He smiled at her, spreading his hands before him.

"I brought a housewarming gift," he said. "Wait right there."

A slow smile spread across her face. Her hazel eyes warmed right in front of him. All traces of fatigue vanished. As a child, Riley had always loved gifts, even the smallest, most off-hand ones. They didn't have to be expensive or come with shiny wrapping paper. It meant someone thought of her, she'd once explained. That someone had remembered her. Her words had cut him deeply, as if anyone could ever forget Riley Layne.

He thought about the ridiculous bear he'd won for her at the boardwalk when they were in high school. That mangy thing had lived on her bed, and she'd called it her 'Luca Bear.' Matteo had razzed him for years, but he hadn't cared. Then he remembered another bear bought by another man, and his smile faltered.

"Luca?" she asked, looking at him expectantly.

"Oh, sorry. Late night. It'll all make sense in a minute." He grinned at her. "Please don't kill me," he said cryptically, laughing when her eyebrows met her hairline.

"Should I be nervous?" she asked, shuffling her feet.

"Too late for that," he called over his shoulder as he reached into his truck. Then he turned to look at her. "Oh, and all sales are final. Now close your eyes and hold out your hands," he instructed.

Her eyes widened. She fisted her hands on her hips and stared him down. He stared back.

"Not sure I trust you enough for that," she said, tone light but her words stung him just the same.

"You're kidding me, right? Who never told Griff it was you who 'accidentally' outed his porn stash to your mother?" he challenged.

Her cheeks pinked as she bit her lower lip, giving him all sorts of other ideas. Porn may not have been the right word for him to say.

"Luca, it happened years ago!" she protested.

"Last time I checked, there isn't a statute of limitations on trust. I never told him, Riley. Now, you either trust me or you don't."

She stared a little longer, maybe the length of another heartbeat or two, then closed her eyes and held up her hands. And he remembered to breathe.

"Okay then. Wait here." He twisted back into his truck, praying the little devil didn't slaughter him. Peering into the tiny carrier, he eyed his opponent. "Let's do this the easy way, shall we?"

Green eyes stared back, never blinking. He swore the damn thing smirked at him. *Was that a thing? Could cats smirk?*

"You do know I just worked a grueling twelve-hour night shift, right?" she complained.

"Sorry, coming," he assured her. He glanced at the tiny kitten once more before opening the door. "Okay, show time. Be good so she'll want to keep you and not kill me so much," he begged the cat.

After scooping it from the carrier, Luca approached Riley, standing there in the sun, eyes closed, hands outstretched. He loved that she still trusted him on some level.

"Ready?" he asked her.

"More than," she answered, grinning.

He stepped closer until he was inches from the tips of

her hands. Even after a long shift, she still smelled of sunshine and citrus, a unique blend that screamed Riley to him. He wanted to wrap himself around her and inhale.

"Luca?" she asked, a hint of laughter and maybe uncertainty in her voice.

"Sorry, here we go." He placed the squirming ball of ragged fluff in her hands, cupping his larger ones around hers to make sure the little guy didn't fall. Then he waited.

He didn't have to wait long.

Her beautiful eyes sprang open. She stared at their joined hands then up at him.

"Who is this?" she breathed before lowering her face to the demon's.

"Wait, be careful..."

But instead of hissing or spitting, the little kitten rubbed its tiny head against her chin, purring, then jumped onto her chest and nestled under Riley's chin.

"I believe this is Lucifer," he began, hoping she wasn't angry. "And believe me, he lives up to his name." He lifted his arm to show her two, fading but still angry looking scratches.

She gasped. "You got me a kitten?" she asked in a husky voice. She raised damp eyes to his.

"I got you a roommate. You said you needed one," he reminded her.

"You got me a black kitten, just like I mentioned the other night," she said, stroking its tiny head.

Watching her fingers run through the kitten's fur, he had to fight a weird sense of something. Jealousy? Could he really be jealous of something that weighed two pounds?

"Despite being raised by the most superstitious woman on the planet, you know I don't believe in fate or signs or anything like that, right?" he asked.

"Of course, Luca. I haven't been gone that long. I believe in science. You believe everything is random. Mama believes everything happens for a reason. What does that have to do with Lucifer?" she asked, pointing her chin toward the tiny ball of fluff.

He told her about finding the stray cat behind the restaurant right after her talking about adopting a black cat.

"I mean really, how odd is that?" he asked.

"Pretty weird, I guess," she admitted, laughing. Her laugh hit him right in the gut. "Although it sounds like excellent timing on his part." She held the cat in front of her face, so they were pretty much nose to nose. "Did you know I was waiting for you?"

"So, you're not mad then?" he clarified.

She turned to face him, grinning. "I should be, Luca. I'm exhausted and really just want to sleep. Now I have to go kitten shopping." Then she kissed the little baby on his head. "But how could I be angry about this?"

"Oh! I forgot. Hold on." He jogged back to his truck and grabbed the bags and a huge thing of cat litter before coming back. "Got you covered."

Riley stared at him, mouth hanging open. "What did you do?"

He grinned. "Well, I couldn't just drop off a kitten, now could I?"

"Let's go inside," she invited.

He followed her up the crushed shell path to her porch. She cooed to the tiny thing the whole way, making him smile even more. He'd definitely made the right call with this kitten. Following her inside, he dropped the bags and looked around.

"Nice place. I like what you've done," he joked.

"Hush now, Luca. Haven't had much of a chance to get things done yet since all I do is work," she said.

"I'm sure your family would help if you asked," he suggested.

She narrowed her eyes at him, making him aware he'd said the wrong thing.

"Or not…"

She sighed and put down the kitten who promptly pounced on the ends of her shoestrings with its claws.

"Of course, they would. They'd do anything I asked of them." She raised a hand and waved it around. "This place needs some work, which is why I got such a good price. I want to paint every room. I don't own any furniture other than what you see." She dropped her arms. "There's a lot to do."

"And you want to do it yourself," he guessed.

"Got it in one," she confirmed, smiling. "I love them, you know I do. They're just so much sometimes. I came home from work, my very first day mind you, to find my dad here with a roofing contractor. He was so sure I'd been 'taken' that he wanted to prove it to me. Didn't believe I'd had the foresight to have an inspection." She shook her head. "They still think I'm seven or something."

"They love you, Riley, even if they can be a bit, well, smothering."

"I know, and I'm grateful. But I've been on my own a long time. What did they think I was doing?"

He shrugged. "Maybe it's hard because they didn't see you doing it? I don't know. Maybe they'll calm down after you've been home for a little while," he suggested.

"Maybe," she echoed, not sounding convinced.

"Have you tried talking to them?"

She rolled her eyes at him. "Have you met my family?" she joked. "No, it's fine. Honestly, I'm so busy with work, just settling in there." Her face lit up. "With the population growth in the area over the past few years, our volume in the department has skyrocketed. They've asked me to take a look at all things related to pediatrics, from protocols to the physical layout in the department."

He reached out and hugged her. The second she was in his arms, he knew he didn't want to let go of her. She felt *right*. Her head fit just under his chin, like it always had. The warmth of her body, pressed against his, stirred something within him. He eased back, setting her away from him again.

"That's amazing, not that I'm at all surprised. They're lucky to have you, Riley!" he praised her.

"It's just that I love working with kids, and most of my colleagues don't. At least not as much. They prefer their adult patients."

"Don't do that," he scolded. "Don't sell yourself short. You've worked so hard to get here. You deserve this," he reminded her.

"You're right, I have." She shrugged her shoulders. "Being home is so much harder than I thought it would be." She dropped her eyes to the floor. Maybe it was to watch the kitten, but he wasn't sure. "On so many levels," she whispered.

And then he knew. He was part of the problem. He'd destroyed a lifetime of friendship in a single night, with only a few words. He needed to fix it somehow.

She covered a yawn.

"I really should get some sleep. At least a 'cat nap' before this one wants to play," she joked.

"I know how to paint," he blurted before he could stop himself.

She stared at him, hazel eyes huge in her face. "What?"

"Painting. I'm good at it. Did my own house. Ask Griff. I helped with his, too." He waved a hand around the room. "I could help you with yours. If you want. I mean, I'm not family, so it would be kind of like you did it yourself."

"Oh, uh, I hadn't even thought about colors yet. Well, other than light, airy ones to go with the beach theme. You know, I used to dream about the ocean when I lived in the desert." Her face suddenly grew pink. "Well, of course you didn't know that. How would you know that? Ugh, I really need to sleep. I'm just saying as much as I loved Arizona, I missed this. I mean the ocean, not you."

She stopped talking. Stopped looking at him. May have even stopped breathing, he couldn't be sure. Luca tried hard to not laugh. *This* was his Riley. The girl who talked in run-on sentences. The quiet girl the world saw who always had a lot to say to him. Maybe, just maybe, he hadn't ruined things between them after all.

"You're tired, so I'm going to go. Pick your colors, Riley, then pick a day. I'll be back. And let me know when. My number hasn't changed."

He turned and left her home before he did something

stupid. Like kissed the breath out of her. Or him.

*****

She followed him out, not to watch his fine butt or anything, but to lock the door behind him. That's what Riley told herself. Then she turned to face her new roommate.

"Well, Lucifer, looks like we're going to be painting the walls soon," she muttered.

She crossed to the bags he'd dropped on his way in earlier. Peering inside, she bit her lip. Luca had thought of everything. She pulled out dishes, food, both dry and wet, treats, an impossibly small collar, and a staggering array of toys. She grabbed an envelope with a sticky note on it.

"You'll see I had the little bugger checked out by a local vet. Dr. Andrews has been a customer of ours for years. Comes highly recommended. Lucifer is healthy as a horse despite his less than stellar beginning to life. Doc thinks he's about eight weeks, give or take. He's had his shots and been dewormed. I made a follow up appointment for you. Info is inside in case you need to reschedule. Good luck with Lucifer. -Luca P.S. He hates me..."

She laughed as she read it a second time before peering down at the tiny kitten.

"You don't hate Uncle Luca, do you? He rescued you from a terrible fate on the streets. How could you hate him? Maybe he's being dramatic. Men do that." The tiny kitten tilted his head back and forth as though listening, making her laugh harder.

She opened the envelope and perused the brief records. Then she laughed even harder.

"Did Uncle Luca miss the part where you're a girl? Well, I'm still calling you Lucifer. Maybe I'll shorten it to Lucy like in the show. His brother calls him that. What do you think? Do you like Lucy?"

Lucy tilted her head and meowed, so Riley took that as a yes.

"Well, Lucy, how about breakfast and bed? I'll get some

things set up for you in the guest bathroom for now, then it's night night for me."

Riley did that, setting up the litter box and some food and water with a few toys and an old towel she unearthed from one of her as of yet unpacked boxes. After settling Lucy in the guest bath, she scarfed down a quick breakfast, took an even briefer shower, and collapsed into bed.

As sleep pulled her down into that warm and comfortable place, Riley thought about Luca and how much she'd missed him over the years. And how much she hadn't allowed herself to even think about him. Now she was back, and he would be here, in her home, painting her walls apparently.

How was she meant to survive that?

Chapter Eight

"Mistakes are always forgivable, if one has the courage to admit them."
-Bruce Lee

That Friday night, the place was packed, always a good thing, but Luca's mind kept drifting back to a certain, feisty ER doctor. He shook his head. Even though he'd never doubted she'd make it, he had a hard time reconciling the Riley he grew up with the professional woman she'd become.

"Luca, wake up," was the only warning he got before his mother whacked the back of his head with her hand. He glanced down at her. "Sorry, did you say something?"

She muttered in Italian under her breath.

"Where is your mind today? I asked if the order was up for table ten." She pointed a thick finger in his face. "I asked for the third time, Caro." Then she pointed at the pot he stirred. "I think the alfredo is done," she said with a laugh.

He glanced down, only then realizing what he'd been doing. He pulled the large spoon from the sauce and laid it aside.

"Let me check on your order, Mama. One second."

"Never mind, I'm on it," Nico yelled from across the kitchen. He hiked a thumb in Luca's direction. "That one may as well go home. Useless this week," he grunted, grinning. "Seems ever since a certain someone moved back home."

Mama glanced between the two men, eyes narrowed.

Then her face broke into a huge smile.

"Ah, finally! Is there something you need to tell me, Luca? Something I have waited too many years to hear?" she asked.

Nico, bastard that he was, grinned and rushed to take the order out to table ten.

Luca turned to his mother to shut down that line of thinking immediately.

"No, absolutely not, Mama. Riley and I are just friends." He crossed his fingers mentally, knowing they were barely that, but it wasn't something he ever wished to explain to his mother, who thought of Riley as the daughter she never had.

Her expression fell. "But, I hoped, now with my bambina finally home…"

He shook his head. "Friends, Mama, just friends. Leave it, please," he begged.

She threw up her hands, muttering. "Fine, fine. I leave it. Is it too much to ask for some bambinos around here?" she asked before walking away.

Luca sighed, knowing he'd only bought himself a temporary reprieve. His single status, and worse lack of 'bambinos,' was a never-ending sore spot with his mother.

"Yo, Luca, your friends are here and asking for you," Nico said, coming back in the kitchen.

"Thanks," he said, not bothering to ask which friends. He slapped his cousin on the shoulder as he passed him. "Do me a favor. Find a nice girl and get married soon, okay?"

He laughed at the younger man's expression as he left the kitchen. Out in the dining room, he spotted Griff and Jack and their respective women seated in a booth. He headed for them.

"Hey, where's my favorite baby?" he called in greeting.

They all laughed.

"I told you," Jamie accused. "Once you have a baby, no one cares about you anymore. All they want to see is the baby." Her laughter lightened her words.

"My parents have Amelia Grace for the whole night,"

Griff said with a huge grin.

Luca laughed, looking at everyone seated at the table. "Then what are you doing out with these guys?"

"Good question," Jack said. "I asked the same thing. But when he suggested dinner here, well, my mom didn't raise any fools."

"What he really means is Jamie mentioned it to me, and I told Jack we were coming," Sam explained. She patted her flat stomach. "While Jamie craved Mexican food all the time, I find garlic is my new favorite thing."

"Wait, what?" He glanced at their faces. Sam grinned while Jack had the look of a lottery winner. "That's terrific news, Sam. I'm thrilled for both of you," he said.

She and Jack both slid out of the booth so he could hug them.

"Wait until my mother hears. She'll be over the moon. She was literally just harassing me in the kitchen about when I'm going to give her babies." He made a face. "As if that's happening any time soon."

"Glad I could help," Sam quipped.

"Speaking of helping. I have an idea I could use a little help with."

He spent a few minutes filling them in on his plan. After they all agreed to help, and to get Harper and Owen involved, Luca turned to leave with the promise to bring out more garlic bread for baby Hardy.

Halfway back to the kitchen, he felt a tug on his arm. Turning, he found Griff next to him.

"Hey, man, do you have a minute and a place we could talk?"

"Uh, sure, come with me." Luca led him to his tiny office and gestured to the extra chair in front of his desk. He walked around it and sat in the one behind it. "What's up?"

His pulse quickened as Griff rubbed a hand down the back of his neck instead of answering. The two had been friends for years. What could he possibly be worried about asking him?

Unless it had something to do with...

"Well, it's about Riley," Griff began.

Great...

"What about her?" Luca asked, having no idea where he was going with this.

"Does she seem, uh, different to you, you know, since she's been back?" Griff asked.

"Different?" he parroted, trying to buy himself time. This was *not* a conversation he wanted to have with her brother. Not after the conversation he'd had with her the other morning. "What do you mean by different?"

Griff stared at him like he had three heads. "Different, Luca. Do you need the Webster definition? Does my sister seem different to you? It's not really a hard question."

"I may not be the person to ask, Griff," he said instead of answering the question.

Griff leaned forward, placing both hands on the desk in front of him.

"I'm only asking because you pointed out the other day that you were her best friend. You didn't hesitate schooling me then. I figured you would know if anyone did. Does she seem different to you?"

Luca winced, remembering that night.

"We *were* best friends, Griff, a long time ago. When we were all kids. I'm really not the person to ask about her these days," he evaded, not really knowing how to answer the question. Not really wanting to discuss Riley with her older brother.

Griff ran a distracted hand down his face.

"I was really hoping you could help me understand her," he said on a sigh. "You know how much I love my sister. How much I always have."

Luca nodded, not trusting himself to speak. Where was this going?

"Maybe it's because we're the youngest in the family, I don't know, but I've always felt closest to Riley. Even though I'm six years older than her."

"Okay," Luca said, still completely lost in the

conversation.

"But then she left." He laughed, but the sound was more harsh than amused. "Of all of my siblings, Riley is the last you'd think would go so far away. Not to mention stay away for so long. Am I right?"

"Well, in her defense, she pretty much did what she always said she would," Luca pointed out. He shrugged when Griff stared him down. "What? When did Riley ever talk about being anything except a doctor? And she couldn't do that without leaving Palm Harbor. If anything, I'm more surprised she came back at all." The last bit he said more to himself and wasn't sure if Griff even heard.

But Griff shook his head. "No, you're right, man, you're right. She did exactly what she set out to do." Griff leaned back in his chair and closed his eyes for a moment.

Luca stared at him and weighed his words carefully in his mind, not sure if he should say what he was about to say.

"So, Griff, when you're asking me if I think Riley is 'different' these days do you mean do I think she's not the same person who left here all those years ago? Because when you think about it, how could she be? You can't expect her to still be the seventeen-year-old who left for college."

"Why is that so wrong?" Griff groaned before sitting up and opening his eyes. "I know, but seriously, she's like a different person. I don't know how to act around her." He threw his hands in the air. "My parents are worried about her."

Luca bit back a groan. "That explains the roofing contractor they sicced on her," he sniped.

Griff's eyes widened. "How do you know about that?" Then he smirked. "Thought you weren't best friends anymore."

"I brought her a housewarming gift," he said by way of explanation. "Never mind. My point is, she's a grown woman, a doctor for goodness sake with a brain bigger than all of ours combined. She doesn't need, or want, everyone fussing over her."

Griff jumped up and started pacing in the tiny space.

"That's all very well and good, but she's still my sister. I love her, so of course I'm going to worry about her. Just like I worry about Jamie and Amelia Grace."

"And that's great, but does Jamie let you coddle her?" Luca asked. "Somehow, I doubt it."

The corners of Griff's mouth drooped. "The last time I tried to tell her how to do something, she withheld sex for a few days." He shook his head. "Didn't make that mistake again."

Luca made a decision and hoped it wasn't the wrong one.

"She's been on her own a long time, and now she's home. Her choice to be back here. And while I know everyone's glad to see her, she's not the same Riley who left all those years ago. She's not a little girl. She doesn't need, or want, everyone telling her what to do or how to live her life." He stared at Griff to make sure he was really hearing him. "I'm only telling you this because she won't."

Then he stood and walked out from behind his desk. When Griff stood, Luca shook his hand. "She's going to be fine, I promise you. Just give her some breathing room and trust her to live her own life," he advised.

"You're right. I know you are." He started to walk out of the office. As Griff got the door, he turned back. This time, he grinned. "I feel so much better knowing you have her back. I mean you're basically another of her big brothers, but this way she doesn't feel like family is breathing down her neck. Just keep her safe, man, thanks."

Luca watched the other man walk away and wondered what the hell had just happened.

*****

On Sunday morning, Riley awoke to the sound of her phone's text alert. Although she wasn't working, she hadn't turned her ringer off. Bad habits die hard. She rolled over to glance at the offending thing.

Seven thirty!

Someone needed to die. She rubbed sleep from her eyes

before opening her texts. Her heart clenched. Although she had long ago erased his contact, she would never be able to forget Luca's number.

He'd texted her…

"Morning! It's Luca, in case you've forgotten my number. May have bribed Harper for your schedule. Since you're off and Nico is covering for me today, paint day has arrived. Will be there in fifteen with caffeine (because I'm not stupid) and donuts (still not stupid nor forgetful). And yes, the maple kind. Be ready!"

She stared at the text then reread it several times until realizing she'd wasted three of her precious fifteen minutes. Because he was the most stubborn person she'd ever met, there wouldn't be any talking him out of this madness.

Shrieking, she jumped out of bed and ran for the shower.

Chapter Nine

"Remember that a gesture of friendship, no matter how small, is always appreciated."

-H. Jackson Brown, Jr.

Eleven minutes after leaping from bed, Riley dashed into her living room, pulling open the front door as Luca lifted an arm to knock. She grinned at him and tried to ignore the fact that he wore shorts and an old T-shirt way too well for her peace of mind.

"Made it!" she cried. She took a step back, allowing him to enter then shut the door behind him. "Mind you, my hair is still soaked, and I have to feed Lucy, but I am not late. I know how you hate it when people make you late." She stopped talking for a minute to suck in some air then held out her hand. "Now, where's my donut? I earned it."

Luca stared at her for a moment before laughing.

"You are something, Riley," he said before handing over a colorful bakery box.

"Sweet jeepers, are these from Better by the Dozen?" she asked, wondering if drool might already be collecting at the corners of her mouth. "I haven't been by since I've been back in town. You know, I used to dream about these."

She hurried to the kitchen and placed the box on her counter. Picking a maple donut, Riley took a big bite, closing her eyes and moaning as the sugary goodness hit her tongue.

She swallowed on a sigh.

"Wow, they're even better than I remembered, if that's possible," she told him. Opening her eyes, she looked at Luca, who hadn't moved, just stood there, staring at her with an odd, intense look on his face.

"Luca? Is something wrong? "She wiped a hand over her mouth. "Do I have some on my face?"

He swallowed hard then shook his head.

"Nope." He closed the distance between them until he was so close to her, she had to look up to see his eyes. "You made this noise when you were eating the donut. Like you really enjoyed it." He reached out to tuck some wet hair behind one ear. "Made me think of other times you might make a similar noise," he said in a low, rough voice.

Time stopped. Everything stopped. Although she knew better, Riley felt as though her heart stopped beating also.

Was Luca Rinaldi flirting with her?

She thrust the box at him. "You really need to try one of these. Of course, you live here, so you know already. And maybe it's just because I've been away so long. But I don't think so, I mean these are the best ever. There was a place in Tucson I liked but not even close to this. They…"

He took the box from her, and then his lips covered hers. *Luca's lips were on hers!* That was her last rational though before sensation took over. He backed her up until the counter bit into her lower back, trapping her against him. She dropped the donut to the counter and reached up, sliding both hands into his thick, dark hair. She moaned when he slanted his mouth on hers, deepening the kiss. His tongue slid against hers, teasing, taunting, making her want things.

Sensations, like currents of electricity, coursed through her veins. The air grew heavy around them. She pressed herself against him, fitting their bodies together until she wasn't the only one moaning. Finally, he dragged his mouth from hers, the sound of his ragged breathing filled the room. He gently kissed her forehead before leaning his against it.

"What have you done to me?" he asked.

"All I did was offer you a donut," she joked while trying

to pull together the shreds of her sanity.

His big body shook with silent laughter.

"Oh, Riley, how I've missed you," he whispered.

"Mreoooowwwww," sounded from their feet. They both looked down.

"Well good morning, Lucy," Riley said. "Yes, I am late with your breakfast." She slowly pulled herself from his arms and crossed to where she kept the kitten's food.

"Lucy?" he asked, more than a touch of humor in his voice.

"Turns out he is a she. Still calling her Lucifer but Lucy for short," she explained.

"Because you like the show," he confirmed.

"Of course," she said, putting Lucy's breakfast down for her. "Not to mention the fact that Tom Ellis is ridiculously hot." She opened her fridge. "Want a water?" she asked with her head in it.

"Maybe later," he said.

When she turned around, he stood there, leaning back against the counter, arms crossed against his chest, sort of growly looking. She tilted her head. "Something wrong?"

"Wrong? No, what could possibly be wrong?" he replied in a tone that said otherwise.

"Maybe you're hangry," she joked. "You always were a bear when you didn't eat. Have a donut. I mean you brought a dozen. Even I can't eat that many." She tapped a finger against her chin. "Although, it's been a while. I may have to give it the old college try."

"They're not all for you," he said. "Don't you think we should talk about…"

The doorbell ringing cut him off.

She looked at the front door.

"Huh, that's odd. Wonder who that could be," she said before walking toward it.

"The other part of your surprise," he muttered.

Riley opened the door, shocked to find half a dozen people standing there. She grinned when she saw Sam, Jamie, and Harper and their guys.

"Wow, what are you guys doing here?" She immediately snatched the baby carrier from Jamie. "I'll take this little pumpkin, thank you very much! Come in, come in."

She stepped back and waved everyone in. Peering down into Amelia Grace's wide blue eyes, she couldn't help but fall deeper in love, as she did every time she got to see her gorgeous niece.

"I may be biased but is she not the cutest thing ever?" she bragged.

"You are, but she is," Jamie joked. "But then, as her mother, not exactly bias free myself."

"I brought coffee," Sam announced, pointing to Jack and Owen who carried several to-go carriers with various drinks. "Don't worry, only mine and Jamie's are the dreaded caffeine free." She frowned. "Between that and alcohol, it's going to be a long nine months," she griped.

"But so worth it," Jamie consoled.

"True," Sam conceded.

"Hey sis," Griff yelled, grabbing her in a gigantic hug. When he let go, he looked around the room. "Love what you've done with the place," he commented, laughing and pointing to the moving boxes still sitting everywhere.

"Funny," she said. "I haven't unpacked much yet because I wanted to paint first." She tapped her temple. "See, there was a method to my madness."

"Ooh, is that a Better by the Dozen box?" Harper asked. Her eyes grew round. "Those are my favorite! And the real reason I stayed in Palm Harbor. Well, that and Daisey Mae's pie."

"Hey!" Owen protested. "I thought you stayed for me."

"Sure, keep telling yourself that," she said as she selected a raspberry-filled donut. "This is my favorite."

"Please help yourself, everyone," Riley invited. "I was telling Luca before you arrived, I'd be tempted to eat the whole dozen."

Her mind went quickly to what else they'd been doing

before everyone arrived, causing her cheeks to heat, but she pushed the thought aside.

"So, now all we need is the paint," Luca announced. He turned to Riley. "Did you choose your colors?"

"I did. Hold on a second." She walked into the kitchen and grabbed a handful of paint color swatches off the counter. "Here you go. I put a check mark on the ones I like. The initials are for which room in the house each color is for," she explained.

He stood next to her, looking down at the colors in her hand. The clean, male scent of him messed with her mind, making it hard to concentrate. She leaned into the heat from his body.

"Are you sure about this?" he asked, looking into her eyes.

She had no idea if they were only talking about paint anymore, but she nodded.

"Okay then." He straightened away from her. "Who's going to the home store with me?" he asked, grabbing his keys from the counter.

"I will," Jack volunteered.

"Thanks. The rest of you can move the boxes out of the way and get ready to paint," he advised.

"Yes, sir," Griff mock saluted.

"Riley, did you get a kitten?" Harper squealed from the hallway leading to her bedroom.

Luca shook his head. "Let's go," he said to Jack and headed for the door.

*****

"So, what's the deal with you two, anyway?" Jack asked when they were less than a block from Riley's home.

Luca tightened his hands on the wheel and refused to look at his friend. Jack had always been the class clown of the group, but he never missed a thing either.

"Not sure what you mean," he said, avoiding answering.

Confessing he'd just kissed the sister of Jack's best friend seemed like a bad idea. Like right up there with New Coke and man buns.

He felt the weight of Jack's stare.

"So, that's how you're playing it, huh? Okay, cool. For now, at least," he granted. "I only mentioned it because things felt a bit tense when we first got there. And then there's the fact Riley didn't look at you the whole time," Jack threw out, laughing. "Very subtle."

"No idea, man," Luca replied, sticking to his guns. He liked Jack a lot, but he wasn't going there today.

"Whatever," he replied before launching into a funny story about Sam and her inability to deal with pregnancy.

An hour later, fully loaded down with enough paint to cover all of Palm Harbor for sure, Luca returned to Riley's cottage. An unfamiliar SUV sat in his parking space, and yet another car was crammed in behind it. He was forced to park along the street. Griff must have been watching, as he and a few others spilled out the front door as he exited his truck.

"Took you long enough," Griff joked.

"What's with the extra help?" Luca asked, gesturing to the other vehicles with his chin.

Griff looked where he pointed then grinned. "Oh, Harper mentioned it at work, and when people found out it was for Riley, a few more showed up. Poor kid seems a bit overwhelmed in there. Since we have so many volunteers and only so much painting to do, Owen and I decided on some other tasks for them."

Luca gritted his teeth.

"Did you think of asking Riley what she might like to have done?" he ground out.

Griff threw him a look he couldn't quite read.

"Of course, I did. I mean, she was standing right there, after all. A few of the women headed out into the backyard to 'tame' it." He shook his head. "Give me a paintbrush any day."

"Luckily for you, there are plenty in the back of my truck," Luca joked before heading into the house.

He walked in, dropping the paint cans he carried inside the front door, then stopped at the sight of Riley, standing alone in her kitchen. She clutched the tiny kitten in her arms.

"Can you believe they all came for me?" she asked Lucy. She nuzzled the top of the kitten's head. "I mean I barely know some of them, and they just showed up on their day off like we're life-long friends." She shook her head. "I've been away too long, I guess. Forgot what Palm Harbor's all about."

A funny little pain settled in around his heart when she wiped a tear from her eye. He wanted to wrap her in his arms, wipe her tears for her.

"Hey, there you are," the guy from the other night said as he walked up next to her. "Hey, who do we have here?"

Her smile hit him right in the gut.

"This is Lucifer, better known as Lucy, and my new roommate," she told him. She held the kitten aloft toward him.

"What a cutie you are," the man crooned, reaching out to pet the tiny cat.

Luca bit back a laugh when Lucifer lived up to her name, hissing and spitting at the doctor.

"Lucy!" Riley exclaimed. Her cheeks immediately washed with color. Then she laid one hand on his arm, making Luca see red. "Brody, I'm so sorry. Lucy doesn't seem overly fond of men."

"That's okay, maybe I'm just out of practice," he joked, making her laugh.

Luca balled his hands into fists and stalked toward the kitchen.

"We're back with the supplies if you're ready to get started, Riley," he announced.

She jumped a little at his voice, turning to face him.

"Oh, hey, Luca, this is Dr. Brody Matthews, a colleague of mine from work. Brody, this is my friend, Luca Rinaldi. I'm not sure the two of you were properly introduced at the restaurant that evening."

"Luca, I am a huge fan," the other man said, holding out one hand. "Your family's restaurant has saved me from a life of frozen meals or worse, my own cooking."

With Riley standing right there, he had no choice but to be civil. Luca shook the other man's hand.

"Brody, it's a pleasure. I'll be sure to pass along your kind words to my mother." He smiled at Riley before turning his attention back to the other man. "I wasn't aware people from the hospital were coming to help today."

He thought his blood pressure might hit the stroke range when Brody slid an arm around Riley's shoulders.

"Well, I'm sure I don't have to tell you Riley is already a favorite among the staff in the department. When Harper mentioned they could use a few more hands, I jumped right in to help." He smiled down at the woman in question, affection in his face. "She's become an amazing addition to our work family."

"I'm sure she has," he agreed in a less than friendly tone. "Can't tell you how happy we are to have her home again where she belongs."

Riley cleared her throat. He looked at her, alarmed to see her face had grown redder as they talked.

"I'm just going to tuck Lucy away somewhere safe so we can get started. If you'll excuse me for a moment," she said before all but fleeing.

Brody watched her go, a puzzled expression on his face.

"Was it something I said?" he asked.

"You have no idea," Luca muttered.

Chapter Ten

"Do not give in too much to feelings. An overly sensitive heart is an unhappy possession on this shaky earth."
-Johann Wolfgang von Goethe

Happy chatter and laughter filled her small house throughout the day. Riley flitted from person to person, making sure everyone had a drink and was fed but mostly basking in the warmth and joy
of friendship.
Which was much easier than thinking about that kiss…
Nico had arrived around one, bringing a carful of pizzas for her crew of painters and would-be gardeners. She bit her lip to keep from laughing when Luca ordered his younger cousin back to the restaurant after Nico insisted he should stay and help. Apparently, he was a touch too flirtatious for his cousin's taste.

She couldn't remember a day she'd laughed more. The women, including Harper's nurse friend, Amanda, who'd been kind enough to come along and drag her husband as well, kept up a steady stream of 'idiot man' stories. Riley had been all too happy to kick in tales of growing up with Griff, much to Jamie's delight.

All in all, the day flew, leaving her content with the understanding coming home had been the right choice. Now in early evening, with the last helpers gone and all the debris dealt with, Riley stood in the middle of her small house to survey the work. She grinned as she glanced around. Soft, pastel colors reflecting the beach replaced the drab off-white walls she'd inherited.

"Not bad at all," she murmured to herself.

"I'd say it's a little better than not bad," Luca corrected, coming in from the back deck. "Looks pretty damn good."

"Oh!" she startled. "I thought everyone had gone." She grabbed her water bottle, more to have something to do with her hands. Then she raised one hand and pointed to him. "This was all your doing, wasn't it?"

"I may have said something to Griff and Jack when they were in for dinner the other night with Jamie and Sam. Just a suggestion, mind you. Sort of took on a life of its own after that," he admitted. "One of them mentioned it to Owen or Harper, and I'm assuming she brought in the folks from your work." He shrugged. "People like you, Riley, they wanted to help."

She felt tears burn her eyes and wiped them away. She crossed the room and threw her arms around his waist. Burying her face in his chest, she breathed in the scent of him. He was familiar and yet not.

"Thank you," she whispered.

"I would do anything for you, Riley. You have to know that," he murmured against the crown of her head.

"I've missed you so much," she sobbed against his chest, letting the tears she'd held in forever finally go.

"Oh, Riley, don't cry. Please don't cry, baby," he soothed.

She felt him lift her in his arms and carry her to the sofa. He sank into it, taking her with him. She curled against his chest, never wanting to leave the circle of his arms. Could this really be happening? Finally? But was it what she really wanted?

He rubbed her back, continuing to whisper things to her, words she barely heard, his tone more than anything bringing her comfort.

She snuggled down against him tighter, letting the tears

come. For so long, she held back her emotions, always playing it safe, keeping everything inside. Throughout her medical training, she'd had it drilled into her head to not get attached, to keep her distance emotionally. It had spilled over into her personal life, especially after Luca had broken her heart years ago.

She stiffened in his arms. *Luca had broken her heart.* How could she have forgotten that one, little fact? She sat up, brushing the tears from her face.

"Sorry about that. I think I'm just tired. Overwhelmed, maybe," she offered. She tried to slide off his lap, but his arms tightened around her.

"What's really going on?" he asked.

She dropped her gaze to the floor. "Why did you kiss me?"

"Because I wanted to more than I wanted my next breath," he uttered, his voice raw.

That brought her gaze up to meet his. She searched his face, for what she wasn't sure. For any signs of a lie? For the truth?

"Since when?" she asked in a tremulous voice she didn't recognize.

"Since forever, or as long as I can remember anyway," he admitted, staring back at her.

"What? But you said all those things to me. You said…"

He held up his hands, as if willing her to stop.

"Please, don't. I know what I said. Please don't make me remember," he begged, hanging his head.

"Just go," she whispered, her heart thundering in her chest. "It's too much to think about right now." She pushed against him. This time he let her go.

Lucy wound around her ankles, purring. Riley picked her up, clinging to her like a buoy.

"We need to talk," he said, gazing at her again, his dark eyes troubled. "We can move forward. You're back home now."

Still clutching the tiny kitten, she walked to the door and

opened it.

"Please," was all she managed, voice breaking.

Luca nodded. He got up from the sofa and approached the door. She held her breath as he slowed but then passed her. When he made it out to the porch he stopped. Without turning, he said, "I never meant to hurt you."

She watched him drive away. Only long after he was gone did she whisper, "That's exactly what I said to Thomas."

*****

Luca drove home with every intention of getting drunk. He'd earned it. His shirt was still damp with her tears. He could still hear her pleas in his mind, only now they mingled with her desperate ones from years ago. A better man would never have kissed her today. A better man would have kept his distance. He had never been the better man. The only question remaining now was his choice of poison. Would it be vodka or tequila? He drove the last few minutes home remembering today, like snapshots in his mind. She'd been so happy. Her laughter, so pure and beautiful, rang out throughout her home. He'd watched her, talking and laughing with the other women, even with Brody he reluctantly admitted, and his heart had soared.

She was happy. She was content. She was making friends and fitting in. Long gone was the too quiet little girl who'd rather sit in the shadows with a book than join in whatever game was being played. She might not ever grow to love being the center of attention, but the shy seventeen-year-old who'd left here so many years ago was long gone. In her place was a confident, charming woman.

A woman he could fall all the way in love with.

Luca shook his head as he pulled into his driveway. No point in lying to himself. He'd been half in love with Riley Layne since he was old enough to know what the word meant. But their timing had never been right. And always at the back of his mind, he'd known she'd leave. He hadn't known if she'd ever come back. And he was never going to be the reason she gave up on her dreams.

"Argh!" Luca yelled when icy water hit his face. He opened one eye long enough to see Nico standing over him grinning, empty pitcher in his hand. He flung his arm over his head to block the rays of the sun.

"Morning, sunshine," his cousin called in an overly loud sing song voice.

But then anything above a whisper would have been too loud.

"Where the hell am I?" he muttered before wincing. Talking hurt.

"Lounger on the deck," Nico answered a bit too gleefully. "Tried to get you to come in last night, but you weren't having it. Once you passed out, I made sure you were safe and went to bed." He laughed. "You're too big to move by myself."

Luca struggled into a seated position, keeping his eyes closed, and hung his head between his knees while he waited out his stomach. It lurched several times as if debating whether or not to keep its contents before settling back down. He heard a thunk near his feet.

"Is that?"

"Yep, Uncle Marco's miracle hangover cure," Nico answered, laughing full on now. "Never could figure out if it works or really just makes you wish you'd died."

Luca opened his eyes enough to stare at the greenish brown concoction. His stomach roiled just at the sight of it.

Hell, no…

He nudged the glass of offensive liquid away with one bare foot.

"No thanks," he told Nico. "I'll take my chances with the hangover." He dragged his hurting body off the lounge chair, mistake number one, to head in out of the sun. Keeping his eyes squinted against the brightness of the morning rays of the sun, he lurched across the patio and into the kitchen.

"Not sure you want to go in there," Nico warned a

second too late.

The pungent smell of frying bacon still hung in the air, giving his stomach second, and third, thoughts about staying quiet. Luca's head threatened to splinter as he ran for the relative safety of his room. He shut the door oh so quietly and flopped across his bed, burying his throbbing head between layers of soft, downy pillows.

Not even a minute had passed before he heard his door creak open.

"What? Why can't you just let a man die in peace?" he moaned, then instantly regretted it since talking hurt.

"I brought pain killers and water. You know, the stuff I tried to give you last night. Geesh, you'd think a guy would listen to his cousin who's studying to be a paramedic," Gino complained.

"Oh, sorry," Luca muttered, unearthing himself from the pillows to sit up again. He swallowed some pills and drained the glass before trying to focus on Gino. "Thanks, man," he said.

"No problem. Hey, maybe Riley's working. She could give you an IV."

Luca groaned hearing her name, since she was reason he was in this shape in the first place. He collapsed back on his bed, pulling a pillow over his face.

"I'm too old for this crap," he griped aloud.

He winced when the edge of the mattress dipped, knowing Gino had made himself at home. He loved his cousin, really, he did. But the man was like a Golden Retriever. Big and goofy and not always the sharpest tool in the shed. Did he really think *now* was the best time for bonding?

"Hey, speaking of Riley, what happened last night?" Gino asked.

"Lower your voice," Luca commanded from beneath the pillow. "And what does that even mean?"

"Oh, sorry," Gino said in a slightly less headache-inducing level. "You were already several shots in by the time I got home last night, man. That isn't like you."

Luca pulled the pillow from his face and propped it behind his aching head.

"A guy can let loose every once in a while without it meaning anything," he responded, hating the defensive edge to his tone.

"Yep," Gino agreed, grinning. "But your mentioning a certain person's name, over and over again, is a bit suspect. What happened with you and the doc?".

"Nothing," Luca bit out.

"Oh, so it's more about what didn't happen then." Gino rubbed his hands together, grinning.

Great, now he'd started down this conversation path, he thought. Luca would have smacked himself in the head if he didn't already know how much it would hurt right now.

"It's not like that, Gino. It's complicated with Riley," he said sighing, wishing death by hangover was really a thing.

"But it never used to be. That's what no one understands. You and she were like, well, thick as thieves, as your mom would say. I remember growing up, you guys were always together." He grinned at Luca. "Did you know I had the biggest crush on Riley when I was a kid?"

Luca snorted. "Who are you kidding, you still do," he accused without any heat. Gino's face reddened at his words.

"That's not entirely untrue. I mean, look at her. Those huge hazel eyes and all those adorable freckles? What's not to love?" he joked. He flexed one arm. "Who knows? Maybe she prefers her men younger?"

But his joke fell flat. Instead, all Luca felt was an intense desire to pound his cousin into sand. *You love your cousin*, he reminded himself. Killing him would not help the situation. Nico was not the problem here.

He dragged a hand down his face, wincing at the headache that remained.

"She prefers them older, actually. Sorry, man," he said without any real sympathy in his voice.

"Nah, she and that guy are just friends, dude," Nico went on, as usual completely oblivious. "Shame, really. Dr.

Matthews is really a nice guy for an old dude," he said, seemingly unaware Luca had checked out of the conversation.

Just friends?

His burst of elation lasted all of a few seconds. Then the crushing weight of reality sank on him again when Luca remembered her words from last night. He had said some terrible things to her years ago. Until he was able to face them, and explain them to her, there was no hope for them.

He glanced at his cousin, saw his mouth moving but had utterly no clue what he might be going on about. He closed his eyes and thought about Riley. One corner of his mouth curled. Not like he had thought of much else since he'd heard she was coming home.

He needed a gameplan. Once upon a time, before everything had gone to hell, they had been friends. Maybe, just maybe, they could start over, be that again. Friends. Maybe he could prove to her he was worth the risk. Maybe he could prove it to himself as well.

Chapter Eleven

"The mere attempt to examine my own confusion would consume volumes."

-James Agee

"Don't have much to sign out to you," Riley said to Brody when he took the seat next to her a few evenings later. She finished charting while he settled in.

"Okay, I'm ready when you are," he said a few minutes later.

She filled him in on her remaining patients, all awaiting various tests before decisions for their care could be made.

"You'll be happy to know I managed to finish three of my peds cases. Know how you feel about them," she joked. "The last one has to be admitted. Appendicitis going to the OR. Surgery should be here any moment for the poor little thing."

Brody gave an exaggerated shudder. "Thanks for sparing me that. And for the record, I love kids." He laughed at her widened eyes. "I do. It's the parents they come with I'm not fond of," he joked.

She laughed. "I can understand that. I try to empathize, put myself in their shoes."

"Since you love them so much, why don't you have any yet?" he asked.

"Oh, sure, like I've had time for stuff like that," she protested.

She grabbed her lunch bag, throwing it in her backpack.

Her stomach growled, remembering she'd only had yogurt and a piece of fruit since lunch, which was hours ago. She hoped there was something edible left in her fridge. Today's shift had kicked her butt. All she wanted was something to eat, a shower, and a long nap. Not necessarily in that order.

"Okay, granted, your life's been a bit consumed with training up until, well, last month, but you're free now," he said, one eyebrow raised.

She snickered at his expression. "Thought we decided to be friends."

To her delight, his ears turned the cutest shade of pink.

"We did, and I didn't mean me," he protested, mumbling something about women being impossible under his breath.

"All I'm saying is don't wait too long." He sat staring at his monitor for the longest moment, leaving her feeling a bit lost. In the brief time she'd known him, Brody took the job seriously, never anything else. He finally turned back to her, blue eyes flat. "You know more than most there aren't any guarantees in life, Riley." He waved a hand around him. "This place teaches us that. Don't put off what's important to you."

"I'm not, Brody, really. But I've been home for a nanosecond. I've hardly had time to unpack, let alone meet anyone," she assured him.

Then he grinned at her, all traces of his seriousness gone. "Are you sure about that? Because I got the very clear impression someone wanted to rip my head off Saturday morning when he walked in and found us talking." He spread his hands wide. "Just saying. Hey, if you need me to cuddle up to you to make him jealous, I'm your man," he added with a cheeky grin and a wiggle of his brows.

"I'm out of here, you crazy man," she announced, hitting him in the shoulder as she got up. "And for the record, Luca and I are friends. Have been since, well, forever."

"Sure, you are. Because I feel that way about all my female friends," he called to her as she left the department.

She shook her head but kept walking, thinking about her

words as she walked out to her car. The wall of humid air hit her as she left the building, but she smiled. It was an old joke in Arizona, where the summer temperatures daily topped one hundred twenty. She would tell her friends that was nothing, since it was a *dry* heat. They should come out East and try to survive a South Carolina summer. Now, she breathed in the air and grinned. She'd never complain about what it did to her hair again. She was home.

Her stomach growled again, and she headed to her car. She briefly debated going through a drive-through, but she was pretty sure some of Mama's pizza remained from Saturday. Visions of that woman's secret sauce combined with spicy sausage were worth the fifteen-minute drive home.

Thoughts of Mama's pizza naturally brought up those of her son, not that Luca ever strayed far from Riley's mind. She groaned and clenched her hands harder on the wheel.

What was she going to do about that man?

Her cheeks flushed as her mind went to the incredible kiss they'd shared. She had plenty of thoughts about what she wanted to do *to* him. He'd always been part of the fabric of her life from the earliest days. Until, well, until he wasn't anymore. Until he'd ripped himself clear of it.

It was easier, being away, being physically separated from him, to deal with it all. When she didn't have to see him every day, she could move on. She learned to make a life without him in it. Why she'd even gone out and gotten herself engaged. Riley winced remembering the fiasco. Not a great example. But she'd had a life without Luca Rinaldi front and center in it. She could do it again. It just might be a bit harder, living in Palm Harbor, where he starred in all her memories.

She shook her head at the foolishness. Time marches on. She was a doctor with a job she loved. She was building a life for herself here in her hometown. She could do this. She would do this. The time when Luca played front and center in all her fantasies was long gone. She almost had herself convinced.

Until she turned into her driveway and pulled next to a black pickup. A truck that looked a little too familiar. There, on her front porch, sat the man himself. Riley sat stone still in her car, torn between driving away again and beating her head against the wheel.

*****

Luca watched her lower her head to the steering wheel in her car, not really sure what that meant but fairly sure it didn't bode well for him. Maybe she was tired from her shift. Maybe she plotted his death. It could go either way he figured. He decided to wait her out.

She lifted her head, stared through him with those incredible eyes of hers. A few moments passed before she opened her door, got out of her car. A few moments in which he sat still, waiting, not breathing. He stood as she approached.

"I brought you some dinner," he said, gesturing to the large bag at his feet.

She glanced down. "Seems like a lot of food for one."

"Well, it might be for two, if you let me stay. Everyone knows dinner's better when it's shared," he said.

"Sounds like something your mom would say," she guessed.

"Maybe because it is. When she asked where I was going, she made sure to include some of her cannoli cheesecake. Knows it's your favorite."

"I could eat," she said as her stomach made a loud gurgling noise. Her eyes widened. "What? I said I could eat. Come in." She walked by him to open the door.

Lucy rushed her as soon as Riley opened the door, meowing and twisting around her ankles.

"Hello, my little demon child," she spoke to the tiny kitten, lifting her up to her face. "How was your day? No mean old man yelled at you? Lucky kitty."

She placed the kitten back on the floor and walked into her kitchen to grab Lucy's food. Once she fed her, Riley turned back to Luca.

"Just need a few minutes to erase my day. Make yourself

at home. Grab something to drink," she invited before disappearing down the hallway leading to her bedroom.

He nodded and grabbed two waters, draining half of his and trying to not think of her in her bedroom when he heard a shower turn on. And now he needed something a whole lot harder than water to get through the evening.

Recent memories of overindulging returned, and he took another sip. He'd stick to water for the immediate future, thanks. Needing something to keep his mind off her in the shower mere feet away, he took the food out of the bag, bringing it to the table. Then he hunted down some dishes and silverware, setting the table. When that only took a few moments, Luca strolled around the living room, taking in the décor she'd put out since painting day. She'd hung a few pictures on the wall, but the mantle drew him. Framed photos of every size drew his eye. All but one contained various shots of her family, from a recent one of her parents to her siblings to various ones of her gang of nieces and nephews. Even Amelia Grace starred in a cute one.

But the photo that caught his eye was one of the two of them from maybe early high school. It had to be after one of his games. His baseball uniform was covered in dirt. He smiled at the camera. Riley stood next to him, smiling at him. He leaned closer to inspect the photo. She wore shorts and a plain T-shirt and her feelings for him as plain as the freckles on her face.

He remembered that day.

"Hey, Rinaldi, question for you," Robbie Hammond, one of his teammates yelled as he jogged to catch up with him.

Luca turned to greet him. "Yo, man, great game."

"You, too. Those losers never stood a chance against your curve ball."

"True," Luca said with all the bravado of a fourteen-year-old male. "Of course, your homerun with two already on didn't hurt," he said with a grin.

"Also true," Robbie acknowledged. He glanced around the now empty field, almost as if looking for someone. "Where's your shadow?"

Luca's jaw tightened. He hated when people called Riley that. "My what?" he asked, voice a bit cooler now.

"You know, Riley Layne, your 'shadow' as everyone calls her. Anyway, that's actually what I wanted to talk to you about." He kicked at the dirt with a cleat.

Luca's gut tightened. He had a feeling he didn't want to hear the question.

"What about her?" he bit out.

"Uh, I was wondering if you thought she'd go to the Spring Formal with me," he said.

Luca smiled at his friend. The kind of smile that showed a lot of teeth.

"Might be kind of hard, since she's going with me," he said.

Robbie held up both hands, backing away. "Hey, man, sorry. I had no idea."

"Well, now you do," Luca said.

He'd asked her to the Spring Formal that very evening, insisting he wanted to go with someone he'd have fun with. And they had. But he wondered now why it was so important to keep Robbie Hammond from asking her all those years ago.

"Hard to believe that was almost half of my life ago already," she said softly from the doorway to the room. "We were so young then."

He straightened before turning to face her. She wore a pair of soft, cotton shorts and a matching T-shirt. She didn't look much older than the picture. Except her expression wasn't so open now.

"We were," he said, shaking his head. "But even back then, you knew what you wanted, Riley. You were always so focused, so driven."

She gave a soft laugh. "Is that what I was? Maybe one way of looking at it, I guess." She sighed a little and moved toward the table to take a seat. "I'm a little lost now, to be honest."

He followed her lead, joining her at the table. Luca dished up salad for both of them, taking a few bites.

"Lost how?" he asked.

She stopped her fork in midair, staring at him for a moment. He got the feeling she deliberated answering his question.

"You're right about that. I was the driven one. The focused one. I did exactly what I set out to do. Only now that I've accomplished it, now what? What's next?" She set down her fork to drink some water. He had to shift in his chair as she swallowed.

"What do you want to be next?" he asked, almost afraid to hear her answer.

"That's the not-so-funny part. What if I don't know?" She laughed, but it wasn't the funny kind, the kind he loved when she laughed with her whole body, with her spirit. This was harsh, brittle. "What if all I've had all along were goals, Luca? What if I don't know what to do next? What if I'm only good at living for the future? What if I don't know how to live in the present. Maybe Brody was right, maybe I should have a pack of kids," she said, the words coming out in a rush.

Wait, what? What the heck did Brody have to do with any conversation concerning Riley and future kids???

"Excuse me? Brody thinks you should have a pack of kids?" he managed to say in a way calmer tone than he felt. Because right now, he felt like punching something, or maybe someone. "Was he offering?" he asked, instantly regretting the words.

She choked a bit on her water. Setting down her glass, Riley wiped her mouth with a napkin.

"No, he wasn't offering to provide me with a pack of kids, if that's what you're asking, Luca." She shook her head and grabbed a garlic knot. Tearing off a chunk, she shoved it in her mouth then moaned.

He barely resisted the urge to adjust himself. At the rate he was going, he'd need a very cold shower soon.

"You're making it difficult to stay mad at you when you feed me," she said, taking another bite of the bread.

"Good to know," he said with a smirk. "And they say the way to a man's heart is through his stomach."

"Hmm, when he has one," she says with a bit of sass. She pushed aside her salad. "What else did you bring me? I'm starving and rabbit food just isn't working for me."

He threw back his head and laughed. "Wow, how I've missed that sass of yours."

"What?" she asked in a not quite innocent tone. "I say what's on my mind. Always have, always will."

"That right there is what I'm talking about. Life is too short to not speak the truth. I've missed it." He reached into the bag and drew out a carryout pan, setting it in front of her. "I made this just for you."

Her eyes sparkled. "Is this what I think it is?" she asked, sniffing the air. "Oh, Luca, I've dreamed of this for years."

Her throaty confession shot right to his groin. He bit back a groan.

"Well, if you've dreamed of Mama's Cucina's lobster ravioli, then you're in luck." He picked up the container and peeled back the lid, allowing a bit of the savory scent to waft toward her. "Of course, if you don't want any, I can eat it," he teased.

She picked up her fork, wielding it like a weapon. "Don't make me hurt you, Luca, because I will. I wasn't kidding when I said I've dreamed of this."

"Fine but before you do, I have to warn you. I've tweaked the recipe. This is *my* version, not my mother's," he informed her.

Her eyes narrowed. "What does that mean exactly? And why would you mess with greatness?" She licked her lips as he removed the carton's lid. "Does your mother know?"

He chuckled at her seriousness. "Yes, she is aware. As if anything gets by Mama," he scoffed. "A few years back, Matteo and I became full partners in the restaurant with her. It was time. There have been some changes. Small at first. She is not a fan of change."

Riley laughed as he dished up their dinner. "Oh, I know. Remember the time Matty wanted to change the font on the menus? The font, not the whole menu. She acted like he'd committed treason." She doubled over laughing. She looked up, tilted her head when he stopped and stared at her. "What?"

"Your laugh. It's one of the things I missed the most. You laugh with your whole body." He shrugged then finished serving up their dinner. "I've missed it."

"Oh," she said, staring down at her plate. "This really is different. The sauce, I mean, is different."

"It's a saffron cream sauce. I hope you like it," he added.

He sat back, watching her take her first bite. Watched her full, pink lips close around her fork. Watched her eyes widen with pleasure even as she moaned.

"Oh, Jiminy Cricket, this may be the best thing I've ever had in my mouth!" she exclaimed before turning the color of a ripe tomato. "You know what I meant, Luca," she huffed out, reaching for her water.

Because he wasn't a stupid man, he bit his tongue. But he couldn't stop the silent laughter from shaking his shoulders.

"Luca Rinaldi, don't you dare laugh at me," she scolded. "I can't help it if I still blush. That's just the byproduct of fair skin and too many years as the sheltered youngest child. I'll have you know, I am a grown woman and can say anything I want," she declared. "Why I have all kinds of sexual innuendo stored up here," she told him, tapping her temple.

"I'm sure you do," he assured her, again chomping on the inside of his cheek.

"Luckily for you, I'm more hungry than eager to impress you right now," she said with her back up. She took another bite, closing her eyes as she savored the morsel.

Glad for the small mercy, he watched her every move, more turned on than if he were watching porn.

They finished their meal without further incident. Deciding to leave while he still could, Luca turned down dessert. He knew better than to watch her eat his mother's cheesecake. There was only so much a man could take.

"When's your next day off?" he asked her, striving for a casual tone, even if that's the last thing he felt.

She was walking him to the door when he asked. She

stopped, turning to face him. It hurt his heart to watch her search his face for some sort of hidden agenda.

"Simple question, Riley."

She blew out a breath. "I'm off until night shift day after tomorrow. Why?"

"See how easy that was?" he joked. "Be ready at nine in the morning. I'll bring donuts and coffee. Oh, and dress comfortably," he said before walking away from her.

He very deliberately did not touch her. No handshake. No hug. Nothing. Because he knew if he touched her at all, he would never leave.

"I'll be ready," her soft words carried to him on the evening breeze, warming his heart.

Chapter Twelve

"Find ecstasy in life; the mere sense of living is joy enough."
-Emily Dickinson

For someone who'd spent a good portion of her life feeling anxious, the waves of *something* rippling through her belly the next morning weren't that. Anticipation? Maybe. Expectation? Possibly. And maybe, just maybe, happiness.

Riley glanced at her phone for the thirty-seven thousandth time in the past ten minutes.. Nope, still not time yet. Thirty minutes left before he would arrive. She blew out a pent-up breath. She felt something brush her leg and glanced down to see Lucy staring back at her with her gorgeous green eyes. She didn't know much about cats, but this one seemed very quiet. She rarely heard a peep from her. Lucy preferred to tap her with a paw to get her attention.

Leaning down, she scooped up the kitten, nuzzling her under her chin. "Well, good morning to you, too, Miss Lucy. Did you have a good sleep?" Her kitten yawned and stretched before settling into Riley's arms a little deeper. She laughed. "I'll take that as a yes. You can come help me decide what to wear."

She carried Lucy down the short hallway and into her bedroom, depositing her onto her bed. "Now, here comes the hard part. I so suck at this part. What does 'dress comfortably' even mean?" She shook her head. "And why am I asking you? Probably not a good sign that I'm getting my fashion advice from a kitten." She grinned then turned to face her closet.

The grin became a frown and then a growl. A sea of scrubs and other inappropriate this-is-not-a-date wardrobe choices greeted her. "Only a man would say 'dress comfortably,'" she told Lucy, who didn't bother to look up from her morning bath. "Ugh."

Grabbing her phone, before she could talk herself out of it, Riley shot off a text to him.

"Explain what 'dress comfortably' means. Now."

She threw the phone back on the bed and immediately wished she could take back the text. Wasn't it bad enough she babbled in person?

Then her phone chirped.

And she dove for the bed. She swiped her finger across the screen to read his text and was overcome with the joint desire to either laugh or murder him. Or maybe both.

"I'm a simple guy. Thought you knew that. I meant to dress comfortably."

She was contemplating where to hide his body when the little bubbles appeared.

*"Does this mean you're naked texting me? *Winking emoji*"*

"Oooh, that man!" she yelled aloud. "No one has ever made me this crazy, Lucy. No one!"

The thought stopped her in her tracks. When Thomas asked her why she ended their engagement, not all that long after he'd proposed, she'd struggled to find a reason he would understand. How to make him understand, without hurting him more, that he didn't make her feel the things she thought she should? Her heart fluttered wildly in her chest as it dawned on her. Life with Thomas had been fine, but she didn't feel any of the highs and lows. It was all a straight line without any peaks or valleys. Looking back, she didn't really feel *anything* for him, other than a bland affection. Certainly not anything on which to base a marriage, a lifetime together.

Her palms started to sweat as the implications became clearer in her mind. A simple text from Luca had her sweating. She couldn't decide what to wear, knowing she was about to see *him.*

She was in trouble.

"Nope," she muttered and turned back to face her closet. She yanked a simple short-sleeved shirt from a hanger and then turned to her dresser. Reaching into a drawer, she grabbed a pair of khaki shorts. Pulling on the clothes, she marched into the bathroom and brushed her hair, slipping on a headband to keep it out of her face.

She studied her face in the mirror, turning this way and that. She liked her shorter hair once she'd gotten used to not being able to throw it up in a ponytail. Dabbing on a bit of mascara and lip gloss and calling it a day, Riley left the bathroom.

"That's all the effort he gets," she announced to Lucy, who merely blinked in response.

Because she badly needed a pedi, she rooted in her closet for her favorite pair of Vans and slid them on. She glanced down at herself. Comfortable would definitely describe her outfit. She shook her head. When did she start caring about how she looked?

Lucy shot off the bed as a knock sounded on her front door. She pressed a hand to her stomach, willing it to chill, before leaving the safety of her bedroom.

"You've got this," she whispered to herself as she approached the front door. She pulled it open and then bit back a groan.

"Morning, Riley," Luca greeted. He stood there, with the morning sun glinting off his still damp hair, taking her breath away. Wearing old, faded denim cut-offs and a maroon T-shirt molded to his chest, he could have stepped off the pages of a magazine. Without even trying, damn him.

You are so screwed…

Hey, uh, come on in for a minute," she mumbled before turning around and retreating into her home. "Let me make sure Lucy is set for the day."

She checked her water bowl, making sure it was filled with fresh water.

"How is your little friend doing?" he asked, glancing around. "Is she hiding from me?"

"I wouldn't take it personally. Brody seems to think it's a male thing. Maybe she was hurt or abused by a guy," she explained.

"Oh, Brody thinks so, huh?" Luca asked.

His brusque tone caught her attention, so she turned to look at him. "Yes, as did Dr. Andrews when I called to ask him about it."

"Here I thought it was just me," he joked. "Guess I'm not special after all."

"Oh, you're special," she assured him with a smirk. "Just in different ways. Now, you promised me a donut and coffee…"

She grabbed her phone and purse before heading for the door. "Be good, Lucy."

"I'm a man of my word. Iced coffee and donuts in the truck," he promised once she locked her door.

"Mom warned me about guys like you," she joked. "Of course, back then it was strange men offering candy and looking for lost puppies. Now it's donuts and iced coffee in their truck. My how the times have changed," she joked.

He held open the passenger door for her and gave her a hand up. "Luckily for you, I'm not a stranger. Otherwise, I'd have to eat all the donuts myself." He flashed a grin of his own. "You know, to keep you safe and all." He pointed to the familiar donut bag on the seat. "There may be one of your other favorites in there. Wanted to keep a little variety going. Can't let it get boring already."

"Hmmm, if it's not another maple one, that must mean…tell me you brought a strawberry lemonade one!" She closed her eyes "Don't you dare tease me, Luca Rinaldi! You know I just might kill for a strawberry lemonade one from Better by the Dozen right now."

He reached around her to grab the bag, coming dangerously close to her. All thoughts of donuts vanished from her head. The scent of clean, crisp male swirled around her.

Luca always smelled of the ocean to her. A little wild, a little untamed, but oh so familiar. She breathed in deeply through her nose.

He grabbed the bag then turned to face her, inches from her face, grinning. His dark eyes sparkled.

"I have what you want right here, Riley," he teased, holding the bag up above her head.

"Yes, you do," she agreed, never taking her eyes from his mouth.

*****

The temperature in the truck soared but had nothing to do with the summer day. Luca dropped his gaze to her mouth, donut bag in his hand long forgotten. Her perfect lips were pink and shiny and begging for his kiss. The air around them thickened. He stared into her eyes, greener than brown today. But more than that, they were wide, trusting, with just a touch of apprehension. It was enough to halt the kiss he had wanted.

He traced the line of jaw with one finger instead, enjoying the silky-smooth feel of her skin. Then he smiled and backed out of the truck to give them both a little breathing room.

"As if I would ever forget your second favorite donut." He tossed the bag in her lap before shutting the door and walking around to the driver's side. He gave himself an extra few seconds to calm down. "I also remembered you like your iced coffee of the vanilla variety, although how you can drink something that sweet is beyond me."

"You remembered," she whispered.

"Of course, I did, Riley. I remember everything. You were my best friend, you know. Until…"

"Until I wasn't anymore," she finished for him.

"Yeah, that." He started his truck but didn't put it in gear. Instead, he turned to her. "I want us to be friends again. I want that more than anything. I know it's a lot to ask. But I *need* you to forgive me." He exhaled loudly. "Do you think you can do that for me?"

She stared straight ahead, wouldn't look at him. He didn't know what it meant, but it couldn't be good. Blood rushed in his ears, drowning out everything else.

Please just give me a chance...

When he thought he might just lose his mind, the tiniest corner of her mouth curled up.

"Well, you did bring me a strawberry lemonade donut," she said. "Guess that's worth something."

He barely resisted pumping his fists in the air and kept them clenched in his lap instead.

"Happy to bring you one every day, if that's what it takes," he said, not joking.

"Jeepers, no, Luca. I'll never fit in my scrubs," she protested.

He snatched the bag from the truck seat.

"Guess you don't want this one, then, huh?" he teased, holding it out of her reach.

She turned to glare at him. "Not nice, Rinaldi. Hand it over or die."

He reached inside to grab his first before surrendering the bag to her.

"Had to make sure you didn't eat mine also," he said before taking a bite. "Now, off we go. Palm Harbor fun day, part one, awaits."

"Part one?" she asked around a mouthful of donut.

"You didn't think I could reintroduce you to all your beloved hometown has to offer in one measly day, did you?" he scoffed.

She threw back her head and laughed. "Of course, you couldn't. 'Go big or go home.' Isn't that what you always used to say?"

"Still do," he assured her. "It's the perfect saying really. Can cover so many areas of your life."

Riley laughed and lowered her window, laughing harder as the wind blew her hair. She inhaled deeply.

"Oh, I missed this," she said on a sigh.

He glanced at her for a moment, the happiness on her face doing funny things to his heart, before returning his gaze to the road.

"What? Humidity? The feeling of trying to breathe underwater even when you aren't actually underwater?" he joked.

She lightly slapped his arm, sending jolts of sensation down it. He'd forgotten how *physical* Riley had always been. She was a toucher, always reaching out to touch him in some way, whether to ruffle his hair or pinch him. He'd bet she had touched him thousands of times over the years without a second thought. What he'd give for those easy times between them back.

"No, silly, the utter joy in the simple things. The salt air or the feel of sunshine on my skin. I've been so caught up in my goals and my life that I forgot to live, if that makes any sense."

"It totally does," he murmured. "I can relate."

Wasn't he guilty of that as well? He stayed so busy with the restaurant, always making sure everything ran smoothly for his mother, who'd worked so hard after their father died. It had been tough for a while. For years really. His mother had been the heart behind it all, his father the brains, so to speak. Her recipes drew customers in, kept them coming back. His business acumen kept them afloat. When he died so suddenly, leaving them all in shock and completely unprepared, they'd really had to scramble to try to fill his rather large shoes.

He felt Riley's soft hand on his arm and glanced down.

"You're thinking about your father," she said. He loved that it wasn't a question but a statement.

"Yes, sorry, sometimes the thoughts creep in at odd times."

Her hand tightened for a moment before caressing his arm.

"Never apologize, Luca. I miss him, too. Your father was such a lovely man." She sighed. "Your parents were relationship goals. Remember how they would dance in the restaurant after the customers left? Mine, too. After all these years, my parents are more in love than ever." She laughed. "Is it any wonder I'm still single?"

She withdrew her hand, folding them in her lap. He felt her withdraw. She felt a million miles away. Even though she sat less than three feet from him, he missed her.

"I do. I asked my mother once about why she'd never even looked at another man since losing my father. She told me, 'Luca, why would I? I've already found my soul mate.'" He cleared his throat, striving for a lighter tone. "At least you were engaged. I never even made it that far," he offered. Then because he couldn't stop himself, he heard himself ask her the one question he knew he shouldn't. "What happened?"

He stopped at a light and glanced at her. She sat looking out the passenger window. He'd given up on an answer when she started to speak.

"I never should have said yes in the first place. I didn't love him. At least not enough to marry him," she said before going quiet again.

He reached out a hand to touch her, but the light changed. He drove on.

"Then why did you?" he asked. He had to know. Luca thought back to that horrible night, remembered watching her, the panic in her eyes. Wanting to bolt, to avoid seeing her say yes to another man yet not wanting to leave her when she needed him.

She huffed out a laugh and shifted in her seat, now with her back to the door, facing him.

"Probably for the worst reason ever, but saying yes was easier than saying no." She buried her face in her hands and shook her head. "All those people, Luca, just staring at us, me really, waiting for me to say yes. It was expected of me. In my mind, I kept screaming 'no' but how could I? How could I say no and walk out in front if everyone I knew and loved in the world?"

"That must have been horrific for you," he began, but she cut him off.

"And you were the only thing that kept me anchored.

The only person I could rely upon to get me through it. Not Thomas. Not my parents or siblings, but you. So, I stared at you and said yes to a man I had no intention of ever marrying." She threw up her hands. "Is it any wonder I'm going to grow old with fifty cats? At least I'm on my way with Lucy."

"I promise to not let that happen, Riley," he said.

If it were the last thing he did, he would keep that promise.

Chapter Thirteen

"I'm living a dream I never want to wake up from."
-Cristiano Ronaldo

"Are you seriously trying to tell me you haven't ridden the bumper cars since then?" Riley asked for the second time in ten seconds.

He shook his head, laughing. "My answer is still no. Doesn't matter how many times you ask," he answered. "Some of us have been occupied running a business," he huffed, grinning.

She grabbed him by the hand and dragged him toward the ride. "Well, it's way past time to correct this."

"Fine by me, but don't cry when I crash into you," he warned.

"As if," she retorted. "You may want to take your own advice. Have you taken a defensive driving course in a several ton ambulance? No? Didn't think so. I've got mad skills, mister." She burst out laughing at his expression. "Yep, that's right. I've come a long way from the girl who flunked her driving test on the first try," she crowed.

"Aren't you forgetting about the second and third time also?" he reminded her.

She rolled her eyes and tried to ignore her burning face.

"Maybe I was a late bloomer. Ever think of that, hot shot?" She stuck out her tongue at him. "We didn't all have an older brother willing to let us practice on their Camaro. Mine was too busy wrapping me in cotton." She sighed. "Still is."

"What?" she asked when Luca shuffled his feet and glanced away from her.

"Nothing," he said. "I had just hoped that situation would have gotten better by now."

"Ha! In your dreams, Luca. Do you know I once cracked a man's chest and massaged his heart, saving his life? Yes, I did. But Griff doesn't think I can be trusted to even cut my own grass."

"It can't be that bad," he said.

"Can't it? Who do you think showed up at nine one morning the second week I got home to do it? I'll give you three guesses," she fumed.

"Okay, maybe he was trying to be nice or helpful?" he suggested.

"Of course, you'd take his side," she complained, moving up as the line moved.

"Hey, I'm not taking anyone's side. I'm trying to understand. Tell me why this was such a bad thing," he requested.

"Because I worked the night before," she muttered.

"Oh," he said.

"Yeah, oh. Griff would have known if he bothered to ask me if I even needed my lawn cut." She let out a frustrated sound. "Look, you know I love him. He's the best big brother ever. He always had my back growing up. But he needs to get it through his thick skull I'm not seven anymore. Nor do I need his protection." Then she smirked at him. "If he's not careful, I'm going to pull out the big guns and go to Jamie about this."

Luca threw back his head and laughed, something she felt all the way to her toes and all points along the way.

"That might teach him," he said, shaking his head. "For such a little thing, Jamie can be scary. Plus, he's totally wrapped around her little finger."

"As it should be," she said. "I'm not afraid to use the weapons at my disposal if he doesn't back off."

The current group of riders exited the cars, allowing

them to enter the platform. She glanced around as she chose her car.

"Did you happen to notice we're the oldest people here?" Then she laughed. "Well, you're the oldest here," she corrected herself.

"I barely have two years on you," he reminded her.

"Gramps is going down!" a teenager called from behind them.

Luca's head whipped around. He made the universal sign for 'I'm watching you' then grinned at her.

"Seems I don't have to worry only about you," he said.

"Oh, you should definitely worry about me." She made a show of cracking her knuckles. "I'm coming for you."

The ride operator recited the rules in a bored tone before the buzzer blared. Riley pounced on the gas, peeling away from Luca, dodging around a few cars. She turned her head to see his teenaged heckler plow straight into him. She didn't even attempt to stifle her laughter.

She laughed even harder when she let a mom and young daughter catch her, hitting her in the side. The little girl laughed and pointed at Riley, her tiny hands on the steering wheel. Riley's breath caught in her throat watching the family. She wondered what that must feel like. Wondered if she'd ever get to experience it for herself.

Within moments, she was literally bumped from her musing by a pair of teenaged girls ramming her from behind. They turned and sped away, chasing after a guy their age. Then she spotted Luca. His car faced away from hers, heading in the opposite direction. Turning her wheel and stepping on the gas, she cut across the free for all track to catch him. At the last moment, she laughed maniacally, screaming his name.

He turned his head, a smile across his handsome face soon replaced by shock, but it was too late to escape her. Riley's car smashed into his, pushing it into the wall and bouncing back off it. Before he could react, the ride ended, and all power to their vehicles was cut. She sat for a moment to wait until everyone came to a complete stop before exiting.

She wouldn't have been able to exit anyway, she laughed so hard. By the time Luca made his way over to her, tears rolled down her face and she sat there with her arms wrapped around her ribs.

"Man, she sure schooled you," his teenaged critic howled as he passed.

"I s-s-sure d-d-did," she cried, still laughing.

"Your driving has improved, I'll give you that much, Riley." He held out his hand to help her out of the car.

She placed hers in it, immediately struck by the warmth and texture of it. She shivered a little at the sensations that ran up her arm.

"Thank you," she murmured, stepping out of the car.

"Since you won, I'll let you buy me some cotton candy," he announced when they were back on the boardwalk. "You must still love the sticky mess."

"I do, but shouldn't you be buying me some, since I won?" she asked, soaking in the atmosphere around her.

"Well, if you want to get technical, I suppose. But you do make more money than I do now being a big, fancy doctor and all," he said. "And I'm a modern guy. I don't have any problem letting you pay for my cotton candy."

"Good to know," she said with a grin. "But in the interest of transparency, I recently bought a house, and you absolutely do not want to know about my student loans. You'd never ask me to pay for cotton candy again if you knew how much I owed."

He grabbed her hand to pull her into line for the messy treat. "As if I'd ever let you pay," he growled playfully.

"Whew," she said, laying one hand against her forehead. "Because once you mentioned it, I'm afraid I have to have some." She leaned in, staring into his dark eyes. "I crave it."

She bit back a grin when he swallowed hard.

"Really? Crave it, huh?"

"Yep, desire it." She stretched up on her toes to place her lips against his ear. "And once I get a craving for something,

Luca, I have to have it," she purred.

"Next!" called the young girl working the booth.

"That's us," Riley cried, dragging him forward in line and ordering a cone for them to share.

She stepped aside while he paid. She knew she was playing with fire and couldn't care less. Luca was attracted to her, as she was to him. Those feelings hadn't changed or died out over the long years. Riley closed her eyes against the barrage of other memories. Reasons getting involved with Luca wasn't a good idea. She'd lived her entire life doing the right thing, making the safe choices.

Maybe, just maybe, it was her time to color outside the lines for once. Take a chance. She only hoped she wouldn't pay for her choice with a broken heart.

Again...

*****

After throwing his change in the tip jar and running though his grandmother's gnocchi recipe in his head—anything to get himself back under control—Luca turned to Riley.

"You're the devil," he whispered and handed the sugary fluff to her.

She laughed and broke off a large piece, her hazel eyes lighting up with joy.

He'd do anything to be the man to make her this happy.

She popped the treat in her mouth, licking her lips and moaning. One recipe wasn't going to be nearly enough. Since they were in public with families everywhere, he tried to remember all the business classes he'd taken. The ones that made him sleepy even at three in the afternoon. Surely that would help with his current *situation*.

"Don't you want any? Because if you do, you'd better hurry," she advised, swiping another chunk from the cone.

He closed his eyes and groaned. "Seriously, you're killing me."

"What?" she asked, all big eyes and not-so-innocent smirk.

"Really?" he asked.

All bets were off...

He grasped her wrist, dragging her behind the cotton candy booth, which offered him relative privacy. The sounds of the summer day faded as he backed her against the building. Luca stepped into her until mere inches separated them. He raised one hand, fingers playing with the ends of her hair.

"I like it this length," he said, his tone casual as if his heart wasn't threatening to beat out of his chest. "May have forgotten to tell you."

She glanced down at her feet before looking right into his eyes. He swore she could see into his soul. But then she always could.

"I cut it after I gave him his ring back," she whispered. Her tongue darted out to wet her lips. He leaned in even closer. "I wanted a change."

"Change is good," he agreed before closing the distance between them.

He watched her eyelids drift close even as a soft sigh escaped her. Her lips parted, and he swept his tongue inside, plundering. She tasted of spun sugar and something uniquely her. With one taste, he already felt drunk on her.

Could he ever let her go again? Could he ever pretend to just be her friend?

Then she pressed her body to his and all conscious thought fled. Without a deliberate plan, his hands wandered around her back and crept up under her hair. He buried them there, anchoring himself to her. He deepened the kiss, sucking on her lower lip until she moaned. He felt her drop the cotton candy then place both hands against his chest. He swore she branded him, right then and there.

Everywhere they touched, he felt the heat between them, scorching him. Would it ever be enough?

Children's laughter dragged him back to the reality of the situation. He broke the kiss, reluctantly, rested his forehead against hers.

"What are you doing to me?" he asked and struggled to wrestle his breathing back under control.

He felt her laughter all the way through his body.

"Not sure, but you're doing the same to me," she accused lightly.

"Well, okay then. Let's enjoy the rest of our day." He linked her hand in his and led the way back onto the boardwalk.

"You owe me another cotton candy someday since I only got to eat part of that one," she sassed. Then she turned to smile at him. "Not right now mind you, but someday."

His chest warmed at the thought of *someday* with her. He wanted many of those with her. He reached out to touch her face.

"If it would put that smile on your face, Riley, I would give you whatever your heart desires."

"Careful, I might hold you to that," she warned, breath hitching.

"You don't scare me." He raised their joined hands, brushing the lightest kiss across her knuckles. "I'm not going anywhere."

"Me either," she assured him.

They wandered along, taking their time, laughing at memories from their shared childhood. She dragged him to a row of games, pointing to one and laughing.

"Do you remember?" she asked.

He looked at the setup of white bottles where a teenaged boy attempted to win his girl a stuffed dolphin. Change it to a bear and take away fifteen years, and it could be them.

"How could I forget?" he murmured.

"You won Luca bear for me here" she said, grinning. "Looks like they decided to switch things up, go for an aquatic theme now."

Sure enough, the row of dolphins he spotted had company. Other shelves contained mermaids, turtles and even a few stuffed crabs.

"Oh, that one looks a little like Sebastian from *The Little Mermaid*," she cried, pointing to the crab.

With her excited tone and jumping up and down, she may as well have been sixteen again, he mused.

"Is that the one you want?" he asked.

"Well, he's no Luca bear but yes, please." Then she smirked at him, raising his pulse a notch or twenty. "If you've still got it, that is."

He gaped at her before laughing. "Are you doubting me, Layne?"

"You're not seventeen anymore, just saying," she pointed out. She crossed her arms over her chest like she was settling in.

"Dude, it's not as easy as you think," the kid next to him said. "And I'm not even old."

"Gee, thanks," Luca ground out. "And for your information, I'm not old either."

The kid's girlfriend snickered. Riley joined in, making him more determined than ever.

"He's just 'well-seasoned' not so much old," she explained to the young couple which made the three of them laugh even harder.

Great, no pressure or anything…

"Hey, man, are you gonna play or what?" the guy running the game yelled out.

"Why, you in a hurry?" Luca asked. He looked around him. No one else was within fifty feet of them.

"Nah, but I get a lunch break," the man explained.

"All right, I'm coming," Luca said. He stepped up to the guy and handed him money. "This won't take long."

He picked up the first ball, juggling it in his hand for a moment. It had been awhile, but the feeling came back. He lobbed it at the stacked bottles, nicking the corner of one of the bottom bottles. It rattled but stayed upright. Another snicker sounded from the kid next to him.

Luca gave him the evil eye

"I'm getting warmed up," he muttered.

"If that's what you have to tell yourself, man," the kid retorted.

Riley sidled up to him. "You realize you're arguing with a kid half your age, right?" she whispered in his ear. "You've got this." Her conviction warmed him.

Her hot breath on his ear did other things altogether.

His second throw missed the target entirely. As did his third.

"You're a bit of a distraction," he admitted.

"Is that what you old folks are calling it these days?" the kid heckled.

"Hey, some respect," Luca demanded.

"Yes, sir," the girl answered. She leaned over to Riley. "He's pretty hot when he's pissed off."

"He's pretty hot all the time," she admitted with a smile.

He smirked at Riley, kissed her fast and hard then plunked down more money. They guy glanced at his phone before handing him three more balls.

"You have five minutes."

"Won't need the last four," Luca said. He fired all three balls in a row, wiping out all the milk bottles from the table.

Then he turned to his critic.

"And that's how it's done." He turned to the guy running the game. "The lady will have the crab, please."

"Yes, sir," he said before grabbing one from a shelf and handing it to a beaming Riley.

"Thank you," she said to Luca before kissing him soundly in front of everyone. She turned to the teenagers. "Some things get better with age. You just can't appreciate it until later. Have a nice day."

Luca laughed before grabbing her free hand. They walked away from the games and crowds. He found a bench near the beach and led her to it.

"What ever happened to your Luca bear?" He shook his head, laughing. "I can't believe you called it that."

She stared out at the waves, seemingly lost in thought. He waited for her to answer him. Finally, she turned back to look at him.

"I lost him, just like I did a lot of things that meant the world to me, Luca."

Chapter Fourteen

"Some things are best left to memories."

-Bez

Riley clutched her stuffed crab tighter than necessary. Anything to not think about Luca bear and what the man himself had asked her. Then she remembered she was a professional, educated woman pushing over thirty and loosened her death grip.

Get ahold of yourself!

"You didn't answer my question. I didn't understand what that douche bag was talking about on Christmas Eve, when he prattled on about the bear." He raked a hand through his thick, dark hair, making Riley's hands itch to do the same.

"Somewhere along the way, I lost Luca bear. I'm not sure how or when but sometime during residency. One day he was there, and then he wasn't. Apparently, Thomas thought he could, I don't know, 'replace' him." She snorted. "That didn't work."

What she didn't tell Luca was that Thomas wasn't able to replace *him* either in her heart. Better to keep that information to herself.

"Wait. You kept the bear all that time?" he asked, his voice rising by the end.

She closed her eyes for a moment then opened them and stared into his dark brown ones. She often fantasized they were the color of the richest dark chocolate.

"Yes," she said in a low, soft tone and silently willed him to not ask anything further.

But she could practically hear the unanswered questions in his head. He wouldn't let her off that easily...

"But why?" he asked, his head tilted.

She thought about lying. Telling him something other than the truth. But that wasn't who she was. Who they had always been. She sighed.

"Because it was all I had left of you," she whispered.

She would have loved to blame the late morning sun for the heat in her face. More than anything, she longed to hide from his gaze. And the old Riley would have. She would have run and hidden. But this Riley had learned somewhere along the way to stand up for herself. She held his gaze and searched for any sign of pity in it. She could handle anything but that, she thought.

"I was an idiot," he muttered before reaching out to wipe a tear from her face she hadn't even felt.

"That's in the past now," she said.

He shook his head. "It's not okay how much I hurt you, Riley."

"You're right. You broke my heart." She took his hands in hers when he winced. "I don't say it to be cruel. Just in the interest of full disclosure. But we aren't those people anymore. We've both grown up. We're in different places now, maybe better places to be, well, us." She swallowed hard, fighting with every fiber of her being to not look away. "If that's what you want."

"Finally," he said before lowering his head to hers.

His body blocked the heat from the sun but brought another, more delicious heat with it. She met him halfway, leaning into the kiss. His arms wrapped around her waist, anchoring him to her as if he couldn't bear to let her go ever again. She was okay with that.

She traced the seam of his lips with the tip of her tongue, asking for entrance. He growled and pulled her tighter, squashing them chest to chest. She wound her arms around him, raking her hands into the hair at the nape of his neck, loving the feel.

Luca deepened the kiss, sliding his tongue over hers, giving her ideas of things they could do if they weren't on a public beach. She pressed against him tighter until she didn't know where he ended, and she began. Then she dragged her mouth from his. She grinned at his mumbled words of protest before placing her lips against his ear.

"The things I want to do with you were not meant for a family beach," she murmured. Then she stood and extended her hand. "Coming?" she asked with a wicked grin while she slid her shades back into place.

"Yes, ma'am," he said, taking her hand. "And so will you."

*****

Baseball stats from his high school career, his mother saying the Rosary, String Theory if he had any idea what it was other than something he heard on his favorite sitcom. These were all the things running through his head as they walked back to his truck. Anything to chill the heck out. The moment she placed her hot lips against his ear and whispered *that*, he was a goner.

"You okay?" she asked with a grin when they finally reached his truck.

"Never better. Why?"

"Oh, nothing. You're kind of walking funny, that's all," she said, laughing.

"Wait until I get you home. You're going to be the one walking funny when I get through with you," he threatened.

"Promises, promises," she said in a singsong voice.

"That's a promise all right. Actually, more like a guarantee," he boasted.

"Huh, we'll see," she said in an unimpressed tone.

Luca helped her into the truck, giving her one more brief

but searing kiss before shutting the door. He smiled when he saw her touching her lips as he got in the driver's side. He grinned at her.

"There are so many places I want to taste you," he said.

A soft gasp was his only answer.

"But in the interest of getting to your house in one piece, let's talk about something else. Tell me about medical school."

She burst out laughing. He felt her gaze on him. "Goodness, Luca, why would you ever want to know about that?"

"Because it's a part of you I know nothing about. You were gone for so long." He glanced at her for a moment, waving a hand in her direction. "This person who came back is a little different. Another version of the Riley I knew. I want to get to know you again."

"Well, I guess I'm Riley two point oh then," she said with a little laugh. "Honestly, it started the very first day at Clemson. I remember so clearly watching my parents drive away. I stood there in the parking lot, and I knew no one on campus."

Her words gutted him. She was supposed to know someone there. *Him.*

"Riley, you know I would have been there, if I could have," he began, only to have her hold up a hand.

"Don't. I'm not trying to make you feel badly, Luca, just telling you a story. You did what you had to do. I know that now. Heck, I knew it then, only I didn't want to admit it. I was too immature. Too scared. Too selfish."

The memories of that awful time washed over him. He drove in silence for a little while.

"Luca, Griff just told me you're not planning to go to Clemson in the fall anymore. What happened?" Riley asked. Her eyes, brimming with tears, begged him to tell her it wasn't true. "Why did I have to find out from him?"

"I didn't know how to tell you," he said, dropping his gaze to the ground.

"But we tell each other everything," she whispered in a broken tone.

We used to, he thought.

He shrugged. "I can't go." He waved a hand around the restaurant kitchen. "They need me here. There's too much at stake."

"But this was our plan," she cried. "This has always been our plan." She reached out her hands to him.

He hated hurting her, but he didn't have a choice. He stepped back, out of her reach.

"Plans change, Riley. You don't always get what you want," he told her in a flat voice.

"Luca, did you hear me?" Riley asked, dragging him from the past.

"Sorry, no. What did you say?"

"Thought I might have lost you there for a moment." She placed a hand on his arm, her touch scorching him. "I said I'm sorry to have brought up such painful memories. Sometimes, I think they're better off left in the past."

He shook his head and covered her hand with his.

"It's okay. I miss my dad every day. You didn't make me think about him. And his dying when he did certainly changed the course of my life. Sometimes, I wonder what might have been different. But that's wasted emotion. All we have is right now." He turned his head and grinned at her. "Right now is looking pretty great from where I'm sitting."

She squeezed his hand and dragged it to her warm thigh.

"I'm glad you think so. Anyway, as I was saying, that was the beginning for me. The beginning of a new me anyway. It didn't happen overnight, and I still hate public speaking or being the center of attention."

"I remember," he said then regretted his words.

"Oh, that. Well, yes. Thomas was, is still I imagine, a lot more outgoing than I will ever be. Even the new, improved me."

"There was nothing wrong with the old you," Luca all but growled.

She sighed. "Not wrong, per se, but I needed to be more comfortable in my own skin. I needed to change for myself, Luca, not for anyone else. Certainly not for *him*. This started long before I met Thomas. Still, what he did, it wasn't…"

"What you would have chosen for yourself?" he guessed.

"Exactly," she said.

He heard the relief in that one word, as if happy that someone got her. *He'd* always gotten her.

"Feel free to tell me it's none of my business, but why aren't you together anymore?"

He waited while she sat there, not answering, and wondered if she would. Had he pushed too far? Was it really any of his business? There had been a time when they told each other everything. But those days were long gone.

"I wasn't in love with him, at least not like I should have been. I cared for him, loved him in my own way, but I wasn't *in love* with him. And he knew it. We were friends throughout medical school, but nothing ever happened between us until…"

She stopped talking for a moment, and acid bathed his stomach. Luca would bet his last cent on the words to follow. He sat in silence as he drove, dreading them.

Riley slumped in the seat. "When I got back to Dartmouth after seeing you, things changed between Thomas and me. We started a relationship then. But I never felt for him, well, I never felt what I should have for him. I think he believed proposing would somehow push me into loving him." She laughed then, a bit harshly. "Can you imagine?"

"Did he know you at all?" Luca asked. "I mean you might be quiet, but the Riley I know isn't a pushover. No one makes you do anything you don't wish to. Not now, not ever."

She turned to him, grinning. "Right? How did it escape his notice? People confuse shy and quiet for doormat somehow. Well, that's their mistake. The other thing that really ticked me off is Palm Harbor."

"Huh? What does home have to do with this?" He risked a quick look at her before returning his gaze to the road.

"Thomas is from Denver. He comes from a huge medical family. They're all doctors. All of them. And they all live and practice in Denver still. He made it perfectly clear he would never live anywhere else. Well, so did I. Returning to Palm Harbor had always been part of the plan. He followed me to Arizona for residency when I never asked him to. Yet, somehow, he didn't believe me when I said I always intended to come home one day to practice medicine. Or worse, he thought he could, I don't know, maybe change my mind." She threw up her hands. "Honestly, I liked him a lot more before we got together."

Acid churned in his gut. He would never like the guy. Never. Did not like him on Christmas Eve. Liked him even less now if it was possible.

"When did you know it was over?" he asked. He entwined the fingers of his one hand with hers where it lay on her thigh.

She sighed, stroking his hand with her fingers of her other.

"It was over before it ever began to be honest. I never saw it coming, the proposal. He blindsided me." She barked out a laugh. "And not in a good way. We were friends who fell into a relationship. I never meant for it to be more than, well, sex, if I'm being honest."

He made a choking noise and gripped the wheel harder.

"What?" she asked. "Do you really think men are the only ones who need sex, Luca?" Her laughter filled the truck.

"No, of course not. I didn't expect you to be so, uh, casual about it. Griff would have a heart attack right now if he could hear you."

"Ewww!" she exclaimed, horror in her voice. "Why would I ever talk to my brother about my sex life?"

"You wouldn't, I'm just saying. Okay, I literally have no idea how this conversation got so out of hand," he admitted.

"Might have something to do with the fact you can't seem to handle the idea of me liking sex so much," she guessed.

"Uh, no, I most definitely want you to enjoy sex. Maybe not with other guys, though."

She laughed so hard, her whole body shook. He knew

he sounded like an idiot but couldn't seem to help himself.

"Why are men so stupid?" she said aloud. "Don't bother to answer. No one can. Let me see if I understand so far. You're driving us to my house so we can have sex, but you're upset when I admitted to liking sex? Is that correct?"

He blew out a breath and wondered how he'd gotten his foot so far down his throat.

"I'm not upset," he ground out.

"All evidence to the contrary," she pointed out. "Okay, let me ask you this then. Are you a virgin?"

"What?" he practically yelled.

"You heard me. Answer the question."

He shook his head. Luca slowed before taking the exit off the highway to bring them back to her section of Palm Harbor, buying him a little time to think.

"It's not a difficult question, and if it helps, I already know the answer," she sassed.

"Of course, I'm not a virgin."

"Okay. Did you think I was?" she asked.

"No?" he said without a great deal of conviction.

Her laughter rang out once again. "OMG! You're one of them!" She stopped talking and buried her face in her hands, laughing so hard, he worried she wouldn't be able to breathe.

"Take a breath," he commanded. "Then tell me what's so damned funny."

It took her a few minutes to regain control. She wiped a thumb under each eye.

"Wow, that felt good. Haven't laughed so hard in a while. It's just the old double standard thing. I never would have suspected you capable of it. It's fine for guys to go out and have all the sex they want. But women? Not so much. Unless of course, we're what? Married?"

"I never said that," he grumbled, although her comment hit a little too close to home. And it was more about her having sex with someone other than him.

"Well, since I think we're about to be intimate, and I certainly hope we are, let me lay it out there for you. My years of medical training were intense. It was nonstop, twenty-four hours a day pressure. I had no desire, nor time, for a relationship. Some did. I had friends who even got married. More power to them but no thanks. I had an 'arrangement' for lack of a better word. A friends with benefits arrangement."

He dragged his hand down his face, not sure he wanted to hear this.

"Go on," he said, figuring if she was willing to tell him, he should listen.

"Thomas became one of those and then he became something else. Oddly enough, I didn't even notice at first. I was always so focused on school and work. When I had time, and our schedules meshed, then it worked out. But then it became dinner and the odd weekend away when we could manage it, though it was rare."

"And then you got engaged," he couldn't help but point out.

"Yep. With all the world to see. And that, my friend, was the beginning of the end."

She stared down at her hand, her empty left hand where the ring didn't rest anymore. He wondered for a fleeting moment if she held any regrets.

"I never intended to say yes, I told you already. Later that night, when we were alone finally, I let him have it. Asked him why he would do something he had to know would make me so uncomfortable." She shook her head. "He never really answered me. I believe he planned it that way, cornered me when he knew I wouldn't make a scene."

"Sounds about right, not like I know him or anything. Did you guys talk about what you would do after residency? Where you would live?"

"Again, I never felt the need because I had been honest with him the whole time. My plan, always, had been to come back here. He knew. Everyone knew. But he didn't listen or worse, thought he could change my mind. You'll find this hilarious. I gave him the ring back on the plane."

"What? You mean on the way home after Christmas?"

he asked, eyes darting to see her face.

"Yep," she said, popping the end of the word. "He spent the little time we had here trying to convince me, and then my family, how happy we were going to be in Denver. How much I'd love it. You know there's no ocean in Denver, right?" she asked laughing.

"One of the drawbacks of living in a land-locked state," he agreed.

"That's what I said!" She clenched and unclenched her hands a few times. "He just didn't seem to get the lack of respect in what he was doing. Thomas truly believed he could talk me into this. Into giving up my dreams and doing what he wanted."

"Guess he sees the error of his ways by now," Luca said with a smirk, feeling the tiniest bit of sympathy for the man for the first time. Not enough to actually care, though. "So, there you were, on the plane," he prompted.

She let out an aggravated noise. "Right. There we were on the plane, and he just would not stop. No matter what I did, he kept talking about how great things would be. His mother had found a 'darling little house' for us. What? I don't have any say in where I get to live? It may have been the last straw. Either that or I feared my ears might start to bleed. So, I took off the ring and handed it to him."

"Just like that?"

"Yep," she confirmed. "Well, not really. You've probably gathered he's a bit determined. Used to getting his own way. I eventually had to threaten a restraining order."

He felt his blood boil at her words, tossed out so lightly.

"Excuse me?" he said, fighting for control.

"Oh sorry, not really. Those were the words I tossed out to get him to back off. He didn't become a bunny boiler or anything. Whew! No, way too dignified. I think no one had ever said no to him is all. Thomas couldn't understand I meant it, had already moved on. The fact I had, without even breaking a sweat, or my heart, told me all I needed to know."

"So, then he stopped?"

"He did. Thankfully, we only had a few months left. And our specialties were so different, there was never any danger of overlapping unless we ran into each other in the hallways. Of course, we did from time to time. He found it harder than I did because I wounded his pride."

"Or maybe you broke his heart," he offered.

She sucked in a breath. "Oh, I hope not. I worry about that, you know. I sleep easier thinking I only wounded his pride. But in the end, I did what I had to do."

He turned into her driveway and turned off the car.

"Huh, didn't realize we were home already. Nothing like the sad tale of my love life to make the miles pass," she joked.

"I'm sorry if bringing this up hurt you, but I'm glad you told me," he said. He took her hand, turning it over to kiss her palm. "I wanted to understand. And you're right, some things are better left in the past."

"Agreed." She undid her seatbelt and reached for him, pressing a hot kiss to his lips. "Come with me. I'm much more interested in the present."

Chapter Fifteen

"It is always good to make new friends."
-Jose Feliciano

Only moonlight creeping around the edges of her shades lit the room when Riley awoke. She wasn't sure what pulled her from sleep, either her stomach or bladder. One was empty, the other full. She glanced at Luca, sleeping on his side next to her. She placed a gentle kiss on his temple before sneaking off to the bathroom. Once she took care of that pressing issue, she grabbed his discarded T-shirt and headed into her kitchen to address the other.

They'd bypassed dinner altogether.

Lucy wrapped around her ankles, almost tripping her as soon as she left her bedroom. She bent down and picked up the kitten, who promptly purred and nestled under Riley's chin.

"Hello there, sweetness. Did you miss me? Or did you miss your dinner? Possibly the first but definitely the latter," she joked.

She placed her down on the kitchen floor and got her some food and fresh water. Then she stared into the fridge hoping to find something easy to eat. No one, at least not her, wanted to cook at four in the morning.

"Hey, what are you doing?" Luca asked, coming up behind her, scooping aside her hair and dropping a kiss on the back of her neck.

"Someone made me miss dinner," she said before

pressing back against him.

"Hmmm, bad someone, although I don't remember hearing you complain."

"Maybe because you were too busy screaming my name?" she guessed and laughed.

"Hmmm, not sure, but I think it may have been you screaming mine," he countered. He hip checked her aside and reached into the fridge. "Want some eggs?"

"Sure. I'll make the toast," she offered. She started to make coffee also. "You know it's only four in the morning, right?"

"Your point? Tell my stomach. I'm famished. Besides, we crashed kind of early."

Her cheeks heated, remembering why they'd crashed early.

He raised one dark brow and chuckled. "I love how you still blush. It's a lost art form if you ask me."

"No one asked you," she said, sticking out her tongue at him. "Trying being taken seriously by patients when you look this young and still blush so easily," she groused.

"Huh, never thought of that," he admitted. "Still, you're doing what you always dreamed, so that must not suck," he joked.

"It really doesn't. It's everything I always hoped for and so much more. They're such a great group in the department. Everyone from my fellow docs to the nurses and techs to all the support staff, every last person has been so welcoming. It's amazing. To have a job you love. Well, it's everything!"

"I can relate. Of course, there's the obvious challenge of working day in and day out with my family but I wouldn't trade it. I love how the restaurant has become the place people come not only for family meals but to celebrate important events. I know you were off in Arizona, but Sam and Jack threw a very impromptu surprise engagement party for Griff and Jamie there. And in June, Owen held a super-secret surprise birthday party for Harper. I like that people think of us for their special events."

"As you should," she said, hugging him. "Mama's Cucina means a lot to the community, far more than just a place for fabulous pasta. You guys sponsor so many children's sports teams and other community events. You have so much to be proud of."

"Thank you, Riley, it means a lot coming from you." He turned back to the stove to finish their breakfast.

She watched the smooth ripple of his muscles as he cooked, wanting to run her hands, or tongue, over them. Memories of doing just that not so long ago warmed her cheeks further. She shook her head and grabbed juice from the fridge. There would be time for those thoughts later.

A few minutes later, they sat down to their feast. Her eyes popped at the omelets he'd whipped up.

"I can see the advantages of sleeping with a chef," she joked. "I may be able to save your life, but I can barely boil water."

"Then you're just using me for my culinary skills." He placed his hand over his heart and frowned. "Oh, how the truth hurts."

"Well, that's one of your skills which interests me," she said with a sly smile. "I'm hoping you might give me a refresher on the other after breakfast."

"You may just be in luck," he said, taking a bite of his eggs without ever taking his eyes from her.

Her girl parts stood up and cheered as she grinned.

"Other than work, what have you been up to? Had time to catch up with any old friends? Make any new ones? Heard a rumor you've been inducted into The Coven," he said.

"You did, huh? Which of you goofy men came up with the name? Had to be my brother." He shook his head, not answering. "Well, you better hope we aren't really witches, cooking up spells. We've haven't had a chance to do much yet, but those are some cool women. My brother and his friends chose very well for themselves. Those women keep them on their toes. I love working with Harper when I get the chance. She's an excellent nurse with amazing experience. Always seems to know what I need before I do."

"Wow, it's not every day a doctor is willing to admit it, I'd bet," he said.

"You're not wrong," she acknowledged. "I have no trouble admitting it. She has way more experience than I do in the trenches, and I'm smart enough to learn where I can. I admire her greatly, and the department is lucky to have her."

"Have they taken you for Mexican yet? Sam and Jamie have a favorite place they like to take everyone called La Hacienda."

"Funny you should ask. We're going next week for dinner. Took a minute to sync our schedules. I hear they serve a mean margherita," she said, laughing.

"Not really my drink of choice, but if Sam and Jamie vouch for it, then you should be fine. Will you need a designated driver? I'm happy to be of service," he offered.

She laughed at him. "You don't even know what night I'm going. Don't you have to work? And exactly what kind of 'service' are you offering, sir?" she asked in a husky voice.

His eyes smoldered as he gazed at her. "Doesn't matter what night. I'll make sure I'm available. As for the service, let me give you a sample."

Before she caught his meaning, Luca stood and scooped her from her chair, running down the hall with her over his shoulder.

*****

Two days later, Riley sat in the employee lounge at work, enjoying a brief moment of peace, and a cup of tea, when Brody came in.

"Hey, stranger," she called to him. "Haven't seen you in a few. I was beginning to think you might be avoiding me."

"Nah, I like working with you since you take care of all the tiny humans. I took a few days off to go back home." He grabbed the seat next to her and dropped into it heavily.

He didn't wear his usual mischievous expression. And

his eyes looked haunted somehow.

"Where's home?" she asked.

"Middle of nowhere, Alabama near the ocean. I haven't lived there in years, but I go back every year this time."

"Oh." She placed a hand on his forearm. "Is this the anniversary?" she asked.

This brought his head up quickly. Something flashed through his eyes, too brief for her to really see it. Greif? Surprise? She wasn't sure. He nodded but didn't say anything.

"I know it doesn't really help to hear it, but I'm sorry for what you went through, Brody. If you ever need to talk about it, I'm always here," she offered.

The very corner of his mouth curved up. "Thank you. You're a kind soul. I'll be okay in a day or twenty. You know it's been a few years, and most days, I am fine. It's just hard this time of the year."

"Of course, it is. Anniversaries are always hard. I imagine they always will be if you loved her." She threw up her hands. "I'm really the worst person to talk about this. I'm hopeless when it comes to love."

He tilted his head, a slow grin spreading on his face. "Not hopeless. Maybe you just need a little push?" He shrugged. "But then I think it's what most of us need."

"Not so sure. Most days, I feel like I don't have a clue when it comes to understanding other people," she confessed.

She thought about Luca and wondered what exactly they were doing. The sex was off the charts. But he was also the man who had broken her heart a few years ago. Did she really trust him to not do so again? And what if he did? She couldn't run away to hide this time.

She took a sip of her tea and willed away such bleak thoughts.

"Seemed pretty clear from where I was standing," Brody said with a chuckle. "Seriously thought the dude was going to rip my head off when he came in and found us chatting in your kitchen."

"What? Luca? No, he's just always been, well,

overprotective of me. We grew up together," she explained.

Brody shook his head. "It was not a back-off-from-my-sister vibe. That was a man straight out marking his territory. He has it bad. Maybe he hasn't mentioned it to you yet, but trust me, he will." Then he laughed as she felt her face warm. "Okay then, maybe he has. Good for you."

The door opened and one of the day shift nurses walked in. "Hey, Riley, I was looking for you," she called.

"Hey, Sarah. Sorry I was hiding for a minute. What's up?" she asked.

"Oh, it's not about a patient, sorry to bother you," the nurse said.

"No bother, Brody was only harassing me, so you're a welcome rescue," she explained.

"Hey, I resemble that remark," he said, making them laugh.

"Speaking of rescue." Sarah slid her phone from her pocket. "I heard someone mention you might be looking for a kitten. Is it true?" She turned it to show Riley a picture of a tiny, white kitten with huge blue eyes.

"Oh goodness, who is this ball of floof?" Riley gasped.

"He is the last of a litter of kittens I have left. I work with a local rescue and fostered the pregnant momma cat. She and all of the litter mates have been adopted. This little guy is special needs, which of course makes him harder to adopt out. So, I was wondering…" she said with a grin.

Riley sighed, knowing she just got one cat closer to being the crazy lady with fifty cats.

"Well, I did just get a kitten last week, but I was thinking because of my crazy hours about getting her a friend. And it looks like they'd be about the same age. Tell me about his special needs."

Sarah pulled up a chair. "Oh my gosh, you'd be a lifesaver. He has a congenital deformity in his one front leg. The vet assured me it doesn't cause him any pain, and he gets around okay with it. He does have an interesting gait because of it. Kind of looks drunk to be honest. There may be further complications as he grows, so it'll have to be monitored." She bit her lip. "I know, it sounds like a lot."

"Not really. I mean, I am a doctor. I can certainly take care of him and make sure he gets the professional help he needs." She sighed. "I am going to become the crazy cat lady. I went from zero to two cats in a week."

Sarah leaned in and hugged Riley. "You're the best. I can bring him to you whenever you're ready. He's up to date on all his shots and ready to go."

"No time like the present," she said with a grin. "Are you off at seven? I could follow you home and get him."

"I am, and that's perfect." The phone in her pocket rang. "Oh, I better get back out there. I'll see you," she said and ran out of the room.

"You're a pushover," Brody accused, laughing.

"I'm really a dog person, but don't tell Lucy and Gabriel." She laughed at his expression. "Lucy you met already, short for Lucifer. This one I'm calling Gabriel, as in the Archangel. At least this way, I'll have the balance of good and evil living in my house."

"You really are a mess, Riley. Why didn't you get a dog if it's what you wanted?" he asked.

"I didn't feel like my weird schedule allowed for one. You know, our hours are long, and I live alone. That isn't changing any time soon." She pointed a finger at him. "Stop with the look you're giving me."

"What look?" he asked all too innocently.

"That's exactly the look my brother always tried to give my mom after eating the last of the cookies," she said on a laugh. "He never admitted it either, even though she always knew everything we did. Scary woman, my mother. Luca and I are, well, I have no idea what we are. It's neither here nor there. What I am is a woman well on her way to fifty cats." She finished her tea. "Better get out there."

"I'm coming. Time to start my shift," he said, holding the door for her.

*****

Across town, Luca stood in the kitchen of Mama's Cucina, smiling as he worked through a busy dinner rush. This never fazed him. Some people lost it when the kitchen got this busy, but not him. It meant they were doing everything right.

"What's with the sappy grin?" Nico said, entering the fray. "You finally getting some?" he guessed.

"Hey, watch it," Luca muttered, slapping the back of his cousin's head as he passed.

"Sorry, man, I figured since I haven't seen you at home the past few nights..." Nico held up his hands as if in surrender.

"Nah, my bad, forget it, man. Just cool it with how you talk about Riley, okay?" he asked.

He stood there, waiting for the bomb to go off. The hundreds of questions.

Nico, smug bastard he was, grinned. "About time, don't you think?" Then he grabbed some orders and exited the kitchen, leaving Luca staring at the swinging door.

"What's wrong, are you sick?" asked his mother, feeling his head. "Do you need soup?"

"What? No, why would you ask me?" He snapped back to attention.

Then he laughed. No matter what was wrong with anyone, food was his mother's answer. Broken leg? Have some pasta. Cold? Have some soup. Fever? Again, soup's the answer. Broken heart, she swore by her fettucine alfredo. His family joked Mama should work for the UN. She'd solve the world's problems in a week.

"It's a busy night, and you're standing in the middle of my kitchen, staring into space. Either you've taken the drugs or you're sick," she diagnosed. "If it's the first, I'll get my wooden spoon and beat you to within an inch of your life. This ought to do the trick. If it's the other, than my wedding soup should cure what ails you." She eyed him up and down, standing there, hands on hips. "So, which is it?"

"Ma, I'm fine. I've never done 'the drugs' as you like to

say, and I feel fine. I was only thinking about something. Now let me get back to work. It's crazy busy out there."

She crooked her finger at him, causing Luca to sigh. It could only mean one thing. He leaned down until they were on eye level. At barely five feet even, Mama Rinaldi stood more than a foot less than her two sons. It didn't mean they weren't afraid of her.

She took his face in her hands and stared into his eyes long enough to make him want to squirm. Then she smiled in a way that made him want to run. Anywhere.

"Ah ha!" she cackled. "I knew it. Very good. Back to work with you," she ordered, dismissing him.

He shook his head, knowing better than to ask. Whatever she thought she had seen in his eyes was enough to get her off his back. For now, anyway. He wasn't stupid. His single status was the 'bane of her existence' as she liked to remind him. A lot. She'd be back. But for now, he had a lot of cooking to get to.

He glanced around to see where he would jump in when his phone buzzed in his pocket announcing a text. His heart galloped, hoping it was from *her*. Their intense schedules didn't make it easy, and he hadn't seen her since that night, or early morning.

He read the text, said heart almost stopping.

"There's a new man in my life…"

Then a picture popped up of a tiny, fluffy kitten. Bubbles followed, indicating she was sending another text.

*"At the risk of becoming that woman, meet Gabriel. Want to come over later to meet him? And maybe take a nap? *Winking emoji* I've missed you."*

He felt lighter, reading her words. She missed him, too. Good, he wasn't in this, whatever it was, alone. He typed back immediately.

"For the record, send the picture first next time. Almost needed your CPR skills. What time are you off shift? Happy to bring your favorite dish. And my PJs. Oh, that's right, I don't wear any."

"Chef, I need two of tonight's specials and an order of

veal piccata," one of the waiters called, dragging him back to the present.

He slid his phone back in his pocket, whistling. He had no idea what they were doing, but he was happy. For now, it was enough.

Chapter Sixteen

"It is the sweet, simple things of life which are the real ones after all."

-Laura Ingalls Wilder

Riley awoke to the feeling of being watched. She smiled, stretched, and murmured, "Good morning," before even opening her eyes.

Two pairs of eyes met hers, One blue. One green. No chocolate brown eyes in sight. She glanced around the room. No sign of Luca.

"Where is he?" she asked the kittens. Not being very helpful, they didn't answer. "Well, you probably want your breakfast, don't you?"

She got up and threw on a short robe before following the delicious scent of coffee and something freshly baked into the kitchen. The sight of flowers on her counter stopped her in her tracks. She grabbed the note propped at the bottom of the vase.

"Hated to leave without waking you, but duty calls at the restaurant. Got you caffeine because you're a beast without it in the morning, sugar because you're sweet and have a huge sweet tooth, and flowers just because. Miss you already. -Luca"

She smiled and reread the note and then again. He knew her, and she loved it. She was a beast without her morning dose of caffeine. She sniffed the white cup, breathing in the rich roast with a hint of cinnamon as she loved before taking a healthy sip. Next, she opened the white box from Baked with Love, a local bakery in town since before she'd been born. Their cinnamon rolls were to die for. Could he have? She peeked in. Yes! She popped the box in the microwave for a few seconds to warm it, taking the time to sniff the gorgeous blooms on her counter.

Riley tried to remember when someone had done something so thoughtful for her and failed. She grinned thinking about everything he done for her last night also. Then her body warmed, remembering. No wonder those long-unused muscles protested this week.

Her phone chirped as the microwave dinged. Hmmm, which to answer first. She grabbed her phone and headed for the other, taking out her treat and inhaling the delicious aroma. Sitting at the breakfast bar, she pulled apart the gooey goodness with her fingers, popping a chunk in her mouth and moaning in appreciation.

She slid open her texts to see one from the man himself. A picture popped up of a shirtless (speaking of yum!) Luca cuddling Gabriel to his chest.

*"Good morning, Bella. Hope you've found your treats by now. As you can see, I have won over one of your little monsters. The other remains a mystery. Both have been fed. You're on your own for the litter box. *Gagging emoji* This is where I draw the line, even for you. Have a great day!"*

Riley set the phone down, laughing. Not a huge fan of it herself, she understood. She glanced at the kittens, who had leapt to the bar stool next to her and sat staring at her while she ate. She rubbed each of their little heads.

"Good morning, my friends. Nice try, but I have it on good authority you've already been fed."

Then an idea struck her. She picked up her phone and took a selfie, something she normally hated, of herself eating a piece of the cinnamon roll. She wore a huge smile. She texted it to him with the caption, #BreakfastOfChampions.

She heard a clatter and looked down to see a tiny, black paw swiping at her plate.

"Oh, no you don't, you little devil," she scolded Lucy. "I see you were aptly named."

She placed her on the floor and finished eating before rinsing the dish and putting it in the dishwasher. Then faced with a day off and no plans, Riley thought about how to fill the hours. She looked around her house, knowing she had many unpacked moving boxes yet lacked the desire to tackle them today.

Her phone chirped once again.

"Glad you enjoyed it. Dinner tonight? Wear something sexy!"

Her heart sped up at the thought of dressing up for him. She'd never done it in all the years they'd known each other. Yes! No! Riley raced down the hall and into her bedroom, kittens at her heels, before halting in front of her large and mostly empty closet. The sight did not encourage her.

Scrubs in every color of the rainbow? Check. A seemingly endless supply of T-shirts. Got them. Jeans, capris, and shirts. Yep. Something sexy? Not even close. She scrunched her eyes shut and threw herself on the bed. What was she going to wear? Do?

Then it hit her. Sam! Even though she barely knew the other woman, no one ever looked as good and put together as she did. She jumped up and ran back into the kitchen, balls of floof once again in hot pursuit.

"Let's think of this as our cardio for the day, shall we?" she said to them.

She grabbed her phone and dialed. She didn't have to wait long.

"Hey, Riley, what's going on this morning?"

She glanced down at her phone, realizing the time.

"Oh, Sam, I'm so sorry. I forgot you're at work," she started.

"No worries. Nothing earth shattering I'm in the middle of," the other woman assured her.

"Whew. I have an emergency only you can help me with," she said.

"Uh, what kind of emergency? I mean, you are the ER

doctor, so…" Sam drawled, laughing.

"A fashion emergency," Riley answered.

"Ah, now it makes way more sense. Hold on, I'm putting you on speaker. I want Jamie to hear this," she said. "Okay, go ahead. Jamie, Riley's on the phone, and she's calling me with a fashion emergency. I thought you should hear this."

"Hey, Riley!" Jamie called from the background. "Hold on a second."

Riley wasn't sure why this would take both of them. Then she heard what sounded like her niece snuffling.

"Is that Amelia Grace I hear?" she asked

"Say 'hi' to Auntie Riley," Jamie told the baby.

"Hi, pumpkin," Riley said. "Hey, Jamie, if you're busy, I really just called to pick Sam's brain about something."

Whatever Jamie might have said was drowned out by the sound of Sam's laughter. Riley got more confused.

"Uh, okay, it wasn't that funny," she muttered.

"Sorry, did you think I put Jamie on to help?" Sam asked. "Oh, honey, you should try an open mike night somewhere. No, I wanted her to hear someone asking me to help them with something fashion related. She always acts like I'm killing her whenever I try to even suggest something."

"And by 'suggest' she means burn my entire closet," Jamie grumbled.

"Again, how many Margaritaville T-shirts does one woman need?" Sam asked.

"Uh, maybe we could discuss this at dinner. Right now, I need help," Riley interjected.

"Go ahead, Riley. Sam is practically salivating," Jamie quipped.

"Kind of true, snarky but true," Sam agreed.

"Okay, here goes." She took a deep breath. "So, I have a date, and he texted 'wear something sexy' which sounds great, but I basically own scrubs, jeans, and shorts. Help!" she wailed.

"And by *he* you of course mean the delectable Luca," Sam purred.

"Sam!" Jamie cried. "I'm telling Jack you said so," she

joked, laughing again.

"Go ahead. He's the one who knocked me up, setting me adrift in a sea of pregnancy hormones. You could have warned me, Jamie," she accused.

"I would have thought all the times I mentioned wanting to climb Griff like a tree would have been fair warning," Jamie rebutted.

"Oh, eww, TMI! TMI! He's my brother. And while I am ever so thankful for my amazing niece, I do not, ever, want to think about how she got here," Riley cried. She blew out a breath. "Ladies could we just focus on the task at hand please? I need something sexy for tonight. What do I do?"

"Easy. Threads & Things," Sam replied.

"Go to Threads & Things," Jamie said at the same time.

Both women laughed.

"And what exactly is Threads & Things?" Riley asked.

"Jamie had to go take care of the princess. It's a vintage clothing store in town. Been there a few years now. It's where we got Jamie's wedding dress and my maid of honor's gown. Mind you, the week before the wedding. It's a fabulous boutique run by a really nice woman named Sadie. Tell her we sent you. She won't steer you wrong."

"Are you sure, Sam? I'm horrible at this stuff. I spend my life in scrubs and am way more comfortable in them," she said on a sigh.

Why was she making this so difficult? This was Luca. She'd literally spent her entire childhood with him. He'd seen her at her very worst.

And that was exactly why…

"Trust me. The woman is amazing. We walked in there and had our dresses in under an hour. She looked at me and said, 'I have just the thing,' and came back carrying the dress I wore for Jamie's wedding. I mean who can do that?"

"Wow! Of course, with a body like yours," she muttered.

"Hey, none of that. Luca is having dinner with you, Riley, so he obviously sees something he likes. Trust me, go to Threads & Things. Sadie will not steer you wrong," she advised.

"Okay and thanks," Riley said.

"And we want to see pictures of this sexy outfit," Sam joked before disconnecting.

Riley glanced at the phone. Better get this over with before she chickened out.

Forty-five minutes later, freshly showered and still unsure, she stepped inside the small boutique in the middle of town. Riley didn't know where to look first. Clothing of every shape and size filled the space. Walls covered in light blues and greens, reflective of the seaside town, soothed her frazzled nerves a bit. She took a few deep breaths and headed toward a rack of dresses.

"Good morning and welcome to Threads & Things. I'm Sadie. How may I help you?" said a woman with a sunny smile coming toward her.

"Oh, thank goodness," Riley blurted then slapped a hand over her mouth. Her shoulders lightened when the other woman laughed.

"You look like you might need some help," she suggested. "Maybe if you give me an idea of what you're looking for, we can start there."

"First, I'm thrilled you're Sadie," Riley blurted, once again wishing the ground would open up and swallow her.

"Huh, can't say I've ever heard that before," the woman joked. "Although, most days, I'm pleased to be me."

Riley waved a hand in the air. "You'll have to excuse my runaway mouth. It gets the better of me at times. My friends Sam and Jamie sent me to you, swore you could help me," she explained. "I'm Riley Layne, by the way, Jamie's sister-in-law."

Sadie's light blue eyes lit up at the mention of the other women's names. She clapped her hands.

"Oh, I love them! It was such an honor to help with Jamie's wedding." She leaned closer to Riley. "Though I'm not going to lie. When she told me her wedding was the same week, I about lost it."

"Well, this is not for a wedding, mine or otherwise. I need something sexy to wear to dinner tonight." She shook her head. "Who am I kidding? I need a whole closet full of things, but I'll start with dinner tonight," she joked.

Sadie eyed her from the top of her head to her feet and back up again. Her intense stare left Riley wanting to hide, but she stood her ground. Then Sadie's gentle smile put her right at ease.

"I get the feeling you don't ever think about clothing. Am I right?"

Riley burst out laughing. "Not more than 'what color scrubs am I wearing today,' no. Sorry, not my thing." She waved a hand around the store. "This is gorgeous. What you've done here is amazing. You clearly have an eye, something I obviously lack."

"I imagine Sam told you how easy she was," Sadie said, laughing. Riley nodded. "But women like Sam are easy because they're confident in who they are. She has spent her whole adult life developing her fashion sense and style. This hasn't been important to you. And that's fine. But now it is. At least for tonight. Am I right?" she asked gently.

"Hit the nail right on the head," Riley answered.

"Okay, so we start from scratch. I promise this won't hurt. Do you mind if I ask you a few questions first?"

"Uh, no, I guess not. I mean you are the expert," Riley answered, wiping her damp palms on her shorts.

"Just remember to breathe, Riley. Start by telling me about yourself. What colors do you prefer? What fabrics? What makes you feel comfortable? Do you want to know the key to looking sexy? It's feeling sexy. If you aren't comfortable in what you're wearing, it'll show."

"That makes sense. I never thought of it that way, I guess. I like to be comfortable. I like soft fabrics that flow, nothing tight or constricting. I love the ocean. I just moved back home and had been living in the desert for a few years." She grinned at Sadie. "I was so homesick at first, so I filled my apartment with everything I could find on the internet to remind me of home. I had a flip-flop shower curtain and little turtles everywhere. My one sister even sent me shells from the beach here. I had them strewn throughout."

"That explains it then. I saw your face when you first walked in today. You wore a sort of panicked look. But then you calmed right down." She pointed at the walls. "The colors relaxed you. I find them quite soothing myself. Been a beach bum my whole life," she said with a grin.

"Me, too, until I moved away for school. But I'm back now and couldn't be happier." She glanced around. "Not gonna lie, I found this a bit overwhelming."

Sadie threw back her head and laughed. "I'm a bit of a pack rat, I'm afraid, when it comes to this place. I can't resist whenever I come across pieces I just know someone will love." She tilted her head, studying Riley again. "With your coloring, you're a dream to dress. Take a look around, I'm going to pull a few pieces for you to try. Be back in a moment."

Riley glanced around, no idea where to even start. Deciding to stay outside her comfort zone, she stuck to the area with skirts and dresses. She drifted around a few displays, allowing her fingers to glide over the various materials she encountered. She thought about Sadie's advice and grinned. She'd never taken on clothes shopping this way before, always facing it, dreading it really, from a practical standpoint. Have an interview? Buy a suit. Have a dinner date? Buy a dress or skirt. But now she looked at the various offerings with different eyes.

She sought out the colors that called to her. The blues and greens of the ever-changing ocean. The pinks and oranges of the sky at dawn or sunset. She loved the outdoors, always had. Even as a small child with her nose pressed in a book, Riley had always preferred to do so outdoors, where the breeze played with her hair and the sun kissed her skin.

Before she knew it, several pieces found their way into her hands. She did a little victory dance and kept going.

"I see you took my advice," Sadie said, rejoining her.

"I did. You're like a magician or something," Riley

praised. "I've literally never felt this comfortable clothes shopping before."

The other woman beamed. "It might be the nicest thing anyone has ever said to me." She tilted her head toward the far corner of the store. "Come this way. I hung a few items for you to try in the dressing room."

Riley followed her, carrying the items she'd picked also. She stopped right inside the door and stared at a dress hanging on the wall.

"What is this?" she cried. She rushed forward, fingering the layers of filmy material in a riot of pastel blues and greens.

Sadie grinned and pointed to the dress. "That is going to be perfect for you!" she answered. "Try this on and come out to let me see," she said as she slipped from the room.

When the door clicked shut, Riley shed her shorts and shirt before slipping the dress from its hanger. She sighed as she slid the silky material over her head. The dress fell into place, hugging her curves but not making her feel constricted. She turned to face the mirror. And blinked. And blinked again. Was it really her looking back?

The muted swirl of pastel colors set off her glowing tan. Her toned calves peaked out from the handkerchief cut of the hem. She said a quick thanks she'd taken up running in medical school as a way to deal with the stress. The thin straps didn't allow for a bra, but the bodice came with built in support, so she wouldn't need one. Riley turned this way and that, watching the dress swirl around her. She couldn't find a single flaw.

She ran out of the room in search of Sadie. "You're a genius," she called, almost running into the other woman who stood a few feet outside the door.

"Wow, girl, look at you!" the other woman said, seeing her. "Turn around," she commanded, gesturing with one hand.

Riley pirouetted, feeling a little like a ballerina as the silky material flared around her bare legs.

"When I came in looking for something 'sexy' I would never in a million years have picked this," she confessed.

Sadie grinned. "See? What did I tell you? Sexy starts with how you feel in something. We're all trained to think of sexy as something black, tight, or low-cut. Anything can be sexy if you wear it right and it makes you feel that way."

"You've got mad skills, my friend. Mad skills." Riley grinned. "Hey, I have a great idea. What are you doing tomorrow night?"

"Well, let me see." She tapped a finger against her chin as if considering. "There's always inventory, of course. Curse of owning your own business. And then there's my perpetual back up plan of comfort food and Netflix. Why?" she asked, eyes dancing with humor.

"I'm having dinner with the others at La Hacienda, and I think you should come. You're a perfect fit with the rest of them," she added.

"And by the rest of them, how many are we talking?" Sadie asked.

"Oh, not as many as it sounded. Sorry. Sam and Jamie will be there, and you already know them or have at least met them. Then there's their friend Harper. She's lovely and a nurse in the ER with me. I think that's the whole Coven. So far anyway." She laughed at Sadie's rounded blue eyes. "We're not actually witches. Well, maybe certain times of the month we are. My brother, Griff, invented the name as a joke."

"Ah, brothers. Have a few of those myself, so I get it. If you're sure I'm not intruding, I'd love to come. Truth is, when you run your own business, it can be pretty solitary. I spend so much time here, I forget to have a life," she admitted.

"I'll let the ladies know ahead of time, but I know it's not a problem. Sam was thrilled to send me to you," she joked. She glanced down at the dress again, brushing her fingers over the soft material. "Now, let me go see how much more damage to my credit card we can do."

"I'll never say no," Sadie agreed with a grin.

Chapter Seventeen

"Crikey means gee whiz, wow!"
-Steve Irwin

Luca walked up to her door, wiping his suddenly damp palms on his trousers. He shook his head. This was Riley. There was no reason to feel like this. Like his heart might just beat right out of his chest at any moment. He stood on her porch for a moment and gathered himself. This was Riley, he reminded himself again. And then it struck him why he was so nervous.

This was Riley...

Even though they'd already slept together, this was dinner out, in Palm Harbor, for anyone and everyone to see, with Riley. The woman he'd spent more than half of his life being more than half in love with. He straightened his shoulders.

Let them look.

He raised his hand to ring the bell as she opened the door. And all conscious thought fled.

"Hey," she said in a soft tone.

He said nothing in return, staring at her in a dress designed to torture him. He remembered learning somewhere along the way you can't actually swallow your own tongue. Didn't feel like it right now.

Her soft laugh filled the evening air. "Would you like to come in for a moment while I grab my things?"

"Sure," he responded, snapping out of his lust-induced

fog.

No more than three steps in the door, a tiny, white fluff ball pounced on his feet. Luca scooped him up.

"There's the other man in her life," he greeted the kitten, who head-butted him and purred. "Where's your feline companion? You know, the one who hates me."

"Lucy does not hate you," Riley scolded. "She's just not as openly affectionate."

Lucifer, as he preferred to think of the cat, darted out from under a chair to wind herself around Riley's ankles, purring loudly.

"I rest my case," he snarked.

"With men," Riley amended. "She's not as openly affectionate with men. She's warming up to you," she suggested in a hopeful tone.

"If by this you mean she hasn't drawn blood in a few days, then sure," he joked.

"Okay, kids, be good. No hitting the liquor cabinet while mom's gone," she cautioned. She shook her head. "Ugh, I'm well on my way to crazy cat lady. Someone get me a dog, quickly," she moaned.

"Thought you were afraid your hours didn't mesh with having a dog?" he asked.

"They don't. But I feel like I might not get any more cats if I had a dog," she admitted. "I didn't say it made sense."

"But cats aren't like potato chips. You can have just one." He smirked at her. "Or in your case, two."

"Very funny, not. Good thing you're cute. Now, can we go, please?" she requested, walking toward her door.

"Cute, huh," he muttered. "Sexy? Sure. Ruggedly handsome? Hell, yeah. Cute is for puppies and babies, maybe even baby goats in pajamas, though I'm not sure I get it. No grown man wants to be thought of as cute."

"Okay, hot, delicious, sexy man, let's go."

He walked outside and waited until she locked her door. Then he spun her against it and kissed her breathless. When neither one of them could see straight, he lifted his head.

"I like that much better, thanks."

"Ugh!" she cried in a faked tone. "You're all impossible."

"Not quite what you said last night," he whispered in her ear, as he opened her door for her.

Riley resisted the urge to fan herself even as she clenched her thighs under the dress. Barely.

"You make a good point," she conceded. She waited until he got in the car and started driving before reaching over and sliding her hand into his lap. "But two can play at this game." She smirked at him. "Now, since I'm all dressed up, something I never do, where are you taking me for dinner?"

"There aren't enough words for how you look tonight. I would have told you earlier, but I momentarily lost my ability to speak. As for dinner, it's a surprise."

"You clean up well, yourself, Luca."

And he did. The white button-down made his deeply-tanned skin glow, while the pressed black dress pants showed off some of his other assets quite nicely she thought. He'd rolled up the cuffs in deference to the heat, and with both hands on the wheel, the musculature of his forearms caught her eye. And made her want to do things to him.

"The infamous Layne Family Labor Day Picnic is almost upon us," she reminded him. Not that he needed it. The two families had been friends since before either had been born. Luca's family had attended forever. His mother's antipasti always graced the buffet table, not to mention the desserts the Rinaldi family brought. Her mouth watered remembering them.

He snuck a glance at her quickly before returning his gaze to the road. "Not likely to forget, since I've been to it every year since, well, probably since I was conceived. Any reason you're acting so weird about it now?" he asked.

"No reason other than my mom has made it her mission to see me 'settled' as she likes to put it. She's mentioned all kinds of eligible young men for me to meet. You know, the son of one of my dad's clients or the nephew of their neighbor's chiropractor. Being the youngest and only single one left, she can't handle me on my way to being an old maid. Wait until she hears I have another cat." She laughed aloud in the truck. "It may send her around the bend."

She snuck a glance at him, noticing how his knuckles tightened on the wheel.

"Any reason you haven't mentioned us to her? Seems like her trying to match you with the neighbor's barber or whoever might have proven a convenient time, Riley," he grated.

"Have you mentioned *us* to your mother yet? And for the record, I wasn't aware there was an *us*. This thing, whatever it is, is really new. I didn't feel the need to tell everyone yet." She blew out a breath. "Besides, you know how my family is. Mom will grill you on your 'intentions' the second she finds out."

His grip on the wheel loosened, and he exhaled.

"Sorry. Didn't mean to snap your head off. No, I haven't mentioned anything, pretty much for the same reason as you. You've met my mother. She'd be planning the menu for the reception because food is life." He pulled into the parking lot of a seafood restaurant at the beach and turned off his truck then turned to her. "I don't know what you and I are doing right now. I do know I have all these feelings jumbled inside for you." She nodded. "And I know this. I do not want your mother fixing you up with anyone else, even if they are the cousin of her hairdresser's friend."

She laughed then leaned in and kissed his cheek.

"I love what we're doing, Luca, whatever this is. I've been home about two minutes. I don't need to define it. As long as you and I are happy, what's the problem? I only brought it up because Labor Day is right around the corner and…"

"And when we show up together at your family party, everyone will know. I have no problem with this. Let them know. Let them ask questions. Let the sons of all the cousin's half-brothers cry in their beer for all I care," he said, laughing.

"When we show up," she said, smiling. "I like the sound of that." She leaned forward and glanced at the building. "Did you bring me to From the Sea for dinner?" she squealed. "You know I used to love this place."

"How could I forget? We celebrated your sixteenth birthday here. Remember they took your picture with the lobster hat on?" he asked on a laugh.

"Remember? I think the picture very well might be still gracing a board on the wall of my childhood bedroom at my parents' home." She shuddered. "I swear, my old room is like a shrine to me, and I'm not dead."

"Oh, honey, they're just proud of you," he explained. "If it makes you feel better, my mother has a similar room in her home. I'm sure you can picture all the baseball trophies. I've begged her to toss them, but she won't. Grumbles every time she has to dust them but won't get rid of a single one."

"Then you know," she said, nodding. "Which is exactly why I bought a house unseen before moving back here. There was no way I was moving back into that room. Now, when I have a spare moment, I'm going to gut it so my mother can finally turn it into, well, something else."

"Maybe she'd like a craft room and then I could get mine to do the same," he suggested. He leaned over and brushed her lips with his.

She kissed him back before sitting up straight. "Let's go. First official date starts right now."

He shook his head before jumping out and walking around to open the door. Riley sat there waiting, smiling.

"No? What do you mean no?" she asked, voice a bit shaky. Her hands shook when he took one to help her down from his truck.

"Our first date already started when I showed up at your door and you stopped my heart with this dress. *That's* when this date started," he corrected. "And I'm so freaking glad." He clicked the key fob to lock his truck before holding out his arm to her. "Shall we?" he asked.

"We shall," she agreed, lacing her arm through his.

*****

"What?' Luca asked as she sat staring at him across the table.

A smile played on her lips as she thought how to answer his simple question.

"Oh, it's nothing and everything at the same time, I guess," she said, smile growing. She laughed and reached for her water as confusion washed across his face.

"Was that one of those female answers I'm supposed to understand but don't?" he joked. "I really wish I had sisters," he muttered.

"Careful what you wish for," she advised. "I have three brothers, as you know, and don't know a thing about men."

"Help a guy out," he begged. "Give me clue at least."

"I was just thinking about you and me and how similar and yet how different things are." She laughed again at his face when his eyes rounded. "You and I are, on some levels, the same as we always were. The conversation flows, things are easy in a way I feared they never would be again. Does that make sense?"

This time, he smiled. "Yes, it does, even though I'm as surprised as you are. So much time passed, and I didn't know how things would go," he confessed.

"Exactly!" she exclaimed. "The flip side of the coin is how things are also so different. We're such different people now. We've had a whole slew of experiences which didn't include each other in them. It never happened when we were kids. It's a little, well, disconcerting."

He tilted his head. "Give me an example."

"Well, right now for instance. We walked in here, and the owner greeted you by name. When did that happen?"

"Oh, that makes sense. John bought the place maybe three, four years ago. Palm Harbor may be growing, but it's still a small place. We know each other from the small business bureau and the restaurant softball league. Course, if he looked at my date for a second longer, that wouldn't have counted for anything," he muttered.

She laughed, more than a little turned on by his inner

caveman.

"The last time you and I spent any time together, Luca, we were both kids. Now, we're not. It's not a bad thing. It just is what it is. It'll take some getting used to. Somedays, I feel like a fraud, showing up for work in the ER when I should really be hanging out at the high school baseball field."

Her reached across the table and took one of her hands in his, rubbing his thumb across her bounding pulse. "You always were my number one fan," he murmured. "But then, I was yours as well."

"I was your *shadow*," she said, hating the word used to describe her all those years ago. "You were my everything, Luca. My best friend. My protector. My first love," she whispered.

She had wanted him to be her first *everything,* but fate dealt her a cruel hand.

He opened his mouth to speak, but their waiter appeared at the table. "Good evening, everyone. Can I start you off with something to drink from the bar?" he asked.

"I'll have an ice water with lime, please," she requested.

"Same," Luca bit out. "And we'll need a few more minutes before ordering, if you don't mind."

"Of course not, sir. I'll be back with your drinks," he said before departing.

Was it too much to hope he hadn't heard her? She glanced out at the waves, always comforted by their timeless coming and going. No matter what happened in her life as a child, she could always count on the tide doing its thing.

"Surely you know I never saw you that way," he asked, a pleading note to his voice. "I hated it when people called you that. You were never my shadow. You were my everything." He brought her hand to his lips, kissing her palm. "I'm sorry they hurt your feelings. I always wished you didn't know about hat stupid nickname."

Fire raced through her blood, burning her from the inside out. Only the ocean breeze kept her from incinerating on the spot.

"How could I not?" she asked when rational thought returned. "You were Luca Rinaldi, star baseball player, captain of the team as a junior, varsity since freshman year. And I was, well, no one."

"You were someone, Riley, always. You were *my* someone. You were the smartest, sweetest someone on the planet."

"To you, maybe, and trust me it was enough. But to everyone else I was a quiet, shy no one who *dared* to be best friends with you."

She flashed back to a painful day, freshman year, in the girls' bathroom. She'd been in the stall when a couple of girls came in talking about him. One of them, a cheerleader named Cindy, went on and on about Luca and how *fabulous* he was and wouldn't they make a great couple at the Spring Formal. Then her tone grew cold when she mentioned Riley, AKA Luca's shadow, and 'why didn't the little nobody get a clue already?' After all, there was no way someone like Luca could feel anything but pity for someone like Riley. She'd waited until the girls left, and her tears dried, before leaving the restroom.

"Where'd you go just now?" he asked giving her hand a squeeze.

"Nowhere important," she assured him. "I'd rather stay right here, right now, with you."

"Good answer," he said, grinning. "Maybe we should peruse the menu to be ready when he comes back."

"Also, a good answer, although I know what I'm getting," she said, shutting hers.

"Let me guess," he said, rolling his eyes. "The lobster."

She burst out laughing, remembering with horror the night of her birthday. The sixteen-year-old version of herself had no idea ordering a whole lobster meant picking the actual lobster from the lobby tank. She'd actually picked the meal for its price and sticker shock. It took Luca twenty minutes to calm her down and get her back in from the beach.

"I will have you know I have never ordered it again. But I am having lobster, only in its mac and cheese form. I had this once in Vermont and thought I'd died and gone to Heaven," she confessed.

"I see what you mean," he said. "We are the same yet different." He leaned in to brush an errant hair from her face, tucking it behind one ear. "I look forward to learning more about Riley two point oh."

Chapter Eighteen

"They say that the way to a man's heart is through his stomach. It's the same with women…or at least the ones I want to be with."
-Ian Somerhalder

"You can glare at me all you want, Lucifer, but your mistress likes me. That's all that matters," he told the black kitten currently hissing at him from under the kitchen table. Unimpressed, she continued her death glare. Gabriel, on the other hand, wove around his ankles, as he stood at the stove making breakfast. "See, he likes me."

Great, now you're talking to kittens…

"Good, it's not just me," Riley muttered as she dragged herself into the kitchen wearing his T-shirt. His heart stuttered. "Tell me there's coffee and I might keep you around."

"My momma didn't raise any fools. It's the first thing I started." He waved a hand at the coffee maker than took a sip of his own. "I'm almost as bad as you in the morning. Not quite but almost."

"Hmmm. Do I have ten minutes for a quick shower?" she mumbled into her coffee.

"I'm feeling generous this morning. You have twelve," he joked, swatting her butt as she walked by.

She raised one brow. "And frisky, apparently. Have to get ready for my shift. Lord, six-thirty start times, what was I thinking?"

"I'm always frisky," he called as she moved back down the hall.

He flipped the pancakes before slicing some fresh fruit to go with them. He poured juice and set out plates. Everything was ready when she came back out, fresh from her shower. She smelled of sunshine, the ocean and something uniquely herself. Something he found himself becoming obsessed with. So much so, that he leaned in and stuck his nose in her damp hair and inhaled.

Her laughter filled his soul.

"Did you just sniff me?" she asked, still laughing.

"Yep, not even gonna deny it." He waved a hand toward the table. "I know you're pressed for time, so breakfast is ready. And the travel cup is next to your keys and badge," he offered, pointing to the breakfast bar.

She stared at him, a suspicious moisture in her eyes. Luca froze. Had he done something wrong? *Think!* She didn't seem angry, and it was just breakfast after an amazing night.

Riley closed the distance between them, wrapped her arms around him, and squeezed. She held him for a long moment. He swore he could feel her heart thumping. Maybe it was his? Then she reached up, planting a kiss on the underside of his jaw.

"Thank you," she whispered before sitting at the table.

"You're welcome," he replied, still not so sure what had happened.

He took the seat across from her. Lucifer, who had been watching him from underneath the chair, hissed and hurried closer to Riley.

"One day you'll figure out I'm not such a bad guy, little one," he crooned to the angry kitten.

Riley stuffed a huge bite of pancake in her mouth. "Maybe if she tasted these, she wouldn't distrust you so much," she quipped. "Oh my!" she moaned as she chewed and swallowed. "Seriously, how are you still single?"

"I'm not," he answered, deciding to not go for the easy,

funny answer as usual.

Her head snapped up from her plate. "Oh. I meant, you know, up until now. But, for the record, I don't consider myself single either. So, tonight, if you're still interested, I'd love a ride home from dinner with the girls when I'm several margaritas in and too tipsy to drive." She winked at him.

Winked!

He felt it all the way to his toes and one particular place further north.

"I think we can arrange it," he drawled.

"I can have one of the ladies take me there if it's easier," she offered.

"Either way works, but yeah, probably easier so Nico doesn't give me crap for running out during the dinner rush," he joked.

"No problem. I'll call Harper or Jamie. Neither of them will be drinking tonight. In fact, now that I think about it, I may be the only one having a few. Hmmm. Interesting. Now, I sound like a lush," she muttered. She took another bite of her meal.

"Hey, there's nothing wrong with having a few. And believe me, if Sam weren't pregnant and Jamie wasn't breastfeeding, they'd be joining you," he assured her.

"Oh, I invited Sadie along. Maybe she'll have a drink with me." She told him about meeting the vintage clothing store owner.

"Now you're recruiting for The Coven, I see," he joked.

"Very funny. I liked Sadie, right off the bat. She was kind and funny, a little different. She'll fit right in."

It warmed his heart hearing how she'd put herself out there. The Riley he'd known as a child would never have done that.

"Good for you! I look forward to meeting her when I come to scoop up your drunk butt tonight," he informed her with a grin. He glanced at the wall clock. "Now, as much as I hate to say it, you need to dash."

"Ugh, whoever scheduled me for the early shift needs a

good talking to," she muttered before scarfing down the rest of her pancakes. She blushed when she saw him grinning at her. "What? I'm not wasting any food cooked for me. And besides, you've seen me eat like a million times. I'm not going to start pretending now I'm one of those women who exists on salads and sparkling water." She scrunched her nose to tell him what she thought of *them*. "And now I have to go."

He cleared their plates while she ran down the hall to her bathroom. When she came back, she stopped to pet each kitten, cuddling them for a moment and wishing them a good day. Then she grabbed her keys, badge, and to-go coffee mug. He handed her a small lunch bag.

"What's this?" she asked, eyes widened.

"This is your lunch. You work hard and deserve a good lunch to keep you going. Saving lives isn't easy."

Her eyes grew damp. Not the first time this morning. She sniffed a little.

"Don't cry, Riley, it's only linguine with Bolognese, nothing fancy," he said, trying to lighten the moment.

"It's so much more than that, and you know it, tough guy." She leaned up and kissed him, a hot, searing kiss. "It's the fact you cared enough about whether or not I got lunch in my busy day today." She looked him in the eyes. "Thank you. No one has ever done this for me before."

"Well then, it's long past time," he murmured. He kissed her briefly before walking her to the door. "Have a good day. Be safe. Text me when you need a ride home. Have a good time with the ladies."

*****

"Did I mention he packed me lunch today?" Riley all but yelled to the table of gathered women. By her second strawberry margarita, the hectic workday was long forgotten, and she wasn't feeling any pain.

Rowdy laughter met her announcement, everyone nodding.

"This might be the third time," Sam commented.

"Or is it the fourth?" Jamie quipped.

"We're much more interested in what else Luca has to offer," Harper mentioned, grinning. "He has such big hands." She wiggled her eyebrows, setting off the women once again.

"So, I'm guessing the dress worked its magic, huh?" Sadie asked.

"Oh my gosh, yes!" Riley exclaimed. "Oh, shush," she corrected herself. "I do tend to get a bit loud when I drink," she giggled.

"You don't say?" Sam joked.

"Well, Sam and Jamie, I am so glad you sent me to Sadie's place, Threads and well, something. She is amazing! She knew just what I needed to knock the man's socks off." She leaned in and whisper-shouted, "Not to mention a few other articles of his clothing."

Harper rubbed her hands together, grinning. "Now, we're getting somewhere. Tell us more."

"A lady does not kiss and tell," Riley said, laughing. "Besides, no reason to make you all jealous. The man has moovvveeesss." She laughed so hard at the expressions on their faces, she almost fell out of her chair. "I may need some food to balance out the liquid portion of my night."

"I have no reason to be jealous," Sam announced. She patted the tiny bump in her stomach. "This little one and the accompanying hormone soup keeps me quite horny. Jack is more than happy to accommodate," she informed the group of women.

Jamie nodded. "I remember very well."

"Well, I may not be pregnant nor newly no longer pregnant, but Owen and I do just fine, thank you very much. You wouldn't be making me jealous at all if you cared to share some spicy details," Harper assured her.

"Okay, that is so not fair," Sadie protested and threw up her hands. "No discussing sex lives when I'm the only single one at the table." She shook her head and reached for a chip. "At least I still have carbs."

"We need to find you a man," Riley cried. She turned to the others. "You guys must know someone good enough for the amazing Sadie! I mean I could try, but I've been back in town for like a minute."

"You are such a lightweight," Sam muttered.

Javier stepped up to their table with another waiter. "Sorry for the delay, ladies, but I have brought your dinners."

"Just in time, too," Jamie quipped, pointing at Riley. "Someone needs some calories to balance out her alcohol."

"That I can help with," he assured them.

The two men passed out everyone's meals and excused themselves. The women dug into their meals, and for a few moments, only the sounds of chewing and a few moans could be heard.

"Seriously, don't y'all know anyone for her?" Riley asked. "Then she'd have a sex life to not tell us about."

"Do you really think that's a good enough reason for me to find someone?" Sadie asked, fork halfway to her mouth, grinning.

"No, but orgasms on demand is," Sam decided.

"Sam!" Jamie exclaimed

Sam turned to her best friend, one red brow raised. "Don't even try to deny it."

Jamie sat there, cheeks flaming, but remained silent. The other women howled with laughter.

"Sounds great but nothing like the last man I was involved with, so I might like it in writing before I try again," Sadie muttered.

"Sounds more like the wrong man," Riley suggested. "Oh, did I say that out loud?" she gasped before slapping a hand over her mouth.

"Funny, when I asked Griff to describe you, he always said quiet. Honestly, that might be the last word I would think of," Jamie posed. "Bright, kind, wicked funny, cheap date? Yes. Quiet? Not so much."

"Thank you!" Riley exclaimed, leaning over to hug her sister-in-law. "He's clueless. But, in his defense, he hasn't spent much time with Riley two point oh." At the round of confused looks on their faces, she felt a need to explain herself.

"The Labor Day party is right around the corner. It'll be the perfect opportunity," Jamie suggested.

"I guess," Riley agreed. "I've been so busy since I got back, throwing myself right into the new job."

"And right onto the new man," Sam added.

"Uh, yeah, that, too. I haven't even unpacked all of my moving boxes yet. I'm still living out of them, which is getting very old." She sighed. "I need a couple days in a row to focus."

"Why haven't you said something to Cheryl? She'd more than happy to help. Gosh, your mom has been a godsend with Amelia Grace," Jamie exclaimed.

Riley buried her head in her hands. "I know I should. I don't want to." When no one said anything, she looked up. "It's hard being the 'baby of the family,' especially in mine. Everyone was so active and outgoing when I was a child. It didn't help I was the youngest by far also. They still treat me like I'm six. What does it say to them if I can't unpack a few boxes without help?" she groaned.

Sadie laid a hand on her arm. "Been there, done that, sister. I am also the youngest and only girl. I have four older brothers. Can you top it?"

Riley shook her head, mouth dropping open. "No, nor would I want to. There are five of us, and I have three brothers and a sister. Wow, I thought I have it rough."

Sadie threw back her head and laughed. "Why do you think I moved up here from Florida? Don't get me wrong. I love my brothers, even when I want to strangle them. Which is pretty much daily. But I needed space. All of them are either in law enforcement or the fire service." She laughed when the other women's eyes bulged. "Yeah, that's a lot of testosterone. Let's just say I love them even more dearly from a distance."

"Well, I'm back to stay so I have to figure this out," Riley groused.

Jamie reached over to grasp her hand. "Maybe give your mom a little credit. She hasn't really had the chance to get to know you as an adult. At least not more than your flying visits home for a few days or weeks. This is just a suggestion, and you can tell me to butt out, no harm no foul. But maybe invite her over to help you out around the house. Maybe a little one-on-one time would be good for the two of you?"

"Huh, maybe. I never thought of it that way." She took another sip of her drink, the icy goodness going down so smoothly, giving her a little buzz.

"Back to more interesting topics," Sam said with a smirk. "What are you and Luca doing? I mean beyond the obvious."

"Not sure other than hanging out and having a great time," she said. She poked at the rest of her meal, suddenly not as hungry. She really didn't have a clue what they were doing.

"Makes you sound fifteen," Harper observed.

Minus the blazing hot sex, it was them at fifteen.

"I've only been back in town a little bit. We're, I don't know, getting to know each other again." She laughed then. "And not just that way. Get your minds out of the gutters, ladies. Funny, he and I had this conversation at dinner. We're getting to know each other as adults. We were best friends as children, right up until I left for college, but you know time passes. Things happen. People change." She played with her napkin, searching for the right words. "We're not the same people we were. How could we be?"

"I think it's wise," Sadie offered. "Of course, you're different. A ton of time has passed, not to mention a ton of life experiences. You are two completely different people. It makes sense you need to get to know each other again."

"You're right, yet underneath all of it, we are the same people we were back then. At the core of who we are, I guess. It's so easy to talk with him. To just *be* with him." She lowered her voice. "I was so afraid we might have lost that."

"Oh, honey, no," Sam stated. "I saw how he looked at you."

"What?" Riley asked, confused.

"At Jamie and Griff's wedding. I know you were only in town briefly, and goodness knows I had my hands full with her crazy family and my mother. But the man had eyes for no one but you."

"Oh," she said. Her breath felt trapped in her lungs. She couldn't think of anything else to say.

"And I'm sorry to bring this up, truly I am," Sam said. "But at Christmas… Well, he looked gutted."

Riley sank back against her chair then rubbed at her temples. Would she ever live down that night?

"Wasn't exactly great for me, either," she said. Then she turned to Sadie and Harper. "So, the Cliffs Notes version goes like this. Stupidly, I brought my boyfriend home with me this past Christmas. A boyfriend I wasn't very serious about but apparently, he was. A boyfriend I had been honest with all along about coming home after we finished our residencies. Completely unbeknownst to me, he planned a surprise proposal. In front of everyone. At Luca's restaurant." She reached for her glass again, having earned a big gulp.

The women gaped at her.

"I really should sell the rights. Sounds kind of like a Lifetime movie, doesn't it?" she quipped. "And the absolute worst part is how much I hurt Luca. As much as I've changed over the years, I still loathe being the center of attention. When Thomas dragged me to my feet in front of everyone, I felt paralyzed. I stood there, frozen smile on my face, with him kneeling in front of me. Luca was all I could see over Thomas's shoulder. I stared at him, and only him, as another man asked me to marry him. I stared at Luca as I whispered 'yes' to Thomas. Only because I just wanted the whole thing to end." She wiped at the tears sliding down her face. "Luca is the only man I've ever truly loved. Luca is the one I should have been saying yes to."

"Oh, honey, he put you in an impossible situation," Jamie soothed.

"How long did your engagement last?" Sam asked.

Riley laughed. "Not even as long as our flight back to Arizona. Somehow, he was shocked by my decision." She laughed harder until the tears came for another reason. "What is it with men and their colossal egos?"

"Now there's a question for the ages," Sadie snarked.

"Who knows?" Sam muttered at the same time. "Riley, have you told Luca about any of this?"

"Yes, we've talked about it all. It was important for him to know." She sighed. "He's a good man, and I love him. I've been in love with him since I was twelve. I just don't know if I can trust him with my heart."

"Only one way to find out, sadly," Jamie offered. "I don't say it lightly because I've been there and not so long ago."

"Same," Sam said. "Love is the scariest thing of all. Risking yourself, your heart, to another human being?" She shuddered. "I had no intention of ever doing that. Especially after watching my parents and their endless rounds of foolishness. Then the right person comes along, makes you rethink your plans."

"Since it's still so new for me, this is all I can tell you," Harper added. "I had a life that worked. It might have been a little empty, less than satisfying, but it worked. Until the moment I saw how much better it could be with Owen. And it was a big step, admitting it, even to myself. I had to learn how to let go of some things while holding on to others. I had to learn how to let him in. No easy feat for the girl who'd been on her own for way too long, but oh so worth it."

Her phone buzzed from her purse. Riley bent down to fish it out. A text from Luca brought a smile to her face.

"Done here. Let me know when you need me. ;-)"

"Let me guess, Prince Charming?" Sam laughed.

"Close. Luca," she responded. "This has been so much fun. We have to do this again soon. In fact, when my house looks like I'm not camping there, y'all can come over."

"Agreed," Jamie said. "And Sadie, consider yourself the newest member of The Coven. You're stuck with us now, I'm afraid."

"Well, never so happy to be 'stuck' so I guess it's mutual," she said, smiling.

Riley dashed off a quick response, telling him she was

ready to go when he was. They chatted a little longer while they paid their bills and chose a date for the next get together.

"There she is," Luca announced as he approached their table a few minutes later. "Good evening, ladies," he addressed the other women.

"Good evening, Luca," Sam returned, grinning. "We were talking about you earlier."

He raised one dark brow. "Oh, really? All good I hope." He stood behind Riley, hands on her bare shoulders. "I'll assume you discussed how I'm the luckiest man in Palm Harbor?" He dropped a kiss on the top of her head, making her melt.

She raised her face to look at him and winked. "There may have been some discussion of your 'attributes,' but don't worry, I kept it PG13."

His jaw dropped as the other women laughed and nodded. He pointed to her now empty glass.

"How many of those did she have?" he asked the table.

"Only two, be glad," Sam joked.

"Now you see why I don't drink," Harper joked. "Who knows what I might spill about Owen."

"Jack's probably pissed I can't right now," Sam joked.

Sadie laughed. "These women are a hoot. I'm so glad I came."

"Oh, you're the newest member," Luca said, turning toward her. "Hi, I'm Luca Rinaldi. Riley has told me lovely things about me and your store. I would love to personally thank you for the dress she wore."

"You are most welcome," Sadie answered with a grin. "Repeat business is thanks enough. Plus, with her body and coloring, Riley is a dream to dress."

"Riley is a dream, period," Luca murmured. He glanced down at her. "All ready?"

"I am indeed. May be a tad on the woozy side, just to warn you. Apparently, I'm a cheap date," she said, giggling then winked at Jamie.

"That she is," Jamie confirmed.

"Well, in that case," Luca exclaimed, helping her to her feet then throwing her over one shoulder. "Goodnight, ladies!" he called before striding out of the restaurant.

Chapter Nineteen

"Choosing to remain vulnerable and sensitive despite disappointments or heartbreak helps me stay authentic to my life. It is the hardest part."
-Sobhita Dhulipala

When he pulled into her driveway, Riley remained slumped in the passenger seat of his truck. Adorable, soft snuffling noises came from her. He hated to wake her but couldn't leave her here all night. Getting out, he walked around to her side and opened the door. She never moved. He looked in her purse for her keys, grabbed them, then undid her seatbelt.

As smoothly as possible, he slid his arms under her and lifted. Without waking, she curled into his chest, her warm breath fanning the hair there. A feeling of peace settled over him. He carried her to the porch, balancing his precious load while he opened the door. Both kittens greeted him as he entered. Lucy from a safe spot under the entry table. He hoped Gabriel wouldn't trip him as he carried her through to her bed.

He lay her on it then stood back to gaze down upon her. With only soft moonlight peeking in, her beauty robbed him of his breath. A small ache settled in his chest. Love for her filled his every cell.

So why haven't you told her...

Good question. But the image of her shocked, hurt face years ago always stopped him cold. How would they ever get past it?

She stirred on the bed, pulling him back from the past.

She'd rolled to her side, her legs caught in the long, gauzy skirt she wore. That wouldn't do. He walked into her closet and grabbed the shorts and tank set she preferred for sleep. Settling onto the edge of the bed next to her, he first slipped off her shoes and then jewelry. Next, he slid down the skirt over her hips gently and then replaced it with her sleep shorts. Easier said than done. Finally, he sat her up to remove her shirt and slip the tank over her head.

But instead of lying down, she curled against his chest, arms wrapping around his abdomen. He sat there for several long minutes, stroking her soft hair, and wishing for the courage to tell her everything in his heart. He kissed the crown of her head before laying her back down on the bed and pulling up the sheet to cover her. He turned to leave the room, intent on seeing to the kittens when she grasped his wrist.

"Please don't break my heart again," she whispered. Her hand fell from his, and she rolled over as her breath evened out once again.

Picking up the shards of his own heart, he left the room.

*****

Her mouth feeling like the desert she'd recently left woke her. Darkness filled the room. Riley glanced at her phone on the bedside table. Three in the morning. Whew. She needed at least a few more hours. She didn't have to go in until this afternoon, so she was in luck. Next to her phone sat an unopened water bottle and pain relievers. She swallowed two tablets with half the bottle before heading into the bathroom. After taking care of business and brushing her teeth, she stared in the mirror.

She looked 'rode hard and put away wet' as her late grandmother would say. She gently dragged a brush through her hair and removed what was left of her makeup. Then she returned to bed. Crawling back into bed behind Luca, she tried to remember how she'd gotten to bed in the first place. Her last, coherent thought was his arrival at the restaurant and maybe him carrying her out of there. Wow.

Note to self, lay off the booze…

She splayed one hand against his back, needing a connection to him. The feel of his warm, soft skin over corded muscle sent zings of electricity up her arm. It had never been like this with anyone else, not even Thomas. Least of all, Thomas, which had told her all she ever needed to know about her doomed relationship with her former fiancé.

"Hey," he whispered in a sexy, husky voice before rolling over to face her. "What are you doing up?" He brushed some hair from her face. "How's your head?"

"Hey, yourself," she whispered back. "My bladder woke me. Either that or the pound of sand in my mouth." She leaned in and kissed him softly.

He smiled at her in the near darkness. "What was that for?"

"For the water and pain relievers. And for taking care of me," she answered. "Mostly, for being you."

He inched closer and dropped one arm around her waist. "Happy to be of service. I'm glad you had fun tonight, but I'm not gonna lie. I missed you."

She laughed at his words. "It was one dinner. I'm sure you survived. Besides, we both have crazy schedules. It's bound to happen."

He rolled onto his back, taking her with him.

"I never cared before about my crazy schedule," he confessed.

"Mine's actually easier than it's ever been," she said. "Well, it will be once I get settled. As much as I loved school, I cannot tell you how glad I am to be done."

"I can't even imagine. I'm so incredibly proud of you, Riley. You did exactly what you said you were going to do, all those years ago." He pressed a kiss to her forehead. "How many people live their dream that way?"

"You are, too, Luca. I mean as much as you can be

without your dad still here. I know it's not quite the same, without him by your side, but Mama's is a thriving family restaurant, thanks to you guys and your dedication and hard work. You have to be proud of yourselves."

"We are, believe me. There were some tough times, a few years really, after my father died. Times we weren't sure how things would work out. I was so afraid of letting him down. Matty and I were so afraid Mama would not survive losing Dad and the restaurant."

She held him tighter, knowing he needed to feel her right now. Her heart wept for the young man with so much responsibility on his shoulders.

"I wish I could have been here for you, Luca," she whispered into his chest.

"I couldn't ask that of you, Riley. You had your whole life in front of you. I couldn't ask you to give it up. And even if you'd stayed here for undergraduate, it wouldn't have mattered. I literally worked around the clock. We all did."

"Still, leaving felt horrible. Like I abandoned you," she admitted through a tear-clogged throat.

He stroked a hand up and down her arm. "No, don't do that to yourself. Things went the way they were meant to go. We can't change the past, Riley, but I am exactly where I want to be right now."

"Me, too," she whispered, feeling herself drift. "I think I might need a little more sleep."

She felt his arms tighten around her. Another soft kiss landed on her temple.

"Go to sleep. I've got you," he promised.

The next time she opened her eyes, a pair of bright green ones stared back.

"Hey, Lucy," she greeted her kitten. "Where's your better half?"

Getting out of bed, she wandered out of her room and followed the amazing twin scents of coffee and bacon.

"Keep this up and I may just have to marry you," she

joked.

Luca turned from the stove so fast, he startled her.

"Oh, I, uh, was only kidding," she mumbled and passed him to inhale her first cup of the day.

"Maybe you shouldn't play with a guy's emotions like that," he warned her. "And for the record, I'm a bit old-fashioned. Blame it on the Italian blood. When I get engaged, I'll do the asking." He turned back to the stove.

"Okay, good to know," she murmured, not really sure what had happened.

He brought their breakfast to the table, ending the conversation. After a few moments she picked up her phone and thought about texting her mother but then set it down again and sighed, unsure if she wanted to jump right in as Jamie had suggested.

"What's up?" he asked, putting down his fork and giving her his full attention.

"Oh, it's silly really." She told him about wanting to unpack finally and Jamie's idea to have her mom come help, to give them a chance to bond, so to speak. When she was done, she grabbed her coffee mug, more to have something to do with her hands. "Told you it was silly. Why should I be so nervous about spending time with my own mother?"

Luca reached over and took the coffee mug from her hands. After setting it down, he wrapped his around hers and squeezed. "There's nothing 'silly' about it if you're hesitating even texting her. I know the way they've always treated you, Riley. I was there to see it. It's not that they don't love you."

"I know," she rushed to assure him. "My family is the best! They've been super supportive of me the whole way through my education." She shook her head. "It's hard to put it in words without sounding stupid. They just still see me as the person I was when I left. As a seventeen-year-old."

"Then this might be a great first step. Spend some time with your mom, here in your space, surrounded by your grown-up things. You can tell her about work." He grinned at her. "You can even tell her about us. Nothing teenager about either of those."

She ducked her head as heat surged into her face. "Ugh, you're the worst."

"Yeah, but I'm yours," he said, grinning broader. "But seriously, they aren't going to change their perspective of you until they're confronted with it. Show her who you are, Riley, who you've become over the past decade. Let her get to know the amazing woman I see before me."

She stared at him, shaking her head. "Seriously, you're going to ruin me for all men."

Her heart clenched as the grin disappeared from his face.

"That's kind of the plan," he murmured before resuming his meal.

Not knowing how to respond, she dashed off a text to her mom, asking if she was available tomorrow to help her around the house. Within seconds, she got a very enthusiastic reply. Riley's stomach flipped a bit.

"Well, let's hope you're right. She's coming tomorrow," she groaned.

"Great. And maybe not have that look on your face when she gets here," he said, pointing to her. "You look sort of like you may puke."

"I do not!" she yelled. He might have a point, but she refused to admit it. Then she burst into laughter. "Fine, maybe a little. I just want, need, this to go well. I love my mom and I've missed her, my whole family, so much. But I need them to see me for who I am, not the little kid they seem to think I still am."

"Then tell her. Tell them all. I don't have any sisters, as you know, but I can imagine how protective I would feel about them. Your family means well."

She waved a hand. "It'll be fine. That's enough about that. What's on your agenda today?"

They talked some more about everything and nothing, finished their breakfasts, and lingered. Riley found the more time she spent with Luca, the more she wanted to. The harder it became to say goodbye. But eventually, he had to go. Real life called. She walked him to the door.

Before she could open the door, he pressed her up against it, covering her body with his own. She felt him everywhere. Her heart raced. For a long moment, he did nothing other than stare into her eyes, his own dark ones mesmerizing. Then he kissed her, a burning hot kiss that vanquished all thought. She moaned into his mouth, squirmed closer, needed to be as close as possible. To memorize the feel of him. The scent of him. Her hands slid into his hair, pressing him closer still.

Finally, he broke the kiss.

"Just so you don't forget me today," he whispered, peering down into her eyes again.

"No danger of that happening," she replied, through swollen lips.

He dragged a hand through his hair. "I have to go. Right now. Or I'll never leave." With one more kiss, he turned and left.

She stood there, fingers pressed against her mouth. Then a smile bloomed on her face. He may have broken her heart years ago, and they may not have dealt with it yet, but they were different people now. The smile grew larger. They would be okay.

*****

The opening strains of from Niall Horan's "This Town" caught his attention as Luca drove home. His older brother always tortured him for having the artist's song downloaded on his phone, but from the first time he'd heard the lyrics, Luca felt they'd spoken directly to him. Although the song about losing their first love to another could apply to many, the words seemed to jump out at him every time he heard it. When he heard the part about dancing with you, his gut tightened.

He drove home on autopilot. Even though her words had been offhand when she'd joked about marrying him earlier, he swore his heart had stopped. Shock had been the only thing stopping him from dropping to one knee and asking her right there and right then.

Wait, what?

He took a deep breath and released it slowly, lowering the truck window for some fresh air. He needed to get ahold of himself. No need to rush things. She'd been back in town less than a month. They were a thing, for lack of a better term, for less than that. What was he doing?

Yet, it wasn't panic he felt. No, it felt more like right. This was right. They were right. This is what they always *should* have been before, had the universe not gotten in the way. He'd spent most of his life more than half in love with her. Because of that, he'd done the hardest thing he'd ever had to. But she was back now. Nothing stood in their way. They had nothing but time. So, he could just slow the heck down and not mess this up, right?

He glanced at himself in the rearview mirror. Saw the indecision in his eyes.

But why wait? He'd known what he'd wanted, who he'd wanted, since he was a kid. When all that was within reach, finally, why wait?

Luca slammed his hands against the steering wheel, practically growling in his inability to decide. Then a thought occurred to him. After pulling into his driveway, he reached for his phone and shot off a text to Griff. Since he was Riley's brother, it had to start with him.

Somewhat settled for at least making a step in the right direction, he went inside to get ready for his day.

Late in the evening, Luca entered Dusty's, glancing around for Griff. The local bar, a favorite of his friend, seemed as good of a place as any to have this conversation. Public place might not be bad, he thought, considering the topic. Griff probably couldn't kill him here.

He waded into the summer crowd, searching for his friend.

"Hey, Luca, over here," came the familiar voice.

Turning, he spied Griff, and several others, around a

large table in the back corner of the room. He groaned, knowing he was about to spill his guts, and heart, for an audience. Knowing he had no other choice now, he wound his way through the tables.

"Hey, guys," he called, hoping he sounded more enthusiastic than he felt when he reached their table.

"What'll you have, Luca?" Stella, the waitress, asked from behind him.

"Oh, hey, Stella, didn't see you there. I'll take whatever local you have on tap tonight, please."

"Coming right up," she said. "You guys need anything?"

When they all declined, she whirled away and disappeared into the crowd.

"So, what's up, man?" Griff asked. "Not that we ever need much of an excuse for a beer."

"Hell, no," Jack agreed.

"Didn't have to twist my arm either," Owen joked.

"I just wanted a break from the restaurant. Thought a guys' night out might be fun," Luca finished lamely, knowing he wouldn't be having the conversation he meant to have now. Not that he even knew what the conversation might have entailed exactly.

"Hmmm," Griff murmured, taking a sip of his draft. "So, it didn't have anything to do with Riley then?"

Luca wondered if this was what they meant by the blood draining from your face. He'd heard the expression before, maybe read it in a book. He'd just never experienced it. Until now. He was glad he had already taken a seat.

"I, uh, well." He stopped talking. The other three burst out laughing.

"Wow, man, I've never seen you so pale," Jack guffawed.

"He doesn't have a gun, Luca, you're safe," Owen advised.

"Not with me at the moment," Griff clarified.

"You boys are gonna keep it civil, right?" Stella asked, dropping off Luca's beer. She winked at them before leaving the table again.

Luca drained a third of his glass for courage. "I'm not even sure why I'm here. But you and I have been friends for a long time, Griff." He nodded at the others. "Well, you guys, too, just wasn't expecting you tonight."

"Sorry, not sorry," Jack said with a grin.

"Fine. This is obviously about Riley. I know you asked me to keep an eye out for her, welcome her back and all, but it's gone way beyond now." He took a deep breath. "I won't tell you about my feelings for her since I haven't even shared them with her yet. I won't disrespect her."

Griff laughed. The others joined in until all three laughed long and hard. Luca sat there, staring at them until they finally got it under control.

"What? Did I miss something?" Luca asked.

Griff grinned at him. "Did you think what you said, or tried hard to not say, is in anyway a surprise to me? Really?"

"But," Luca sputtered. "How? I mean, what are you talking about?"

"Dude, come on," Jack started, grinning. "You've been in love with Riley since, well, forever."

"Yeah, you can't possibly think this comes as a surprise to any of us," Owen added, biting back another round of laughter.

Griff shook his head. "You two were always together when you were little, and it didn't change as you grew older. Even when you became the big baseball star, and God knows Riley can barely walk without tripping over her own feet, I thought for sure, things would change. But there she was, day after day, sitting in the stands with whatever book she happened to be reading."

"You know the only game she missed is when she had her appendix removed?" Luca said more to himself than the group.

"If memory serves, it was the only game you missed also," Griff reminded him.

The memory of her too pale face, freckles popping out in

stark contrast, assailed him. He begged his mother to take him to the hospital to see her. And she did, knowing even then how much Riley meant to him. And Riley had been so cool, so tough. Even though she hurt, she told the ER nurse exactly what was wrong with her. Her appendix needed to come out, she said to anyone who would listen. And damn if she hadn't been right.

"I'm not even sure what my point is anymore, Griff, to be honest. Just letting you know I care about her. A lot." He stopped talking before he buried himself even further.

This had *not* gone as planned…

"Listen, Luca, no one likes to think about their sister, even worse little sister, with a guy. But we're all adults now. And you're a good man." The three other men nodded. "So, if it has to be someone, I'm glad it's you. That's all I'm saying."

"Are we done or is hair braiding up next?" Jack asked.

Griff cuffed him up the back of his head, never taking his eyes off Luca. "I think we're done here. Who wants to see the latest picture of my daughter?" he asked, pulling out his phone.

Everyone groaned but also leaned in to see Amelia Grace. As the first baby born to the pack of friends, she already had them twisted around her tiny finger. Luca sat back and let the conversation flow around him. He half listened as Jack and Owen fought over who claimed the title of 'favorite uncle.'

Relief swept through him having survived this conversation with Griff. But it was short-lived. If Griff had any idea how badly Luca had broken his sister's heart five years ago, things would have ended much differently.

Chapter Twenty

"I think as mothers we are all just trying our best."
-Gisele Bundchen

Riley sipped her second cup of coffee, or maybe third, and stalked around her house awaiting her mom. Lucy and Gabriel mistook her nerves as play and pounced on her bare feet every time she passed them. She scooped up both kittens, nuzzling them.

"Good thing you're cute," she muttered before placing them back down.

She hated feeling like this. Like her skin might be too tight. She got this way when anxiety crept back in. But this was her mom for goodness sake. No reason to feel like this. She stopped pacing and walked into the garage to pull some boxes into the living room.

She might have felt better this morning if she'd gotten more sleep, she thought. Sleeping without Luca next to her had proved surprisingly difficult after only a few days. She'd missed the warmth of his body next to hers. The scent of him on her sheets.

Wait. What?

Where were these thoughts coming from? *Slow down*, she told herself. He'd be running for sure if he could hear her thoughts after what she blurted out yesterday morning. Even if she had been joking.

Sort of.

A soft knock on her door caught her attention. The herd of butterflies in her stomach took flight. She ran a hand over her hair and walked to the door.

"Hey, Mom," she called and pulled open the door.

"Darling!" her mother cried, hugging her as if she'd just returned from war. She released Riley and stepped further into the house. "The colors look amazing, honey. I love your choices," she enthused.

"Oh, thanks. Wait until you see the rest of the place. I would still be painting for months if they hadn't all come to help," she admitted.

Her mother stroked a hand over Riley's cheek. "That's what family and friends are for, my darling girl. You don't always have to do everything by yourself, you know. There's no shame in asking for help."

That didn't take long…

"I know, Mom."

Her mother fixed her with a look that said differently, but she let it drop. Instead, she handed her a small gift bag. "I wanted to get you something for your new home."

"Thanks, Mom. Come on in and have a seat." She waved at the couch. "Can I get you a drink?"

"Not right now, but thanks. Goodness, who is this gorgeous creature?" she asked, picking up a purring Gabriel. "Aw, look at your poor, little paw. Well, didn't you find the perfect home for yourself. My daughter, the doctor, will get you the very best care, little one," she crooned to the kitten.

Riley's heart warmed at her mother's words.

"This is the most chill cat on the planet. I named him Gabriel to offset Lucifer," she joked.

"Where is Lucy?" her mother asked.

"Oh, she's around somewhere. Probably making sure you're not Luca." Riley froze, unable to believe what she'd just uttered. Maybe her mother hadn't heard her. Maybe she was too preoccupied with the ball of fluff in her hands.

"So, Luca's been spending time here, has he?" she asked in her not-so-innocent-don't-even-think-of-lying-to-your-mother tone.

"He has," she said, willing the flames in her cheeks to go away. "We think, and by we I mean the veterinarian and I, a man may have abused Lucy before I got her. She is not Luca's biggest fan." Then she smiled, thinking about all the ways he tried to get the tiny kitten to like him. "Not yet anyway."

As if knowing she was the topic of conversation, Lucy sidled out from under the couch between Riley's feet. She sat and stared at her mother with her bright green eyes.

"Well, you're gorgeous, too, aren't you?" her mother cooed. Then she looked up at Riley. "Go on, open your gift. You know you want to."

"You're right." She pulled brightly colored tissue paper from the bag, tossing it to the cats who immediately pounced on it. Peering inside, she pulled out two sets of hand towels, one with flip-flops on them, the other with seashells. "Mom, thanks, these are so cool," she gushed.

"You'll be amazed the things you need in your first home, Riley. The list is practically never ending. And while I know you probably have a bunch of your own stuff you brought back with you, I figured this would be good for my little beach baby."

The reference brought happy tears to Riley's eyes. "Wow, haven't heard that in a long time," she said, sniffing.

"Well, you haven't been home for more than a heartbeat in a long time." Her mother got up and crossed to where Riley sat, joining her. "I can't even begin to tell you how excited I am to have you back, Riley Jane. How excited we all are."

Riley threw her arms around her mother. "As excited as I am to be here?" She sat back, sniffed some more then laughed. "How silly am I? It's been so much since I've been back. New job. New house."

"New man?" her mother suggested, grinning.

"Mom!" Riley protested weakly. Cheryl Layne always had eyes in the back of her head. That's what she'd told them when they were kids. When Riley had been very little, she thought her mother meant it literally. It certainly seemed true since she always seemed to know everything.

"What? Don't 'Mom' me. You know Maria Rinaldi is one of my best friends. I get daily text updates about what a great mood he's been in at work." She winked at Riley. "Have you been away so long you've forgotten how small Palm Harbor is? There aren't any secrets here."

Riley groaned. "It's not a secret. Or at least, I didn't mean for it to be. We just haven't put a name to it, whatever it is we're doing."

"Of course, my dear girl. And you've been back home for no time at all. I'm not trying to rush you." She stared at Riley long enough to make her nervous.

"What is it, Mom? Please, whatever's on your mind, just tell me all ready," Riley implored.

"I just don't want to see you get hurt. Again. I know you two have always had something, well, special. I can't even begin to define. Not sure you two can. Thick as thieves as children you were. Maria and I used to joke we'd finally be family." Her face fell. "Then Angelo died, and everything changed."

"Funny, Luca and I talked about that recently."

"It's not only that," her mother said. "Something happened your last year of medical school, when you came home to tell us you'd matched with your top residency pick."

Riley closed her eyes for a moment, as if to ward off the pain of those memories.

"Honey, I'm not trying to pry. Or to tell you how to live your life. I don't want to see you hurt again, that's all."

She placed her hand on top of one of her mother's. "I don't either, but Mom, you can't protect me forever. And I'm not a little girl anymore."

"Oh, I know. In the blink of an eye, my children are all grown, some with children of their own. It happens so fast, darling, you can't even begin to imagine." She wiped a tear from her eye and smiled at Riley. "I only want all the good things for you in life. If I could protect you from pain, I would, but I know it's not reality."

Riley squeezed her mother's hand and decided to go for broke.

"Here's the thing, Mom. I get it, I do. But I'm not a little girl anymore. Dad can't panic because I bought a house and come running over here with a roofing contractor."

To her shock, her mother burst out laughing.

"Yes, my darling, he can. It's how he shows his love. You know he's never been big with words." Riley nodded. "But he'll make sure you have a safe roof over your head. And no one clapped louder or harder at any of your graduations." Riley nodded again, tears blurring her vision.

"He certainly did. The dean of the medical school did not look pleased," she joked.

"Oh, poo, who cares? My point is that's what it is to be a parent. It doesn't end when your child turns eighteen. It never ends. The situation merely changes," she clarified.

"But I had an inspector, Mom. I'm not stupid. Although I bought this place sight unseen, I wasn't taking any chances," she explained.

"Your father knew that, honey. If it helped him to sleep better bringing in his own guy for a second opinion, what did it hurt?" she asked.

"Nothing, I guess," Riley admitted. She blew out a long breath. "I just always felt like no one in the family trusted me to make it through a day without dying when I was growing up." She almost laughed at the sight of her mom's eyes bugging out. "Oh, come on, you know what I mean. Y'all treated me like I was made of spun glass. Like I would break."

"Oh, my dear girl, you have no idea," her mother cried, throwing her arms around her. "Did you ever wonder why there are so many years between you and Griff?"

"Not really, but now that you mention it, the gap seems a bit odd. The others are all so close in age," she admitted.

"That's an understatement," her mother said, laughing. "Your father wasn't joking when he said he wanted a big family. Of course, telling me on our first date might not have been the best move. Good thing I don't scare easily, huh?"

"Wow, first date? Never knew that."

"Anyway, the point is, we wanted one more child. And we tried. And tried. After having four in quick succession without any issues, it never occurred to your dad, nor me, there would be any difficulties. But there were."

"What kind of issues?" Riley asked. "Why haven't I ever heard this before?"

"I lost two pregnancies in between you and Griff, honey. One early on, but the second was full term." She closed her eyes for a moment and just sat there. Then she opened them again and smiled at her daughter. "When you came along, it was like the universe was repaying me for all the pain I had endured. Your father and I had given up after the last loss, you see. I couldn't go through it again. But you, my dear girl, had other ideas."

Tears flowed down Riley's face as a newfound respect blossomed for this woman.

"I had no idea, Mom. But I still don't understand why you never told me."

Her mother shook her head. "All I can say is after all the pain, we had you, and I didn't want to think about it ever again. And although we didn't talk about it, I'm not sure we didn't let the memory of it taint us a bit."

"How so?" Riley asked, gripping her mother's hands.

"It took me a long time to not be afraid, Riley, after losing my baby. I used to sit in your nursery and watch you breathe. Just watch you breathe to make sure you still were. I know it wasn't healthy, and eventually I got over it." She shook her head. "It took a long time."

"I can't imagine, Mom, really. I've seen what loss does to families in my work, but to live it, to survive it personally. No, I have no idea."

"And I hope you never do," her mother fervently added. "It was so hard to not smother you, Riley. You were such a precious gift, and I knew you were our last baby." She shrugged. "Someday, you'll understand."

"It certainly explains a lot," she admitted. "Emily always

treated me like a living, breathing doll."

Her mother laughed. "You're not wrong. The poor girl! All she ever wanted was a sister after all the boys. I think she'd about given up hope by the time you finally arrived. And it was hard because everyone was so much older than you. Having you almost felt like starting over again. Not that we minded, of course," she rushed to explain.

"No, I get it. It helps to understand," Riley said.

"But honestly, the hardest thing about raising you was, well, you," her mother admitted.

"Okay," Riley said dragging the one word to several syllables.

"Oh, dear girl, we were so unprepared for your big brain," her mother laughed. "Right from almost the start, we knew you were different. You met all your milestones earlier, faster than your siblings. You never wanted anyone to show you how to do anything either. Miss Independent, you were."

"Pretty much still am," Riley offered. She waved a hand around her house. "It's why I came home the way I did, Mom. I couldn't handle y'all doing everything for me. I had to prove I could do it on my own. Does that make sense?"

Her mother's eyes shone with unshed tears. "I'm so sorry we made you feel you had anything to prove, dear." She hugged Riley before letting her go. "Well, that's enough confession for one day. Put me to work."

Riley wiped her own eyes, so glad she'd listened to Jamie.

"That, I can do."

Chapter Twenty-One

"The bond that links your family is not one of blood, but of respect and joy in each other's life."
-Richard Bach

Days passed in a blur of work and blissful hours spent with Luca, and suddenly Labor Day dawned sunny and hot. More often than not, except for nights Riley worked in the ER, she slept beside him, content in the feel of his warm, hard body snuggled next to hers.

They didn't talk about it, didn't define what they had, just lived. If the doubts continued to creep back in every once in a while, well, she did her best to shove them right back out.

Lips pressed against her neck, blowing away the last dregs of sleep from her brain. Her body lit up under his expert touch.

"Mmmm, wonder who that could be," she teased.

"Were you expecting someone else?" he demanded. "You're in trouble now," was the only warning she got before he pounced, tickling her sides.

"No!" she shrieked, laughing as he hit the most sensitive spots. "Please, anything else."

He stopped tickling her but didn't lift his hands away. Rather, he slid them up her sides, oh so slowly. She swallowed thickly, never taking her eyes from his.

"Anything?" he asked in a low, deep voice.

She nodded, words beyond her.

He leaned down, about to kiss her, then stopped. One brow quirked.

"Unless you're more flexible than I give you credit for, we have company," he said.

"Wait, what?" she asked, staring at him.

"Someone is licking my ankle," he informed before he burst out laughing.

Riley whipped her head around to see Lucy sitting at the bottom of the bed with Luca's bare foot in between her front paws. Her tiny, pink tongue darted out to, indeed, lick him.

"Aww, she likes you. She's bathing you," Riley cried.

Luca glanced down. "Either that or she's marinating me. It could go either way," he joked.

Hearing his deep voice, Lucy froze, mouth open, tongue sticking out, and stared at him. Neither human said a word. Then she darted from the room.

"It's progress at least," Riley commented. She snuggled against his side. "Now, where were we?"

He raised himself up on his elbows above her. "Right about here," he said before kissing her.

She wound her arms around him, pulling him closer until all she felt was him against her. Everywhere.

She could get used to this.

"Meow!"

His laughter vibrated all throughout his body and hers followed by his groan.

"Are you kidding me right now?" he moaned

She peeked around his shoulder into Gabriel's unblinking, blue stare. She pressed her mouth into his bicep to smother her giggle.

"I think someone's hungry," she announced.

"Someone is," he confirmed, wiggling his brows.

Riley giggled harder before swatting him. "Not you and not *that* kind of hunger."

Luca dropped his head, shaking it. Then he swung around to stare at Gabriel for a moment. "How about if you give me, say, an hour? I promise you a gourmet breakfast later."

"Meow!" the kitten replied, seemingly not impressed with the offer. Gabriel stalked up

the bed and sat next to their faces. "Meow!" he repeated with more urgency.

"Great," Luca said with a sigh. "Cock-blocked by a something weighing less than five

pounds." He leaned down to kiss her fiercely one more time. "I blame you for this," he joked.

"You and your crazy need for pets. I'll start breakfast."

She sat up and watched him get up, throw on shorts and a shirt then scoop up the tiny cat before striding from the room. Riley lay back against the pillows for a moment. Not having to do anything but show up at her parents' home later gave her the morning to chill. She should probably get up to help with breakfast. The thought made her laugh. Get someone's heart started again? Absolutely. Scramble an egg? Not even on the best of days. She yawned and stretched, feeling a delicious twinge in certain places. Still, she could make coffee at least. Or watch him make their breakfast. Luca cooking in her kitchen…

That was always worth the price of admission.

*****

Luca pulled up to Riley's parents' home. Or at least to within a block or so. It was as good as he was going to manage with parking already at a premium. He'd spotted his family's various cars parked along the street. He pulled on a baseball cap and turned to smile at her.

"Ready for this?" he asked, grinning.

"What's to be ready for? This is the first one I've managed in, well, I'm not even sure. Way longer than I care to remember," she said. "I still can't believe I'm home. Sometimes, I think I should pinch myself to be sure I'm not dreaming."

"I'll be happy to pinch you later," he growled before jumping down from his truck. He walked around and opened her door. Giving her a quick kiss, he helped her down. But he didn't release her right away. "What are we telling them?"

"Telling them?" she asked, nose scrunched. "About what?"

He stared for a moment, a slightly icy sensation skating across his skin despite the sunny day. She wasn't answering his easy, direct question.

"Telling them about *us*," he said in a simple, slow tone she could not ignore.

Riley dropped her gaze to the ground. "Oh, that. I hadn't planned to tell anyone, anything. We're adults, so it's no one's business, really." She glanced up at him then away quickly. "Is it?"

He ran a hand through his hair, absently wondering when the last time was he'd gotten it cut.

"Not really the point I was making. Are you avoiding telling people about us for some reason?" he asked, not sure he wanted to hear her answer.

She hesitated for a moment, almost stopping his heart. "No, of course not. But we haven't exactly defined what we are. Or what we aren't for that matter." She shrugged. "Maybe we could do this another time?"

He blew out a breath he didn't realize he held. "If you'd rather," he agreed, knowing this conversation could not be put off forever. "Let me grab the food."

Luca walked around to the back, lowering the tailgate to grab the cooler. He took a moment, trying to get back the joy he'd felt earlier, waking in her arms. Each morning starting with her made him a little happier to be alive. And each night, he thanked his lucky stars she'd come home.

And yet, a small chill wrapped itself around his heart. Something lurked between them, preventing the closeness he desired. Something rooted in the past. Something he had wrought. Luca hesitated to bring it out into the light of day just yet. Had she forgiven him? Could they get past it?

"Do you need any help?" she called.

He forced the dark thoughts from his mind. Today was

about family and friends. She was both.

"No thanks, I've got it. You just bring your cute self," he added, grinning.

"You're a mess," she scolded.

"Maybe, but I'm your mess," he countered.

She went up on her toes and kissed his face. "Yes, you are. Now let's do this."

"Let's," he agreed.

Because he'd been coming to this for as long as he could remember, he walked around the side of the Layne house to the back patio. He nodded as several people waved and called out to him. Riley dashed ahead of him and opened the slider into the kitchen.

"Riley! Luca!" Mrs. Layne called in greeting. "Welcome to the annual madness." She glanced around the kitchen. "Just put it down wherever you find an inch of space." She wiped her hands on a towel and hugged her daughter. "Honey, be a dear and grab more of the table cloths from the dining room, please."

"Sure, be right back," she said before heading in that direction.

Mrs. Layne walked up to Luca after he set the cooler down. She wrapped her arms around him. "Thank you for making her so happy," she whispered before kissing his cheek." She turned back to the vegetables she'd been chopping without another word.

He stood there, staring at her for a moment, words out of reach. She grinned over her shoulder at him.

".What? Did you think I didn't know? Didn't approve? Maria and I have only wished for this since you two played in the sand together," she said with a laugh.

"Are these the ones, Mom?" Riley asked, walking back in the kitchen. She glanced from her mother to him, head tilted. "Did I miss something?"

"No," her mother said. "I was just thanking Luca for making you so happy. I'm sure Maria will say something similar to you." She laughed before taking a drink of her tea.

"But you know her. It'll be much more colorful."

"No doubt about it," Luca agreed, swallowing hard. He glanced at Riley, glad to see she hadn't paled under the scrutiny. "What else can I help with, Mrs. Layne?"

"Oh, I think we're long past the formality, aren't we? Cheryl will do just fine. Why don't you go see what Tim and the boys are up to out near the grill?" She winked at Riley. "It's always easier to leave the men folk to the grilling. Keeps them out of our hair. Your sister should be here any second. Give us Layne women a chance to catch up." She made a shooing motion with her hand. "Make sure you take a drink with you, it's hot as Hades already out there," she advised.

"Thanks, I will." Luca crossed the kitchen and kissed Riley before grabbing a water from the fridge. "See you later," he called before stepping outside.

He glanced around the big backyard before spotting her family grouped around the massive grill along with Jack and Owen. Her father and all of her brothers in one place. Great. And even though Griff was one of his best friends, he was still her big brother.

Okay then, he could do this.

"Luca!" Mr. Layne yelled in greeting the moment he spotted him, making Luca cringe just a little. Even in his sixties, the man was not to be taken lightly. He handed a grill tool to his oldest son and walked toward Luca, wrapping him in a bear hug. "Make her happy and we're good. Make her cry, they'll never find your body."

"I would expect nothing less," Luca answered once his heart started again. The Laynes owned the biggest lawn business in Palm Harbor. He had no doubt no one would ever find his body.

"Hey, Griff," he called to his friend, who grinned at him.

"He's not kidding," Griff mentioned.

"I'm aware," Luca answered. "No need to worry. If anything, I think Riley will probably break my heart first."

Shoot, why did he say it out loud?

Griff gave him a funny look but didn't comment.

"Of course, we'd be honor bound to help," Jack quipped. "Being honorary sons and all."

"I didn't hear a thing," Owen said, in his best lawyer tone.

Luca threw back his head and laughed. "Wouldn't have it any other way. Now what do y'all need?"

"Luca!" his mother bellowed as she made her way over to him. "Where is my darling girl?"

"I thought I was your favorite," he said, hugging her ample frame.

"You're the youngest, not the favorite," his brother, Matteo, said. "I'm the favorite."

"Well, not so sure about that. Aunt Maria always wanted a daughter, so Riley may be the favorite," Gino snarked, earning himself a smack on the back of his head from Luca and Matteo. "What? I speak the truth."

"He's not wrong. Where is my girl?" Maria asked, glancing around. She turned her gaze back on Luca, narrowing her eyes. "You'd better be good to her."

He threw up his hands, laughing. "Why does everyone think I'm less than perfect to Riley? Everyone should now how much I lo-care about her by now."

Whew, that was close, he thought. Confessing his love for her to them before he had a chance to tell her would not go over well. Nope. Best to stay busy.

"And now that your interrogation is complete, what needs doing?" he asked to the crowd in general.

And just like that, the spotlight shifted. Upwards of a hundred people or more would descend within hours. Plenty to accomplish before then. Everyone got busy, setting up tables and chairs, making sure the bar was set up, putting out games and activities for the hordes of children attending.

Before he knew it, two hours had passed with him barely saying a handful of words to Riley. She'd stayed inside with the women, fussing with food preparation, something that made him laugh. She would be the first to admit she lacked any culinary skill. Maybe he could find some time in their busy schedules to give her a few lessons.

Luca headed inside to use the bathroom. He spent a few minutes cleaning up from his sweaty work setting up chairs and tables in the hot sun. When he walked back outside, he saw Riley, his Riley, cornered on the patio by a blond man with his hands on her.

Something dark and a little scary settled in his brain. He made a beeline for the unsuspecting man. As he started to intercede, he stopped to listen.

"There must be some confusion," she told the other man. "I'm here with someone." She stepped back slightly, shaking his hand from her shoulder. "And even if I wasn't, you might want to think in the future about putting your hands on a woman uninvited. I may be small, but I pack a mean punch. Now, excuse me."

She turned and almost slammed right into Luca, who grinned down at her.

"Oh, I didn't see you there, honey," she drawled, grinning.

"I was about to come to your rescue, but I can see you didn't need rescuing," he explained.

She glanced over her shoulder at the man, who had paled.

"Certainly not," she confirmed. "But I do need a kiss," she murmured. She leaned up on her toes to kiss him before whispering in his ear. "Or a quickie to remind me whose hands I do not mind on me."

His heart seized at her words.

"Never a problem, Riley," he assured her.

Chapter Twenty-Two

"If you aren't in the moment, you are either looking forward to uncertainty or back to pain and regret."
-Jim Carrey

September brought more of the same for Riley. She thrived at work, becoming more comfortable with her coworkers, and learning every shift she spent in the department. Unlike what TV shows liked to portray, most days were fairly routine. She saw her fair share of common illness and minor traumas. But she'd also had a few noteworthy cases also. She and Brody often worked on the same shift, and she enjoyed his ridiculous sense of humor, even though she knew it covered a pain and loss underneath.

Although she was the last one to ever play matchmaker, and loathed anyone doing it to her, she wished she knew someone for the affable doctor. Still, she had introduced him to her brother and his friends, so at least he had other guys to bond with.

She sat staring at her monitor when she should be typing up discharge instructions for one of her pediatric patients. Thoughts of Luca, never far from her mind, intruded once again. He'd been on a mission since her return to reacquaint her with all Palm Harbor had to offer its citizens.

You'd think he was running for mayor.

Between their crazy schedules, they didn't get to spend as much time together as she would have liked, but maybe it was for the better, she thought. She tried to push down the thought, but unease slithered through her mind.

She'd already made the mistake of making him the center of her life once. Was she willing to risk it again? She closed her eyes for a moment on the memory of the horrific pain.

"Cat napping on the clock, are we?" came a gruff voice next to her.

"What?" she cried, her eyes popping back open. Brody's handsome, smiling face floated inches from hers. She swatted him with the back of her hand. "Very funny. I was gathering my thoughts before discharging my patient, if you must know," she informed him archly.

"For the little guy in five? The one with the ankle sprain?" he asked, shaking his head. "If it requires you to 'gather your thoughts' then how do you plan to pass your boards, kiddo?"

"Ugh, don't mention those," she begged. She finished typing then got up to retrieve the instructions as they printed out. After handing them off to the patient's nurse, she returned to her seat. "Any tips on that, by the way?" she asked. "Since you're a veteran and all?"

"Ha! Is that your way of saying I'm old?" he asked.

"Not so much old as older," she said with a grin. "Normally, I don't worry about standardized testing, but this has me freaked."

"Well, with your big brain, you've nothing to worry about. Just don't psych yourself out," he advised.

"Huh, like I would ever do that," she said with a laugh. "At least I have a few months left. I've been pacing myself, making notes of which areas I'm less confident in."

He shook his head. "No, not freaking yourself out at all. Weren't you top of your class in medical school?"

She felt her cheeks warm. "Uh, second, actually."

"And we still hired you?" he joked. "Wow, our standards are slipping. Seriously, Riley, this smart and double boarded, you could have written your own ticket. Why here?"

She shrugged. "This is home. I never considered going anywhere else. I dreamed of coming home for so long, I couldn't wait to get here," she confessed.

"And is it everything you thought it would be?" he asked.

"Everything and more," she said with a grin.

"Then you made the right choice. Not everyone can say that you know. Not everyone finds their niche," he commented. His voice dropped at the end so much, she almost had to lean in to hear him.

"What about you, Brody? Are you happy here? Do you think you'll stay?"

"I'm as happy here as I am going to be anywhere, I guess. I know it sounds terrible, and I don't mean it to. I love it here, really, I do. Palm Harbor is my home now. I could never go back to Alabama. Too many memories. And thanks again for the Labor Day invite. I enjoyed meeting your family. I just, well, you know," he finished without really saying anything.

"I don't but I do," she said, heart breaking a bit for him. "You have friends here, people who care about you. I'm glad to hear you consider this your home. I'd miss you. Because you know, I don't already have enough big brothers," she joked.

"Said no woman ever," he agreed. "My sister anyway. I used to harass her something fierce in high school, making sure the boys treated her right. Of course, I was doing it for her own good. At least, that's how I remember it. She might remember it differently, as I'm sure you do from your high school days."

She shook her head. "I had a different experience from the sound of it. There weren't any boys, per se, just Luca. And we were friends."

She hoped he somehow missed the wistful note attached to her voice.

"Was he an idiot or just blind back then?" Brody asked.

Riley barked out a laugh. "Neither? Both? Who knows? It was a long time ago. Doesn't matter now, I guess."

He turned his body to look at her. "From your tone, it seems like it might. What's going on, kiddo?"

She huffed out a sigh. "Not sure," she said as honestly as she could. "Things with us are great. Better than I ever allowed myself to imagine."

"And yet?" he asked. "Because something seemed lacking in that statement."

"There's history between us, stuff that isn't so easy." She dropped her eyes to the desk, unsure what else to say or if she even wanted to say anything. "Honestly, this is a conversation I should have with Luca."

"Agreed. The question is why haven't you?"

She threw her hands in the air. "Excellent question. Let me know if you come up with something on that," she joked.

"Fear can rob you of everything if you let it. Don't let it."

"What?" she all but whispered.

He stared at her, his blue eyes filled with nothing but kindness and compassion. "Maybe I'm overstepping, but I think you haven't rocked the boat because you're afraid. Life is short. No one knows better than I do. You seem really happy with him, which is great. But you also seem like you don't trust that happiness, which is no way to live. So, maybe you need to have the conversation." He shrugged. "Like I said, overstepping, but I hate to see you unsure, doubting things. Only one way to find out."

"Dr. Matthews, can I borrow you a moment?" a nurse asked. "The guy in room five seems to think he knows more than you based on his Google search." She rolled her eyes. "Maybe you can explain better than I could why he doesn't need emergency surgery."

"On it, Megan." He got up then placed a hand on Riley's shoulder. "I'm only a phone call or text away if you ever need me." Then he walked around the counter to join the young nurse. "Let's go educate him, shall we?"

Riley couldn't help but grin, wishing she could be a fly on the wall of room five. Brody's words bounced around her head, making more sense as they did. Although she was very happy with Luca, she always felt like she was waiting for the other shoe to drop. Waiting for him to somehow break her heart again. She was tired of waiting for disaster. They needed to have a conversation about what they were doing, what they meant to each other.

She just wasn't sure how to even start such a conversation...

*****

Luca stood in the middle of the bustling kitchen for a moment and smiled. Business was great. They were as busy as they could handle. In fact, he and Mama and Gino had been talking, casually but talking nonetheless, about opening a side catering business. Maybe a destination catering business for events. Something to think about. He smiled, thinking about how proud his father would be.

Then a hand slapped the back of his head. "Ouch!" he exclaimed. He saw his mother glaring at him. "Was that necessary?"

"When my son chooses to daydream in the middle of my busy kitchen, then yes, it becomes necessary." She pointed at his face. "What's with the goofy smile?"

Her ire made him grin harder. "If you must know, I was thinking about how proud Papa would be if we opened the catering business as we've been discussing."

Her face softened. She reached up to pinch his cheeks, which he tolerated because it was her highest form of praise. But truthfully, it hurst worse than the head slaps.

"My Angelo surely smiles down on that idea," she said with a grin. "It might be time to discuss with the girls and Owen," she suggested.

It brought a grin to his face. By 'the girls' she meant Jamie and Sam who managed the books for the business. Owen was their attorney.

"Might be," he agreed.

"As lovely as the thought is, I hoped the daydreaming might be about a certain young doctor," she said with a sigh. She slapped his head once again.

"Really, Mama?" he asked, rubbing his head. "You're going to give me a concussion. Then I'm going to *need* a doctor. What about Riley?"

"When are you going to make an honest woman of my topolina? Do I have to tell you about milk and cows, Luca?"

He shuddered, in no way ever wanting to have *that* conversation with his mother. Gino snickered behind him.

"Aunt Maria, if Luca isn't respecting Riley, I am more than happy to show her how a real man treats a woman," he offered.

Even though he knew his cousin only wanted to get a rise out of him, Luca's blood boiled at the thought of another man touching his Riley. He turned to deal with him when his mother beat him to the punch.

She merely gave him 'the look.' The one his mother had been giving him and Matteo since they'd been smart enough to understand it. Gino shut his mouth.

"Now, as I was saying before being rudely interrupted by that child," she began again. "I do not pretend to know what happened between you guys in the past, but she is back and for good. You seem happy together. She is an extraordinary woman, Luca. Do not make the mistake of letting her go again. Life doesn't give you many do overs, my son."

With those words of advice, she walked away, leaving him to stare after her, knowing she was right. He grabbed his phone from his pocket and dashed off a text to her.

"You're probably knee deep in sick people. Wanted you to know I'm thinking of you. Miss you. Be safe."

He waited for an answer, swallowing back disappointment when it didn't come right away and slid his phone back in his pocket. She was probably busy. He lost himself in the craziness of the kitchen. Thoughts of expanding the business swirled with those of Riley in his brain for the rest of the night.

A few hours later, his phone beeped, alerting him to an incoming text. He grinned like a kid on Christmas morning, hoping it was from her.

*"Sorry, getting crushed tonight. Apparently, everyone in Palm Harbor is making bad choices. Miss you more. And I'm always safe. Coming over later? *Fingers crossed emoji*"*

He didn't hesitate to answer, feeling like a teenaged girl.

"Try to keep me away. Your mattress is comfier than mine. Must be newer."

He grinned at his own foolishness, not caring in the least. The little bubbles appeared, raising his pulse.

"Oh, so it's my mattress that attracts you. Good to know. Glad I decided NOT to drag the old one clear across the country. I'd be sleeping alone...gotta go. Incoming!"

He cringed, not sure what it meant, but knowing it couldn't be good. A bad night for him meant working short-staffed or extra-crowded. He could only imagine what a bad one for Riley looked like.

He caught Gino making kissing faces at him from across the kitchen and put his phone back in his pocket. After saluting him with one finger, he got back to work. Although they spent most nights together when she didn't have a night shift scheduled, he didn't like to assume. Now that he knew she expected him over tonight, the tension in his gut unfurled. He breathed a little easier.

Maybe if things relaxed a bit later, he could sneak into his office and take a look at the plans he'd been fooling around with for the expansion. Time to put his money where his mouth was, in more ways than one.

Chapter Twenty-Three

"If you can act calm, that's step one in trying to convince yourself to be calm."
-Brendan Bottcher

September faded into October, bringing somewhat cooler temperatures and pumpkin-spiced everything. Riley didn't care for the former but loved the latter. She was a beach girl at heart who wanted to wear her flip-flops or sandals each day of the year. However, once the temperatures cooled off enough, she would trade them in for fuzzy socks and comfy boots. She wouldn't say 'no' to an oversized hoodie either.

Her boards written exam now loomed less than a month away, which meant her level of craziness skyrocketed. Luca tried to understand, but really how could he? While he was sweet and brought her study break treats on a regular basis, he didn't get her all-encompassing need to cram every bit of emergency medicine information into her brain. What if they asked her something about a poisonous spider indigenous to Australia?

It could happen.

"Hey," the man in question said, knocking on her home office door. He held up a plain white bag and to-go cup. "In keeping with the theme and despite the current temperature of eighty-five, I come bearing a pumpkin-spice latte and pumpkin-spice cookies for dipping."

"You may enter," she joked in a deeper than her normal

voice. "But only because you come bearing sugar." She smothered a yawn with her fist. "You also happen to know I'm a sucker for caffeine."

"Ooh, I get to enter the rarified air," he joked. He dropped a kiss on her lips, the bag and coffee on her desk and then took a seat near the window. "How goes it, or shouldn't I ask?"

"I might not fail," she admitted. "At least, it's how I feel right at this moment." She shrugged. "Ask me again tomorrow."

"You're not going to fail, Riley. Surely, you know."

She took a sip of her latte to avoid answering his question, hoping he meant it as a hypothetical.

"Riley, come on. With your big brain?" he cajoled. "You're going to be fine."

She plunked down the drink harder than she meant to, splashing some on her hand. Feeling out of sorts, as she had for weeks, she unleashed her temper on the only available target.

"You cannot possibly know. This exam means everything to me, Luca. Everything in my life has led up to this. My job depends on my passing this. And this is just the written part. I have to pass this to be eligible to sit for the oral exam. And we all know how much fun that will be for me." She blew out a breath, sending tendrils of hair flying off her face. "This is important to me," she finished in a smaller voice.

"Of course, it is, which means it's important to me, too. I wish I could help you in some way other than supplying you with an endless line of caffeinated drinks," he joked.

"This isn't a joke," she snapped. "This is my life."

She watched as he stood and paced the smallish room. She might have gone a step too far, but she couldn't help how she felt.

"No one understands how important this is more than I do. I've watched you kill yourself studying day after day. When does it end? At what point do you know everything you need to know? At what point do you admit you might be starting to freak yourself out just a little?" He stopped pacing to face her, breathing hard.

"You don't understand. Please go." She turned back to her notes, not wanting to see his face.

"Are you kidding?" he asked, voice raw with emotion.

"No," she whispered. "I have several more topics to cover tonight. Your hovering doesn't help."

"Fine. Didn't realize my caring about your welfare was 'hovering.' Sorry I bothered you."

He left quietly, the soft click of the study door the only sound in the room. She stared at her notes, words blurring as tears pooled in her eyes. *This was better,* she told herself. She needed to concentrate. She would find him tomorrow and explain.

*****

"What do you recommend for heartbreak, Stella?" Luca asked the waitress when she approached. "I'll take one of whatever it might be."

"Not messing it up in the first place is my best advice," she all but growled. She looked him up and down. "I see it's far too late. I'll bring you a beer instead," she quipped before turning away.

Because he was pathetic, he checked his phone. Again. Still no word from Riley, not that he expected any. She'd made it pretty clear what her priority was. Not him.

"Here you go, Romeo," Stella sniped, plunking down a pint and a single shot glass. "Let's not repeat last time, shall we?"

He winced remembering the fierce hangover. "Agreed," he muttered.

"Let me know if you want any food." The waitress shook her head. "This is the second time you've been in here, drinking alone, in a few weeks. You may want to stop pissing off Riley. May I recommend flowers?" She tilted her head, looked at him as if considering something. "Or jewelry depending on how badly you screwed up."

He grabbed the shot and slammed it back. Vodka. Always a good choice. He took a healthy swig of his beer.

"How do you know I did something?" he asked, risking her wrath.

Stella cocked one hip. She didn't say a word.

"Okay, so it was me. But you couldn't have possibly known that for sure," he muttered then drained half the pint.

"And yet I did," she said with a laugh before walking away.

"Witch," he mumbled to himself before reaching for the next shot glass.

"I heard that," she called over her shoulder, not bothering to turn around.

"Of course, you did. Probably used your witchy, sixth sense."

A few minutes later, she returned, dropping off a plate of pretzel sticks and cheese dip. "You're gonna want these," she said by way of explanation for the food he hadn't ordered.

Since she wasn't wrong, he grabbed one, dipped it, and bit into it, groaning at the explosion of melted cheese and salt on his tongue. He washed it down with the rest of his beer.

Fifteen minutes later, Brody appeared at his table. Every time Luca had seen the other man, he'd always been laughing or joking. Not this time.

"Thought I might find you here," he said by way of hello. He slid into the other side of the booth without an invite, setting his draft on the table.

"Why don't you join me, Brody?" Luca asked. He shoved another bite of pretzel in his mouth to stop himself from saying something else snarky. The other man hadn't done anything to deserve it.

"Should I be betting on your current blood alcohol level?" Brody asked. "We do it at work."

"Really?" Luca asked. "It seems, well, rude."

"No, rude is throwing up on my favorite pair of work sneakers because you can't hold your liquor." He shook his head. "They always seem to be able to sense when I've gotten them broken in just right, too."

"Uh, not that I'm not happy to see you, but what are you doing here?" Luca asked.

"I called Riley to check in," Brody replied. He grinned (grinned!) at Luca's narrowed eyes. "Relax. You know she and I are just friends. I'm worried about her, too. She's making herself crazy over boards."

"That's what I said," Luca muttered. "Right before she told me not to let the door hit me."

Brody smirked. "Sounds like our Riley. What? She's mine, too, just in a different, little sister way. Anyway, she didn't get into specifics, but she mentioned having a fight with you over it." He took a sip of his beer. "I could tell she'd been crying," he finished in a roughened tone.

Luca dragged a hand through his hair. "I don't know how to help her, man. With each day that passes, she pulls away a little more. She's not sleeping and not taking care of herself."

Brody nodded. "I've tried, at work, to help her review without putting pressure on her." He blew out a breath. "She could very easily be the smartest person I've ever met. But she's gotten all twisted up over boards."

Stella slapped a menu down in front of Brody. "Evening, handsome." She jerked her chin toward Luca. "This might take a while. You may want to consider some food," she suggested, before turning away with a swing of her hips.

Luca chuckled at Brody's grin. "Don't bother. The mountain tending bar is her significant other. Dusty's the nicest guy in the world but would snap you like a twig for looking at her the wrong way."

"Thanks for the warning," Brody said with a grin. "Doesn't mean I can't look. It's about all I'm good for anyway," he mumbled into his beer.

Luca thought about asking him what he meant but let the comment go. He had enough to deal with for one night. He leaned back against the booth and closed his eyes for a moment to gather his thoughts. "All I did was suggest maybe, just maybe, she was freaking herself out about this exam. And maybe she should, I don't know, calm down a bit. Cut herself some slack." He threw his hands in the air. "She got all scary calm like women do when they're really pissed and asked me to leave."

"I'm sure she took your advice well," Brody drawled. He shook his head in a way that made Luca's stomach drop.

"But I meant it in a good way," he started, aware of how lame the words sounded. "Riley is the smartest person any of us have ever met. Why should she worry about this after everything she's already accomplished?"

"You don't get it," Brody said. "People expect more from someone like her. *Because* she's so off the charts smart. Because everything comes so easily to her, or so it seems. But everything in life comes at a price. She's young to have accomplished everything she has already. There's a lot of pressure in that, and not all of it is from outside of her."

Luca sighed. "You're not wrong. She's always been her own toughest critic."

"She has less than a month to go before the written exam. This will get worse before it gets better. You need to be there for her, without judgment, without thoughtless comments, no matter how well-intentioned," Brody suggested.

"I need to not be a jackass, in other words," Luca broke it down.

"Well, I wasn't going to put it quite that way but sure," Brody chuckled.

"What'll it be folks?" Stella asked, appearing at their booth again.

Brody ordered a burger and fries while Luca shook his head.

"I'll be back with your order shortly," she said and disappeared into the growing crowd.

Luca pulled his phone from his pocket, but just as quickly, Brody grabbed it from him.

"Believe me, I'm doing you a favor. Apologize when you're completely sober," he advised. He slid the phone in his own pocket. "Plus, you might want to give her a little time to cool down."

"Yeah, good idea," Luca said. He picked at the pretzels and cheese.

Brody held up most of the conversation as they ate, entertaining him with stories from work. He listened but didn't offer much, thinking about Riley and what had happened between them. He definitely needed to make this up to her and support her through these next few weeks as she prepared for the exam.

But later, as they got ready to leave, Luca couldn't help worrying he was missing something larger. Something else looming just under the surface that threatened his peaceful existence with Riley.

Chapter Twenty-Four

"Apologies are great but don't really change anything. You know what does? Action."
-Stella Young

Riley holed up in her home office, empty coffee cup at her side, poring over burn treatment protocol. Not her favorite thing to study but would definitely appear on the exam. She winced remembering a little boy in residency who'd grabbed a pot of boiling water off the stove, upending it on himself. Sometimes, she could still hear his screams and those of his hysterical mother.

She shook her head, willing away the terrible memories. Smothering a yawn, she grabbed her cup and wandered into the kitchen for a refill. Grabbing a pod for her machine, she reached down to pet the 'twins' as she'd come to think of her kittens. Both wound around her ankles, hoping for a treat now that she'd emerged from her cave. Because she was hopeless where they were concerned, she tossed them each one.

The coffee machine spit out the latest of her caffeine-laden lifeline, its savory scent spicing the air. She took a deep breath, enjoying it for a moment. Her phone buzzed from her pocket, alerting her to a text. She stilled. It was *his* ring tone. She hadn't heard from Luca in over twenty-four hours, since asking him to leave. She covered her face with her hands, cringing as she remembered. *Bitch.* No other word for it. Well, there were, but she didn't care for them. Bitch would have to do.

She needed to apologize, knew this, but had somehow never gotten around to it. Between falling asleep on her notes, a grueling twelve-hour shift and now back at studying, time had passed her by. With a shaking hand, she pulled her phone from her pocket.

"Words are easy, but I am sorry. Not trying to make anything harder for you. Listen to this then open your front door."

She touched the attachment to hear the racy strains of Justin Timberlake's "Sexy Back" fill her kitchen. She cranked the volume and clutched her phone, dancing around the room. She laughed and laughed, remembering her ridiculous crush, obsession really, on JT and how indulgent Luca had been. One time, a particularly catty group of girls had cornered her about her 'friendship' with him. When he'd found her crying in the bleachers later, he'd driven her home playing this song on loop the whole way. Just because it made her smile.

She gave herself over to the music, making her way to her door. What could he possibly have left for her? Shimmying her hips in her brief booty shorts and tank, she pulled it open only to find him standing there. Mouth hanging open.

"Oh!" she exclaimed. "I, uh, thought maybe you left coffee," she finished lamely.

"I did," he said, holding up a to-go cup and a take-out bag from Mama's. "I also brought dinner because I know how you get." He shook his head. "Gummy bears are not a meal."

She stopped the music as she felt the heat creep into her face. "I, uh…"

"Hey, don't stop on my account," he suggested.

"Come in." She reached behind him to close the door.

"I only wanted to drop this off. I know you're busy." Luca dragged a hand through his hair. "The last thing I want is to make anything harder for you. You know that."

"I do, of course, I do." She reached out to throw her arms around him. He smelled so good, a mixture of spicy Italian food and crisp male. "I'm so sorry for yesterday. I was so mean to you."

"Can you take a break? Maybe eat something?" he

asked, his tone a little tentative.

Her stomach growled, answering for her. "I believe it's a yes," she said, laughing. "Come sit with me. Have you eaten?"

She led the way into the kitchen. Gabriel pounced on Luca as if he hadn't seen him in months. Lucy sat under the table and glared but didn't hiss. Riley took it as progress.

"I think Satan hates me a little less today," Luca commented as he slid into a chair at the table.

"Huh, funny, I was just thinking that. Maybe *Lucy* isn't plotting your death anymore."

She opened the bag, almost swooning at the scents pouring from it. "Oh my! What did you bring me?"

"Well, I remember what you were like in school and figured this was like that but on steroids. So, carbs and protein, right?" He lifted out a container and placed it in front of her. "Veal parm with a side of angel hair, your favorite of all the pastas." He reached back in and grabbed a smaller one. "Salad with extra veggies because gummy bears aren't an actual food group."

"But they should be," Riley protested. "Especially now."

"You can have some after you eat your salad. I made that for you knowing you've already probably eaten your weight in the bears," he joked.

"You're not wrong," she muttered. "I may have to take up running daily. Or something."

"And last, but certainly not least, from Mama." He whipped out another box and held it aloft.

Her eyes rounded. "Is that?" she whispered. "Oh, please tell me it is."

"It might be turtle cheesecake," he admitted. "But you don't get to find out until you've cleaned your plate, young lady."

"Won't be a problem. We got run off our feet today. Not sure I had anything other than coffee and a yogurt. Brody quizzed me in between patients." She grinned at him. "I got gummy bears for a reward when I was right." She reached for the salad to take a bite.

He smiled back at her, but it didn't reach his dark eyes.

"What?" she asked. She set down her fork and grabbed his hand. "Tell me."

"I want to like him. He seems like a nice guy."

"Okay," she said, dragging the two syllables out to several. "So, what's the issue?"

"Tell me there isn't one. You work with him a lot. I know this. It just seems like your face lights up when you talk about him," he mumbled.

Riley clapped her hands and laughed.

"What?" he groused.

"You're jealous," she crowed. "You're jealous of a man who's at least fifteen years older than me, if not more. Sorry, but it's hilarious."

She went back to eating, realizing how hungry she really was if her growling stomach was any indication.

"I'm not jealous, per se," he said. "I just." Luca blew out a breath. "Fine, I might be a little jealous. You have so much in common with him. What does age matter?"

She stared at him. Couldn't help herself. Could he really feel this way? Worry about Brody of all people?

"Um, age doesn't matter, you're right. But Luca, aren't you missing the obvious here?" she asked.

"What?"

She waved a hand between them. "You and I have *everything* in common. We have history, a shared past. Brody and I can never claim that." She reached across the table to grab his hand. "You are the only man who matters to me, Luca, even when you're being a pain in my butt."

He raised her hand to his mouth and kissed it, releasing a herd of butterflies in her belly.

"Sometimes, I forget," he admitted. He shook his head. "Not forget really but it feels like we're starting over. This, what we're doing now, is different."

"Sort of, I guess," she said. "But it's a part of the past also, don't you think? Or maybe an extension of it. We have *history* together. It's important. I've never had this with anyone else."

And part of their history was terrible and hurtful, she thought. Part of their history ended with her heartbroken and crying for days. That part needed to be brought to light, dealt with. But not until after her exams. This was too important to risk dredging up the past right now. She pulled her hand from his and picked up her fork to take a bite.

"I hope you're going to help with some of this," she invited, hoping to change the topic. "No way I can eat all of it by myself."

"Even the cheesecake?" he said with a smirk.

She pointed her fork at him. "Don't even think about it. Your mother meant it for me."

"That's okay. I had other sweets in mind for dessert," he said with a grin and a wink.

*****

Luca lay awake in the dark, watching Riley sleep. He wasn't sure what had awoken him and cared even less. He took the time to study her. Even in sleep, she didn't look fully relaxed. Her brow wrinkled from time to time as if her brain wouldn't shut down. He longed to soothe a hand over it but feared waking her. She needed her rest.

She needed to get through this board thing, then maybe she could relax a little. He didn't truly understand it, other than how important it was to her career. Maybe he could ask Brody. He didn't want to freak her out anymore. Maybe, after it was finally over, he could take her away for a few days. He smiled in the dark at the idea. Just the two of them alone somewhere. Hopefully naked. Yep, it was a great idea. He snuggled down against her, hoping to fall back to sleep.

He thought about what she'd said earlier. They shared a history like no other. He honestly couldn't remember a time without her in it. Their families were best friends. She was always just there. Because they were both the youngest, they'd been paired off since, well, forever. Having a best friend with such a big brain came in handy, too. Science and math had never been his strong suits, much to her amusement. 'Luca, it's so obvious,' he could almost still hear her say.

Then other words ricocheted around his head. His words from five years ago. Harsh words with claws that shredded her tender heart. Luca squeezed his eyes shut as if by doing so he could block the memory of them. He never meant to hurt her, wanted only the best for her, but he'd gone about it the worst possible way. He rubbed a hand over his face. Nothing he could do about it now.

Riley stirred on the bed, turned toward him in her sleep. He gathered her in his arms, held her to his body.

"I've got you," he soothed in a hushed voice. "I'll always be here for you."

He trailed one hand over her hair and down her back, soothing her. Her breathing evened out again. He envied her. Sleep seemed a long way off for him.

Chapter Twenty-Five

"What nicer thing can you do for somebody than make them breakfast?"

-Anthony Bourdain

"You're spoiling me," Riley said as she strolled into the kitchen the next morning. She didn't have to be at work until ten, so she had time to eat without rushing.

"I'm making scrambled eggs," Luca countered. "Hardly falls under the heading of spoiling." He dropped a kiss on her lips before turning back to the stove.

"Ha! Could have used you all through my medical training when I was lucky to grab a Pop Tart on my way out the door," she told him. "A great day was stopping long enough to toast it."

He cringed. "Please tell me you're joking."

"I wish. Those were actually the good days," she clarified. "Bad days meant coffee or energy drinks."

"Please, I'm begging you, stop. Hearing it makes my chef soul weep," he lamented.

She laughed at his pathetic face. "Knew I should have learned to cook, not that I would have had the time. What I needed was my own personal chef."

Luca turned at that moment with the frying pan in his hand. For just a fleeting second, something she couldn't quite name passed through his eyes. But it vanished as quickly.

"Come sit down, breakfast is served," he announced.

She took her seat, glancing at the plates and juice already on the table. "Wow, how long have you been up?"

"Oh, a while, I guess. Didn't sleep great last night."

"Something wrong?" she asked before taking a bite of her eggs. "Mmmm is that Asiago in there? Wow, see I would never think to do that."

"Yes, it is, and thanks for noticing. Not wrong really, just thinking."

"How did I have Asiago in my fridge?" she asked.

"You didn't," he said. "I brought a few things with me. Your fridge is pretty bare."

"Luca, you don't have to. Make a list. I'm happy to pick stuff up at the store next time I go."

He looked up from his meal, cocked one dark brow. "Really? When's the last time you grocery shopped?"

"Do you think the elves bring me food, Luca? If I want to eat, then I have to shop," she informed him with a bit of heat.

"Ah, grabbing some yogurt, coffee, and bananas isn't exactly grocery shopping," he corrected.

"You forgot ice cream," she mentioned, sticking out her tongue because she felt like it. "Wow, you're such a snob."

"I'm a chef, of course, I'm a *food* snob," he corrected haughtily.

"Whatever, fine, you shop. I can just put money toward it, I guess," she offered.

She knew immediately she'd said the wrong thing. He lowered his fork to the plate. His face darkened.

"Did I ask you for money?" he queried in a tight voice.

"Well, no, but if I'm going to eat, then I should pay," she countered.

"Did I ask you for money?" he repeated.

Riley threw up her hands. "Ugh, no, Luca, you didn't ask for money. Excuse me for wanting to help."

"Good. Glad we settled it." He picked up his fork to continue eating.

She threw her napkin at him, hitting him in the face. "You know you're impossible, right?"

"Nope," he answered, popping the sound.

"Whatever," she ground out.

"Oh, who's McBurney?" he asked.

"What? What are you talking about?"

"You were muttering about someone named McBurney last night in your sleep. Wasn't sure if it was a coworker or what. Seemed important since you said it a few times," he said.

Riley stared at him before laughing. "Huh, maybe I am studying too much."

His look made her think he questioned her sanity.

"McBurney's sign is something we check with patients who come in with abdominal pain when appendicitis is suspected," she explained. She leaned over to poke him in his right, lower abdomen. "It's part of the examination we do, along with labs and a CT scan of the belly."

"Well, look at that, not even nine o'clock in the morning, and I've already learned something new," he bragged.

She shook her head and tried to cover her face. "I'm so over studying for this thing," she muttered. "Can't believe I'm talking in my sleep now."

"Haven't you done it before?" he asked.

"I wouldn't know," she answered, suddenly very interested in her cooling eggs and toast.

"But surely Thomas or someone would have mentioned it," he began.

"I haven't had a lot of 'sleepovers' for lack of a better word. Is that what you wanted to hear?" she huffed out. "In fact, if data is what you need, you're only the third guy I've slept with. One in college just to see what the big fuss was all about." She shook her head. "Wasn't impressed. Then Thomas. Now you." She picked up her juice and took a swig, anything to cool her burning cheeks.

"I wasn't asking but thank you for telling me. Obviously, I know there have been men in your life. I'm not naïve. You're a beautiful woman. Men would have to be foolish to not want to be with you." He cleared his throat. "Honestly, I'm shocked the number is so low, but I also know it is because you chose it to be."

She tilted her head. "Why do you say that?" she whispered

"Because I know you, Riley. I know sex has to mean something to you. You're not the type to just sleep around. Not that there's anything wrong with it if that's your thing. Just don't see you doing it."

She nodded. "Definitely wasn't my thing in college. By the time I got to medical school, I barely had time to breathe. It wasn't a priority. School was my priority." She flipped her hand around. "I know how it sounds."

"It sounds like you were focused and driven," he said. "Nothing more, nothing less."

She smiled at him. Her heart felt warm and mushy. He always got her like no one else.

"Exactly. People used sex, or drinking or other things, to blow off steam. And I get it, but it was never my thing," she admitted. "Then I met Thomas, and we sort of fell into an arrangement. But you know that already."

"Yes, no need to discuss it, or him, again," he said through clenched teeth.

She laughed lightly. "Really, Luca? Care to share your number? I'm sure it's quite a bit higher."

"It is, though probably not as high as you may think. The restaurant has always kept me busy, focused. After the first few years, when we realized we weren't going to drown, I went to school, got my business degree. I wanted to be able to handle all aspects of it. After losing my father the way we did and getting thrown into the deep end, well, there wasn't much time for anything else."

"You've done an amazing job, you and your family," she praised.

"Thank you. It means a lot coming from you. We have plans for the next stage," he said, making her curious.

"Next stage? What does this mean? Are you expanding? Opening another location?" She clapped her hands together. "Oh, this is so exciting."

"Well, yes and no. For the past two years or so, we've talked about opening a catering hall. Someplace to have events, like weddings and such. Mama brought it up, mentioned it being a dream of my father's. Then Matteo sort of ran with it. He's the one really excited about it, interested in running it."

"Not you?" she asked.

"I'm excited *for* it. For anything that helps to grow the family business. But, no, I'd rather stay in the kitchen. I don't want the headache of managing all the details of that side of the business. I want to…"

"You want to feed people," she finished for him.

He grinned at her. "How did you know?"

"Because I know you. It's all you've ever wanted to do. And why shouldn't you? You're amazing at it." She grinned as a bit of red creeped into his face.

"There's something so basic, yet so perfect, about feeding people. I can't explain it. It soothes my soul. And while I don't want anything to do with the day to day of what we're trying to build, I understand it. I want people to come celebrate their big moments with us," he explained.

She nodded. "I get it. I do because it's how I feel about medicine. People come to me for help when they're sick or injured and afraid. They trust me to make them feel better. And while I can't always do that, I can do my best for them."

He shook his head. "How do you do it, though, when you can't help them? How do you tell them? How do you tell their families? I don't know how you handle it."

"It never gets easier, I can tell you. There's a certain privilege to being with someone when they're dying. Even if all you can do is be with them or hold their hand. Sometimes, all I can do is ease their pain. And then, when they're gone, help their families to understand what happened."

"There's a reason I'm a chef and not a doctor," he joked.

"Everyone on this earth is important, Luca. Everyone plays a role," she said. "Mine only seems more important from the outside." She pointed at her plate. "You keep me fed, allowing me to go to work and take care of people. That's important."

"Well then eat up. I might have made you something to bring for lunch also," he said, smiling at her. "You know, so you don't run out of steam halfway through your shift and resort to gummy bears."

She sprang up from her chair and threw her arms around him. "You really are the best!" she exclaimed.

"So, I keep trying to tell you," he joked.

That afternoon, in between patients, Riley flipped through her board review flash cards. With the exam only weeks away, she alternated between wishing it were over already and wanting another month to cram.

"I know you can handle questions about febrile seizures, Dr. Layne," Harper joked over her shoulder.

Riley looked up from her card and smiled at her favorite nurse. "You're right of course, but it never hurts to review. What are you doing here during the day? Thought for sure you were a vampire."

"Living the dream," she quipped. "Actually, filling in for Amanda and earning some overtime." Harper yanked the cards from her hands. "You're going to make yourself crazy," she admonished. She plunked down a tall cup in front of Riley. "Strawberry milkshake, extra thick, like you prefer. You're welcome."

Riley shoved the straw in her mouth and sucked in a gulp, moaning as the freezing yumminess hit her taste buds.

"You might be my new best friend," she cried.

"What do you mean might?" Harper protested.

"Hey, thought that was my title?" Brody added, taking the seat on her other side.

Riley took another long sip. "I don't know, this is hard to top. What do you have to offer, Dr. Matthews?"

"How about my ridiculously good looks and outlandish sense of humor?" he offered, sending both women into peals of laughter.

"Well, he certainly has the humor part right," Harper

joked.

"Hey, now, watch the fragile male ego at play here," Brody cautioned.

"Hmm, not so sure it's all that fragile," Riley questioned.

"Wow, just wow," he grumbled good-naturedly. "So how goes the studying? Or shouldn't I ask?"

"Not really sure," she admitted, frowning. "I just wondered to myself if I would feel better taking it right now or having another month tacked on to study." She grimaced. "Wonder what it means."

"Means I'm glad I'm a nurse," Harper said, laughing.

Brody grinned at her. "You're not wrong. But honestly, it means you're ready. And you're freaking yourself out. Don't do it, Riley. You know better."

She dropped her head onto her arms and moaned. "I know better but not how to stop myself at this point. I want it to be over."

"And it will be soon, I promise," he attempted to console her. "I can only tell you what worked for me. Take another practice test. Then really look at the areas you still feel you need work in. And focus on those. The ones you have cold, let them go. Do not make yourself crazy trying to cram everything you've learned in the past five years. You will absolutely do more harm than good." She felt him pat her on the head like a Golden Retriever. "You've got this. I promise."

She lifted her head up and offered him a small smile. "I know that, really. I just feel so much pressure. I *have* to do well. You understand."

"I do." He caught her gaze. "And so does Luca. Let him in, Riley. He may not be a doctor, but he cares about you. Knows you better than probably any other person on the planet. Don't shut him out. Especially now."

She rolled her eyes at him. "I know, I'm an idiot. It's so hard sometimes."

"To what?" he asked her gently. "To let others in? To admit you're human?"

"To open my heart to him," she whispered. "Again. Not

sure I could survive it a second time."

They both stared at her, neither saying a word. She realized this was entirely new information.

"Forget I said the last part," she begged.

Harper slung an arm around her shoulder. "I'm the last person who should ever lecture about taking chances and letting people in, except maybe I am that person. Until Owen came along, I was perfectly happy with my castle walls and alligator-filled moat. I had a perfectly good life if I didn't look too closely. But he made me want more. He made me want things. And every day since, I am so glad I did."

"At the risk of sounding like a broken record, you know my feelings on the subject," Brody offered. "Life is short. No guarantees. Except this. The answer is always no if you never even try."

"Hey, Riley, medics are bringing in a kiddo from a pedestrian versus motor vehicle. Doesn't sound too bad, alert and oriented, possible orthopedic involvement. Here in five," Sue, their day shift charge nurse, advised.

"Okay, thanks for the warning," she called to the nurse as she turned and walked away.

"I have four open if you want to use that one," Harper offered.

"Sounds good. Unless we see something different when they roll through the door, that's the plan," she responded, already thinking about all the possibilities.

"And she's off," Brody commented to Harper. "Honestly, watching how her brain works is fascinating. And exhausting."

"No joke. Try being her nurse," Harper added.

Within minutes, they heard the wail of the approaching ambulance. Riley said a silent plea to the universe for the child and their family. She'd seen too many families already in her short career torn apart by tragedy.

As the outer doors slid open, a child's cry tore apart the relative silence in the department, followed by a harried mother's pleas for help.

"At least we know there's a good airway," Brody exclaimed.

Riley shot him a look before nodding then heading toward the ambulance bay entrance. What looked like a five or six-year-old boy lay strapped to a backboard. His face, red from screaming, was thankfully clear of blood. His blue eyes shone brightly. She stepped right up next to him and peered down into his face.

"Well, hello there. What sort of silly thing happened to you today?" she asked. "Did a Tyrannosaurus Rex step on you?"

The little boy stopped crying long enough to stare at her, possibly wondering if she had lost her mind, but Riley didn't care. At least he wasn't crying anymore.

"How silly of me. I forgot to tell you my name." She held out her hand to where he could reach it with his arms strapped to the board. "I'm Dr. Riley, and I specialize in kiddos your age. Why don't you come with me?" She glanced at his mother. "Hi there. You can come, too, of course." Then, off she went, pulling the stretcher to room four as Harper pushed from the other end of it. The medics told their story as they all walked.

Once in the room, the team transferred their patient ever so gently to the stretcher. The medic's radio squawked, and Riley assured them they had this from here. She pulled the curtain around the four of them. "Now, since you know my name, it seems only fair I get to know yours." She turned to the bewildered looking parent. "And yours, of course."

The little boy giggled. "You're weird," he announced, before grimacing again.

"Brandon!" the shocked mother gasped. "I'm so sorry, Dr. Riley. Please excuse him. He's had a tough day."

Riley laughed. "Well, of course he has. It's not every day a T. Rex stomps on you, and you live to tell the tale. So, you're Brandon and does your mother have a name, or shall I just call her Brandon's mom?"

"Oh, sorry, I'm Jane. Jane Farrell," the woman responded.

"Brandon and Jane, this is Harper, and she is my very favorite nurse in the entire world. And do you want to know why?"

His large blue eyes widened. "Why?" the little boy shouted, making everyone laugh.

"Well, there are many reasons, but most of all she knows magic. Harper has the ability to take away your pain. Isn't that cool? You won't even feel a thing. Right, Harper?" Riley pulled her aside and gave her a verbal order for pain medication based on the youngster's weight. Harper nodded.

"I sure can," Harper agreed. "Let me get some of my magic tricks gathered together."

"Now, why don't you guys tell me what happened?" Riley suggested.

Brandon's lower lip quivered. "I'm in trouble." One tear slid down his grimy face. "I forgot to look both ways."

At his words, his mother's composure cracked. Her hands shook. "We've talked about the importance of always checking for cars. Always."

"I looked, Mommy. I just forgot to look the other way," he said, voice trembling. He looked at Riley. "I had to get my soccer ball from the street," he explained.

"I looked at my phone for a second. I swear it was no longer than a few seconds," his mother cried, a sob following. "My husband texted, and I answered him. So stupid!"

"Why don't we focus on the good news, huh?" Riley encouraged. "Brandon here is awake and talking to us, which already tells me a lot of very good news." She leaned forward and tapped his head gently. "It means your big, beautiful brain in here is doing great. So let me tell you what's going to happen next. I know coming to the ER is a scary thing, both for little boys and their mothers." She offered both a smile. "Harper and I are going to make it as unscary as possible. Sound like a deal?"

Brandon glanced at his mother, as if looking for permission, and the woman nodded.

"Okay, first, honey we're going to give you some medicine to make your leg stop hurting. Then we'll take some pictures of you, so we can see your bones. How cool is that?" She pointed to his right leg which had been splinted in the field. "Looks like you might have hurt your leg, huh?"

"Yes, ma'am, it hurts a little," he whispered, lower lip quivering. "That's where the car bumped me."

Riley bit her own lip to keep from laughing. *Men!* Even at his tender age, they felt the need to be stoic, never admit to pain. His mother, on the other hand, gasped at the mention of the car. Color leached from her already pale face.

"On it," Harper muttered before shoving a chair behind the mother's knees as she swayed. "Jane, we've got you and Brandon is in excellent hands. I can only imagine how terrified you must be," she whispered to the young mother as she helped her sit. "But know Dr. Layne and I are doing everything Brandon needs." Riley watched as Harper squatted down in front of Jane and grasped her hands. "But what he needs most right now is reassurance from his mom."

Riley held her breath until the other woman nodded. Then she blew out a quick breath and forced a smile she didn't feel.

"So, now that we have a plan, let's start with making you feel better, Brandon. With your mom's permission, I can give you some medicine through the tube in your arm to take away the pain. Sound good, everyone?"

Both Brandon and Jane nodded.

While Harper drew up the medication, Riley had a quick chat with mom to explain what had to be done and the medication she wanted to give for pain control. When she agreed, Riley completed her thorough patient assessment to make sure she hadn't missed any other injuries. Then she ordered a set of x-rays.

"Jane, I can tell already without the x-rays he broke his femur. That's the bone in his thigh. The question now is how badly he broke it and whether or not he will require surgery to fix it. The x-rays will give us a better idea, so I want to get those done. Then I'll have someone from orthopedics come and take a look. Sound like a plan?"

The other woman nodded, glancing at her son lying quietly on the stretcher. She stroked his sweaty hair away from his face, the gesture plucking at Riley's heart strings. She excused herself from the room, promising to come back as soon as they had more information.

Chapter Twenty-Six

"One has to do everything at the right time. That includes motherhood."
-Shamila Tagore

"Do you want children?" Harper asked as they walked back to the desk. Riley took a moment to sign back into her computer before responding. Really, she gave herself time to think about her answer.

"Not sure. You?" she asked in return.

A laugh greeted her question. "Not the answer I expected," Harper said in response to Riley's raised brow. "It's just you grew up in the perfect family, Riley."

It was Harper's turn to stare as Riley snorted. "Hardly!" she scoffed in reply. "You try being the odd ball out in that pack of siblings."

Harper shrugged. "Beats being alone and an adult way before I should have been." She held up a hand to stop Riley from saying anything. "Not looking for sympathy. Merely stating a fact. Your Rockwellish family trumps my childhood hands down, so you not being sure about wanting to have kids of your own took me by surprise. No judgment."

Riley shook her head. "It's not so much not wanting to have kids as much as never really thinking about it. I've spent my whole life laser-focused on my goals, really to the exclusion of all else. Having kids, getting married, really anything outside of medical school and residency weren't even on my radar."

"What about now?" Harper queried. "At some point, you have to start living your life, not living for the future. You'll miss everything that way."

Riley threw her hands up in the air. "I'm aware. I promise. But I have to get through these next few weeks. Get this stupid exam behind me. Then I get to have a life."

She felt the weight of her friend's stare, trying to not bend under it.

Harper smiled. "You were so good in there with him, it made me wonder. That's all," she said by way of explanation.

Riley sighed. "I love kids, obviously, since I chose this specialty. I've spent the past, well, forever, completely focused on my education. On getting to now. I haven't had time to think about anything else. To dream about anything else."

She didn't say Luca shattered those dreams five years ago with a handful of careless, cruel words. No reason for Harper to hate him, especially now since Riley and Luca were whatever they were. She frowned at the unspoken questions racing through her mind. She didn't have time for this right now.

"Why do I feel like there's something you're not telling me?" her friend asked.

Riley dragged her gaze back to Harper's knowing one. "Maybe because you're super smart and intuitive?" she admitted. "But this is a conversation for another time. Right now, I have Brandon's femur to think about."

She clicked on his chart and entered notes for his exam while she waited for his films to show up. Already sure he'd broken his leg, the question remained *how badly* and whether or not he would need a surgical intervention. It could go either way, and the ortho consult would have the final say.

"Hey, how'd your little guy do?" Brody asked as he dropped into the chair next to her.

She pointed at the screen, grimacing, as his broken femur appeared on it. "Look for yourself."

Brody leaned in, peering over her shoulder. "Oh, yuck."

"Nice," she teased, swatting him. "How many years of

schooling to come up with that word?" she teased.

"Glad he's not my patient," Brody grumbled.

"Thanks a lot."

Riley entered a stat ortho consultation then followed it up with a brief phone call. She explained the situation and hung up the phone. After typing for another few minutes, she closed out his chart.

"Never play poker," Brody advised.

"What?" she asked, whirling to face him.

"Your face just now. Either you sucked on a lemon or that was Williams from ortho," he guessed.

She felt her face tighten again at the mention of the cocky surgeon.

"Too bad he's brilliant and super with the kiddos," she grumbled.

"He is a bit much to take," Brody agreed.

"I've only met him once. He stopped just short of patting me on the head. Mistook me for a volunteer, I think. Ugh, I know I look young but really?" She leaned back and sighed. "When are people ever going to take me seriously?"

Brody leaned over to nudge her with his knee. "You're young, yes, but brilliant in your own right. People are going to think what they want. But they can't deny the obvious. Keep showing up, Riley, doing what you do. Be yourself. That's all you need to do."

"You're a good egg, Brody," she told him, smiling.

"All right, enough of the mushiness. I have a reputation to protect," he warned.

"Well, when his highness arrives, I'll be in with my patient," she advised.

*****

After a busier-than-usual lunch crowd, Luca wiped the back of his hand across his forehead and took a long drink of water.

"When can I expect my first grandbaby?" his mother

yelled as she entered the hot kitchen.

He almost dropped the water bottle.

"Geez, Mama, a little warning next time," he muttered before kissing her cheek.

She pinched his. Hard enough to get his full attention. "Always with the smart mouth, this one."

She muttered something in Italian. He heard his father's name, which made him grin. His mother pulled out the big guns only when truly upset with him.

"Mama, Riley's barely back home. Give her a moment to catch her breath," he advised. He mentally crossed his fingers, hoping she would give him a break.

"Last time you gave her 'a moment to catch her breath' she came home dragging the *cretino* with her." She gave him *the look*. It took every ounce of concentration to not shudder. Mama was a force to be reckoned with, even if he was a grown-ass man.

His brother, Matteo, snickered from the corner.

"I seem to remember being the younger of your two children. Maybe we should ask Matty why he hasn't given you any grandchildren yet," Luca suggested.

He bit his lip to keep from laughing as he watched his brother scramble to escape from their diminutive mother. What she might lack in height, she more than made up for with attitude.

A tremendous sigh racked her frame. "Angelo, where did I go wrong? Two healthy, grown sons and not a single bambino to spoil in my old age," she cried.

"Mama, would you like to look at the plans the architect has drawn up for the catering hall?" Matteo asked.

Luca met his brother's eyes over their mother's head and grinned. Diversion meant survival for them.

She clapped her hands. "Of course, Matty, of course. If I cannot rock a grandbaby to sleep, this will have to do."

"I'm going to go check on something at the bar," Luca muttered, slipping out while he could. Although he had staff to do this already, he knew a golden opportunity when he saw it.

Slipping through the swinging kitchen doors, Luca ducked out into the dining room and strode behind the bar. He poured himself a soft drink and sighed in relief. As much as he loved his mother, she was a bit much at times. Things with Riley were great. He didn't need Maria Rinaldi sticking her nose in, good intentions or not.

He leaned against the bar, grinning, and thought about Riley. Despite their odd schedules and her ridiculous study regimen, they stole moments together. His favorites were waking in the middle of the night to find her asleep next to him. Hearing her sigh. Tracing a finger down one bare arm. Watching the moonlight bathe her face in its ethereal glow. Just being next to her was enough for him. For now.

After a lifetime of waiting, of wanting her, of never acting on the feelings he'd harbored forever, he was ready to go all in. They weren't kids anymore. Their timing was finally in sync.

Then what held him back?

Painful memories flashed across his mind. Too big eyes in a face suddenly devoid of color tortured him. Her small hands reaching for him, as though seeking a lifeline in a stormy sea. And all he had done was back further away from her, stepped out of her reach. Because Luca had known that night if he had touched her, even for a moment, he'd never have been able to let her go again.

He shook his head, took a sip, and shook himself from his reverie. They had to go back, back to the terrible night, before they could move forward. Too much had been left unsaid between them. But how? When?

His stomach twisted at the mere thought of bringing up that dreadful time. Other than the stress she felt over this exam, they were in such a good place right now. Did he really want to mess with everything? He blew out a long breath he didn't realize he'd held.

No, but he had to.

Sometimes, though she never voiced it, he felt like Riley held something back, part of herself, from him. Maybe she didn't even know herself. Maybe it wasn't conscious. Maybe she was protecting herself. Whatever the reason, if they were going to go the long haul—and he certainly hoped they would—then he had to speak up. To clear the air.

The alternative didn't bear thinking...

Chapter Twenty-Seven

"If we weren't all crazy, we'd just go insane."
-Jimmy Buffett

Bloodshot eyes rimmed by bruised-looking skin stared back at Riley as she peered into the mirror. She winced and turned away, not wanting to see any longer. Lack of sleep, long hours hunched over her flash cards, and a steady stream of caffeine were taking their toll. With less than two weeks left before her written exam, she wasn't sure she'd make it.

The thought turned her blood to ice.

Everything in her life up until now led to this. Everything! She couldn't fail now. Failure was simply not an option. Yet, with each passing day, she felt her confidence slip away. And yet she thrived at work. Her patients, and their parents, loved her. Each shift brought a mix of the challenging and mundane, and she met it head-on, never faltering. She treated each patient confidently and competently, gaining praise from family members and fellow staff alike.

But the second she picked up a study card, all the warm fuzzies fell away, leaving her with icy dread in the pit of her stomach. Just the thought of them waiting on her office desk, like a deadly snake coiled to strike, made her heart flutter.

Her phone buzzed from the pocket of her cutoff sweats. She sighed and debated ignoring it. Luca most likely, as it had been for the past day. She winced then, remembering the fact she hadn't replied to any of his increasingly worried texts or voicemails. She wasn't ghosting him. Well, not deliberately.

He didn't understand.

This exam meant everything to her, the culmination of her life's work to this point. *She had to pass.* And she would. If she could only get through the next few days. And if it meant ignoring him and his many gifts of coffee, food, and flowers, then so be it.

Her doorbell rang.

Riley threw up her hands. Really? She thought about stomping her feet, not caring if it would make her look the age of her patients. What part of she needed time alone to study wasn't he getting?

Her shoulders tightened as she thought about the last conversation they'd shared, sometime yesterday morning. Or maybe the day before. She'd suggested he stay at his own house until after her exam. She needed to be able to focus only on studying from now until it was over.

He had not taken the suggestion well.

Since then, he'd texted regularly, asking how she was, if she needed anything, and she had only given one-word replies before stopping altogether. She needed time. And space. And for this stupid exam to be over.

The doorbell rang again.

"Are you kidding me?" she yelled into the otherwise quiet space.

Lucy and Gabriel tripped over themselves running to her front door.

"You're not dogs," she reminded them in an acid tone.

She stalked to the door and yanked it open. "What part of I need space did you not understand?" she growled. Then she felt her eyes widen. Her mouth dropped open. "You're not Luca," she gasped.

Mama Rinaldi chuckled. "I have been called many things in my day, Bella, but this is a first." The older woman smiled at Riley, holding a bag bearing their restaurant logo. "May I come in?"

Riley did the only thing she could. She stepped aside and promptly burst into tears.

*****

Luca sat on Owen's back deck, cold beer in hand, scowling at his phone. Around him, the other guys joked and laughed. *He should have stayed home.* He took a long pull of his beer, the icy brew soothing his throat but not his aching heart nor worried mind.

"What's up with Romeo?" Jack wisecracked.

"From the dark scowl and murderous glint, I'd say woman problems," Owen offered. He nodded at Jack. "I think the murderous glint is for your benefit for bringing it up."

"Can't I be concerned about a friend?" Jack asked, not quite hiding his grin behind his own beer bottle.

"Let's all keep in mind the woman in question is my sister," Griff reminded everyone with a groan. He placed a kiss on the head of his sleeping daughter strapped to his chest. "Lucky for me, Amelia Grace is never going to date. Remember what your father says, honey. Boys are evil."

A round of raucous laughter pulled Luca from his dark thoughts. He turned to face Griff.

"Aren't you worried about her, man?" he asked him. "She doesn't eat or sleep much. All she's doing is working and studying. It cannot be healthy."

"Of course, I'm worried. But what am I supposed to do? Riley is far and away the smartest person I know. Always has been. Always will be. How do I give her advice on this?"

Luca raked a hand through his hair. "You don't have to be Einstein to see she's killing herself with this. It's common sense. Not only is she freaking herself out, but she isn't taking care of herself. The not eating and not getting enough sleep isn't helping."

"I'm not arguing with you. I agree, but what do you want me to do? Riley has never taken advice from her big brother. Why would she start now, of all times? Besides, aren't you two close?" He cleared his throat. "I mean we all know you guys are together, so wouldn't she rather hear this from the man who, well, cares about her?"

"Loves her, Griff. Let's be clear. I love her," Luca declared before shutting his mouth after realizing exactly what he'd said.

Silence reigned. Luca glanced around at their faces, all wearing expressions ranging from shocked to grins.

"Well, hell, I called this way back in high school," Jack bragged.

"What?" Luca asked.

"No way," Griff protested.

Owen tilted his head as though contemplating the meaning of life. Then a smile spread across his face. "Oh, makes sense now."

"What makes sense?" Griff asked, eyes wide and shaking his head. "Enough of your cryptic BS."

Owen grinned, not taking offense apparently. "For a smart guy, you can be pretty dense about your little sister. Tell me, how many times have you ever seen her watch a baseball game on TV?"

"Uh, never," Griff answered. "You know she's not a fan."

"Yep," Owen said, popping the p. "Then answer me this. How many high school baseball games did Riley watch in her four years?"

"All of them," Luca answered, grinning.

"And who played baseball all four years?" Owen queried.

"Let's not forget who made all those ridiculous signs with your mother despite not being exactly crafty," Jack added.

Luca hung his head. *The signs!* "How could I forget. I'm very sure she tried to talk my mom out of them," he muttered. "As if anyone could talk Hurricane Maria out of anything." He ignored the snickering. "She means well, but Ma is a force of nature, as you know. She loves hard."

He shook his head remembering the conversation about

grandchildren.

"What?" Griff asked. "You look like someone just ate your last cookie."

"She grilled me again about grandkids. As in when am I giving her some." He reached out to touch the downy hair on Amelia Grace's head. A weird, unsettled feeling drifted through his chest. "Hey, I know. Maybe I could borrow your daughter."

"Get your own," Griff suggested, turning away his upper body, effectively cutting Luca off from his sleeping daughter.

"Right, like that's going to happen anytime soon," he muttered. "Riley and I are nowhere near the 'let's talk about how many kids we want' stage. First, she has to survive this exam. Then, I have to convince her I'm all in." He took a large gulp of his beer, wishing he could take back his last words.

Griff's darkening gaze told him his wish was futile.

"Care to share with the class why she might doubt you?" Griff asked in an overly controlled voice.

Luca glanced up, wondering idly if the other man's jaw might break from clenching it so tight.

"No offense, but that's between me and your sister. It's ancient history that needs to be put to rest, once and for all."

An uneasy silence cloaked the deck. No one spoke, but Luca felt the weight of three sets of eyes. He looked only at Griff.

"I should have told Riley I loved her before I told you. My mistake. I won't further disrespect her by discussing our past with you guys. Know this. I would rip my own heart out before I'd harm one hair on her head."

Griff held his gaze for one long, heavy moment longer before a grin spread across his face. He clapped Luca on the shoulder. "I've always liked you, Luca. I think you're a good man."

Luca released a long breath he didn't know he'd held. "Good to know. Thank you."

Griff grinned at him, showing more teeth than normal.

"Keep in mind while I like you, I love my sister. Hurt her, and they'll never find what's left of you." He leaned down to kiss his infant daughter's head before engaging Owen in a discussion about the Braves' chances in the post season this year.

"As much as I like you, and love your carbonara, I'd feel obligated to help him," Jack quipped. "Sisters, man, what are you going to do?"

"Understood," Luca said, not really sure what had just happened.

*****

"Cara, it's okay, I promise. Come, tell Mama all about it," Mama Rinaldi urged, leading Riley to the sofa.

Beyond exhausted, Riley let her. She couldn't stop the tears anyway and had stopped caring. They flowed freely. Collapsing to the cushions, she allowed Luca's mother to gather her into her arms. The older woman patted Riley on the back while she cried.

"Shhh, Cara, it'll all be okay. My Luca will take care of you. You will see. Soon, there will be grandbabies, and all will be okay," she predicted.

Riley stiffened in Mrs. Rinaldi's arms, sure she must have misunderstood her. She straightened up and away from her, swiping a hand across her face.

"Excuse me, what did you say?" she asked.

"The bambinos you and my Luca will have." She clapped her hands and grinned. "Can you imagine? Your mother and I have wanted this since you and Luca were babies yourselves." She leaned forward to pinch Riley's cheeks. "I told Cheryl one day you would come back to us, to Luca. Was I not right?" she crowed. "Now, I know you have only just returned, but when can we start planning the big day?"

"Big day?" Riley gasped. "Mrs. Rinaldi, I don't think you understand. Luca and I, we, uh…" She closed her eyes for a moment to gather her thoughts. Luca's mother was the human version of a steamroller. She had a heart the size of South Carolina, but Riley had seen her work people over to get her way. *Not this time.* "There seems to be some confusion here," she began again."

"What confusion?" Mama waved her hands in the air as if Riley's words were the most ridiculous thing she'd ever heard. "The only confusion was that man you brought home last Christmas. That man who was so wrong for you. Who insulted my food! The man who was not my Luca."

Riley's cheeks burned at the memory. She nodded. "Thomas was indeed not the right man for me, Mama, and I apologize for him. I never imagined he would, well, do what he did. In your restaurant of all places." She wrung her hands together.

"Child, as if I would ever hold you responsible for another's actions. While I'm sure that man…"

"Thomas," Riley supplied with a watery smile.

Mama harumphed. "While I'm sure Thomas is a lovely man." Her tight lips made Riley think of the time Luca dared her to eat half of a lemon. She'd been six. "He most certainly was not the man for you."

"Agreed," Riley said.

"Oh."

"Which is why I ended the engagement almost before leaving South Carolina air space on the way back to Arizona," she added.

"Well, good." Mama chucked Riley under her chin. "You always were the smartest of us."

Riley smiled, waiting for the other shoe to drop.

"And because you are the brilliant one, I know you can understand why you and my Luca are a sure thing, dear heart," she oozed.

And there it came…

"Mama, Luca and I are, well, I'm not sure what we are. But respectfully, whatever we are is between us. We are adults, Mama."

"My point exactly!" Mama cried. "You are not the shy

little girl with her nose buried in a book anymore, Riley. You are a grown woman who knows what she wants." Mama looked her up and down, giving Riley the idea she was checking out the width of her hips. "You are not getting any younger, my dear. The time for bambinos has come," she announced.

With that, Mama stood. "And now I must go. There are many plans to make. And you have all the studying to do. But then comes the wedding and the baby making."

Before Riley could get a word in, Mama kissed her cheek and scuttled out the door, leaving her more than a bit flustered in her wake.

Chapter Twenty-Eight

"Life is too short to work so hard."
-Vivien Leigh

Griff's words tumbled over and over in Luca's head as he left later that evening. Of course, he never wanted to hurt Riley again. Doing so five years ago almost broke his own heart. Even though his motive was pure, the look on her face burned his soul forever.

Making a snap decision, he flicked on his turn signal and maneuvered toward the beach. He knew she wasn't working tonight, which meant she would be home, holed up in her 'she cave' studying. Not seeing her, or even hearing from her, in the past almost two days had been too much. Enough was enough already. He understood how important this exam was to her future. But did she understand how important she was to his?

If not, then the fault lay totally at his feet.

A few minutes later, Luca breathed a sigh of relief at seeing her car in the driveway. Then relief turned to dread. He pulled in next to it and sat there, wondering what to say to her. How to make her see his point of view. He worried about her. About them. Knowing he was hiding, Luca exited his car.

Surely, he'd think of something brilliant between here and her door…

When he reached the door, and without any mind-blowing thoughts, he knocked. Dismay pooled in his gut. He shifted his weight from side to side before knocking again. His heartbeat served as a timer. When she didn't answer, he rang the doorbell. With each passing moment, his chest tightened, making it harder to breathe.

Did she really not want to see him? Speak to him?

Finally, when he didn't think he could stand it one more second, the door opened.

"What are you doing here, Luca?" she asked in a dull voice.

His first thought, always, was to drink in the sight of her. To be happy to be near her. But the dark shadows under her eyes hurt his heart.

"You didn't answer my texts. I wanted to make sure you were okay. Is it really so strange?" He shoved a hand through his hair. "We've barely gone a day in the past month without seeing or at least talking with each other. Suddenly I don't hear from you in almost two? I was worried."

She nudged the door open wider and came forward a few paces, stepping into the porch light. "Here I am. As you can see, I'm fine. Or I will be once I get through this exam."

"You don't look fine," he noted in a blunt tone.

"Gee thanks," she sniped.

"I'm worried about you. You look exhausted, Riley, like you haven't slept," he accused.

"Well, it's probably because I haven't," she said. "Hard to sleep when your entire future is on the line. Besides, I can sleep when I'm dead."

"Funny."

"This is nothing compared to what I survived during medical school and residency," she assured him. "You have no idea. And anyway, it's just for a few more days."

"You're right, how would I know?" he replied.

"You wouldn't. That's why I'm trying to reassure you, I can handle this." She stuck her hands on her hips. He knew she was mad now. "But if you really want to help, then call off your mother."

He almost missed her words, so struck by the green fire shooting from her hazel eyes. *Almost.*

"What did you say?" he asked, a sick feeling creeping into his stomach.

"You know I love your mother. I always have. But right now, she's the last thing I need. She came to see me earlier. Wanted to know about our 'plans' and 'babies.' Can you believe it? What plans? I'm barely back in Palm Harbor, and she's already got my life planned out for me, complete with marriage to you and a pack of grandbabies for her. Never mind that I have boards to study for."

"Would it be the worst idea?" he asked, heart in his throat, dreading her answer.

"What?" she croaked. "Hardly the point, Luca. Your mother basically came here to ask my intentions. Well, not really ask, more like she came here to dictate them to me." She threw her hands in the air and started to pace. "Oh, I almost forgot the best part. She and 'Cheryl' have been plotting this since you and I wore diapers. Can you imagine?"

Riley started to laugh then, but it lacked any humor. It was the kind of laugh born of equal parts desperation and exhaustion. She laughed and laughed until she folded over at the waist, clutching her ribs.

He stood watching her, unsure how to react. He'd never seen Riley so far out of control. Finally, she stopped, if only to come up for air.

"We really played right into their plans, didn't we?" she asked, when she could talk again. "Maybe I should have asked how many grandkids she wanted. Asked about names."

"You know how my mother is, Riley," he said, hoping to calm her. "She gets a little overly involved." He held up his hands as if in surrender. "She meant well. You know she's always thought of you as the daughter she never had."

"Well, now she thinks of me as a broodmare." She raked her hands through her hair, pulling the band out and shaking it out. "I don't have time for this right now. I have to get back to studying."

She turned to leave, but he grasped her wrist, stopping her.

"Wait. Just give me a moment. Surely you have five minutes to talk to me?" he asked.

She turned back to face him but didn't meet his gaze. Arms crossed against her chest didn't bode well for him. "Well?"

"I'm worried about you," he whispered as he gathered her in his arms. He feathered kisses against her hair. "It's not that I don't understand, because I do. I know how important this is to you. But you're exhausted, and you can't go on like this. When's the last time you ate a decent meal? Not taking care of yourself won't help you do well on your boards."

She stiffened in his arms, and he knew he'd gone too far. Despite his instinct to hold her tighter, Luca let her go when she pushed against him.

"Are you kidding me right now?" she all but yelled at him. She poked him hard in the chest. "Who do think has been taking care of me all these years, Luca? When I was away at school and working crazy hours you can't even begin to imagine? When I was sick, tired, and overwhelmed? How about the days I wanted to quit? When I thought I couldn't do it even one more second? Who took care of me then? I did, that's who. So, the very last thing I need at this point is someone deciding what I need now. You lost the right five years ago."

Her hands flew to her mouth as her eyes grew to the size of saucers.

"I didn't..."

"Yes, you did," he said. Luca lifted a hand toward her then dropped it again. "There it is, Riley, the unspoken elephant in the room that's been between us this whole time. One way or the other, it had to come out."

"I never meant to blurt it out like this, though," she explained. "You broke my heart, Luca. That day." She stopped, squeezing her eyes shut.

A funny, little pain ripped across his chest remembering.

He stood behind the bar, mixing a drink for Sheila Forrest, a woman he'd been casually seeing, when Riley walked through the front door. For a moment, he forgot to breathe. He saw the moment her eyes, scanning the restaurant, found him. She turned and made her way toward him, grinning. Riley had always smiled with her whole body. It was one of the many things he'd always loved about her. Then he saw the moment she noticed Sheila's hand on his bicep. And the way her smile dimmed.

She came to a halt several feet from the bar, wariness in her hazel eyes.

"Hey, Riley, what brings you back to Palm Harbor?" he called. Before she could answer, Sheila turned and introduced herself. "Hi, we haven't met. I'm Sheila Forrest, Luca's girlfriend."

"Oh, hi. I'm Riley Layne. Luca and I grew up together." She held out her hand, which the other woman shook.

"What brings you back to town?" He turned to his date. "Riley's in medical school up north, Sheila. Where did you end up again? Boston?"

Her quick intake of breath gutted him. He knew she went to Dartmouth. Had even driven all the way up there once two years ago. He'd missed her so much, and things with the restaurant were going so well. He wanted to talk to her, just be with her. Somehow get her back in his life. But he'd seen her walking across campus with a guy, laughing and smiling, and he couldn't do it. He still lived a thousand miles away, and it wasn't going to change. What was the point? He'd gotten back in his car and driven home. He'd never told anyone.

"I go to Dartmouth in New Hampshire, actually," she told Sheila in a small, flat voice. "Luca, could I, uh, speak with you for a moment? In private?" She turned and walked away, leaving him no choice but to follow.

He caught up with her in the tiny space they'd converted into an office. She'd shoved her hands in her pockets, a sure sign she was nervous. Her eyes darted around.

"What's up? I haven't seen you in years. What's so important you had to pull me away from work?" he asked in a rougher tone than he meant to use.

She scoffed. "It's three o'clock on a Wednesday, not exactly overflowing with customers. Besides, I'm sure Sheila can spare you for a minute." She licked her lips, ratcheting up his pulse. "Yesterday was match day. I came home to tell everyone my amazing news. I, uh, came here first. You were the first person I wanted to tell. Just like when we were kids. I got the residency I wanted, my first pick!"

He didn't respond for a moment, just stood there, taking in her bright eyes and hopeful smile. His heart pounded too fast in his chest, like it was trying to escape. She'd wanted to tell him first before even her own family!

"Luca, did you hear me? I matched with the combined adult and pediatric emergency medicine residency program at The University of Arizona. Can you believe?"

She grabbed his arm and jumped up and down as her excited voice bounced off the walls. He heard her saying something about it being a five-year program and then the words faded to white noise. All he heard was she would be even further away from him. Riley wasn't coming home.

And in that moment, he made a decision that would cost him.

"Is that it?" he asked in the most off-hand tone he could muster. "Great, Riley, but honestly, a phone call could have sufficed. I mean we haven't seen each other in a while, so why bother now?"

"But I thought…"

"Well, if that's all, I should get back to Sheila. Don't want to be rude. Have a safe trip back." He turned away to leave the room but not before seeing the light leave her eyes.

Luca exhaled loudly. "Riley, about that day," he started, but she held up a hand, stopping him.

"Please don't. You made yourself perfectly clear that day." She straightened her shoulders. "It was foolish of me really when you think about it, after all those years, to think you'd care about my news. My mistake."

"Riley, please, let me explain," he begged.

But she held up her hand again. "There's no need. What's past is past." She waved a hand between them. "I don't even know what this is between us. But I have too much on my plate right now, I can't handle any more pressure. So, I'm asking you to take a step back and not add to it."

He clenched his jaw. "I didn't know worrying about you equaled pressure, Riley. Since when am I not allowed to care?"

"There's no reason to worry. I can handle it. But

worrying about someone is different from telling them what to do. I'm not a child, Luca. I don't need someone to tell me when to sleep and eat. I already have parents. I don't appreciate your attitude, nor do I need it right now."

"Riley, I'm trying to help," he pled, reaching out for her.

But she stepped further away. "If you want to help me then do what I asked. Give me space and time. I know what I need better than you do."

"At least let me bring you some dinner," he added. "I can drop something off. This way I know you're eating."

"You're not listening!" she yelled, throwing up her hands. "That's it. I'm done. I don't want dinner. Or coffee. Or to go for a walk on the beach. Despite what you, and your mother, seem to think, I know what I'm doing." She shook her head. "This was a mistake. It's too hard to make you understand. I have to go."

Luca stood there, arms at his side. He didn't reach out to her. Didn't try to stop her. The finality in her voice stopped him dead in his tracks. The click of the front door lock may as well have been a gun shot in the otherwise silent night. Her words shredded his heart.

She hadn't forgiven him.

*****

Riley threw the deadbolt before pressing her forehead into the heavy, wooden door. Hot tears scalded her eyes, and she let them flow unchecked. What would be the point? There would only be more behind the ones she swiped away. Her heart clenched when she heard his footsteps on the crushed shells of her drive. The sound of his car driving away ripped it from her chest.

But what had she expected? Riley had pushed him away, after all. Boards were making her crazy, but she couldn't blame this on that. With each passing day, the closer she and Luca grew, the more the memory haunted her. Her face burned with the memory of how excited she'd been. She'd matched at her very first choice! Arizona was one of only five programs in the country to offer the combined pediatric-adult emergency medicine residency program. Theirs was the one she wanted. And they wanted *her!* And even though it meant staying away for another five years, to her, it meant being one step closer to finally coming home.

And despite everything, Luca was the very first person she thought to tell. On a whim, she'd booked a flight home, knowing she had barely twenty-four hours off to fly home, tell everyone, and fly back in time for work the next day. Still, she couldn't wait to see him. To share her news.

On the flight home, she'd gone over it a million times in her head. Seeing him again for the first time in years. Sharing her dreams with him as they always had.

It had not gone to plan. His face, so lacking in any expression as he dismissed her, was almost that of a stranger. And his voice, always warm with a teasing note she secretly thought he used only for her, had been cold, flat.

She barely remembered the rest of her time in Palm Harbor that trip. Couldn't get back to the safety of Dartmouth fast enough. The next week, she'd started her Pediatrics rotation and met Thomas.

Riley shook her head and sniffed. She'd cried enough over Luca Rinaldi through the years. She'd worked her whole life to get to where she was. Nothing, and no one, would stop her now.

She slid her phone from her pocket and hit a preset. When the person on the other end picked up, Riley sighed into it. "I need your help."

Chapter Twenty-Nine

*"Guys have a level of insecurity and vulnerability that's
exponentially bigger than you think. With the primal urge to be
alpha comes extreme heartbreak. The harder we fight, the harder we
fall."*

-John Krasinski

Tiptoeing into her living room, Riley stopped near the couch and grinned down at the sleeping form sprawled there. A chunk of more-salt-than-pepper hair swept across Brody's forehead. His feet and a good portion of his lower limbs hung at an angle off the edge. Her couch had clearly not been meant for someone over six feet tall.

She grabbed an old throw from the back and leaned in to place it over him when a giggle stopped her mid-toss.

Harper, stretching awake in the opposite recliner, smothered a laugh. "Don't wake him. Senior citizens need their sleep," she advised, tongue firmly in cheek.

Riley buried the throw against her face to smother a laugh and nodded.

"Hey now, watch it with the age jokes. I'm not as old as my hair would imply," Brody grumbled as he sat up. He placed both hands against his lower back and twisted left then right, grimacing. "You know I love you like the annoying little sister I already have, Riley, and would do anything for you. But you're getting the chiropractor bill."

Riley gave up all pretenses of not laughing and

collapsed onto the couch next to him. "Consider it paid in full," she affirmed. She lay her head upon his shoulder and sighed. "I can't thank you enough for talking me down off the ledge last night." She glanced at Harper. "Both of you."

"I'm only pissed you didn't think to call me first," Harper sassed. "Even if he is a fellow doctor and can truly understand what you're going through," she huffed. Her grin took the bite from her words.

"Be glad I called you," he advised. "Although it was more about self-preservation," he added with a wink. "No need to rile your man. I figured inviting Harper to the party as 'chaperone' so to speak might smooth things over."

Riley's heart sank at his words. She'd called Brody last night out of desperation, seeking advice on how to survive the next few weeks. He'd showed up fifteen minutes later with a smiling Harper in tow. Believing her stress was entirely focused on her upcoming board exam, Riley had made the snap decision to let them go on thinking it.

No need to add to her drama, right?

But lying to these wonderful people who'd dropped everything to come running last night felt wrong.

"Uh, about that. I wouldn't worry if I were you," she said before heading into the kitchen. "Scrambled and bacon okay for everyone? My breakfast repertoire is a bit limited. I have sourdough bread for toast also." She busied herself fetching stuff and waited for the inevitable bomb to go off.

She didn't have to wait long…

"Wait, what?" Harper cried.

"What does that mean?" Brody asked at the same time.

Both crowded into her tiny kitchen. She held her frying pan against her chest like a weapon. Or maybe a security blanket.

"I may have forgotten to mention I ended things with him right before y'all showed up here last night." She waved a hand in the air between them when Harper started to speak. "I really can't right now. I'm already hanging on by a thread. Please."

Harper stared at her before giving the smallest, barely perceptible nod.

Tears burned her eyes, but Riley refused to let them fall. There would be time for that later, preferably alone in her shower.

Brody stepped closer and removed the pan from her trembling hands.

"Luckily for you, I'm not only dashingly handsome and wickedly funny, I'm also an excellent cook. At least when it comes to breakfast. After that, not so much," he added with his trademark grin. Why don't you ladies see to the toast and such while I whip up a meal? Then while you fall in love with me, I mean my cooking, we can make a plan for the next two weeks and you passing the board exam, Riley."

Riley laughed and threw her arms around him. "You mean something other than giving up medicine and selling ice cream at the beach like I decided last night?"

"That's not the worst idea," Harper mused. "There are days in the department when that seems the wiser choice. And it's certainly better than some of the other choices from last night." She held out one hand and started ticking off fingers as she recited them. "Let's see, there was professional poker player, but since we know every thought you have is on your face, nope. Then we had chef, but you still think Pop Tarts are a food group, so that's another no."

"Hey! Don't knock it until you've tried it," Riley protested. "Did you know they have a confetti cupcake flavor?"

Brody whipped around from the stove. "Aren't you in your thirties?"

"Well, I turned thirty at the beginning of the year. Why?" Riley asked.

"Because thirty is way too old to be eating Pop Tarts."

"Preach," Harper cried, toasting him with her glass of orange juice.

"Seriously?" Riley glanced back and forth between her friends. "Pop Tarts come with an age limit? As in, I should be carded at the store? 'Sorry, ma'am, you're too old to buy those.'"

"Hey, maybe we should have put stand-up comedienne on the list," Brody offered before turning back to the stove.

"Nah, she doesn't really have the obnoxious personality for it," Harper commented.

"Gee, thanks, I guess," Riley said.

"You know what I mean. But it would have been better than professional athlete," Harper suggested. "I mean I've never seen someone trip over lines in linoleum before."

Brody burst out laughing, but smart man that he was, did not comment.

"Hey now, we can't all be graceful," Riley protested. "Just because some people in my family got all the athletic prowess and some of us did not."

"At all..." Harper joked.

"Ooh, I know. I probably shouldn't be one of those romance advice columnists. Let's see, I'm thirty, have one broken engagement and have been in love with the same man my entire life. The one I just dumped." She barked out a short, harsh laugh. "Yep, probably should stick to medicine."

A silence fell over the room.

"It's fine," she said. "I'm going to focus on the career I have wanted, and worked for, my entire life. I have great friends and a wonderful family. I have my health. It's fine."

Brody turned from the stove and dished out their breakfasts. He gave her a soft smile, not his usual, cocky grin. "Here's a tip from an old pro. Convincing others of how 'fine' you are goes better when you don't use the word more than once."

This time, she didn't bother to stop the tears as they slid down her face.

*****

"Where's the rest of your gang?" Stella quizzed Luca as he slid into a booth at the back of Dusty's later that night.

Not feeling particular chatty, he shrugged. "Can I get

whatever you recommend on tap and a shot of something to kill the pain, please? In fact, make it several." He tossed his keys on the table. "Took an Uber here. No worries about me driving later."

"As if that would happen on my watch," she sniffed. "It's your liver. I'll be right back."

He closed his eyes and leaned back for a moment. Alcohol was never the answer, at least not in the long run. But tonight, it seemed like a good one. He'd slept like crap last night, if one could count lying in bed, staring at the ceiling, and reliving the same scene on her porch, over and over, sleeping. No matter how hard he tried, Luca couldn't think of a way to make Riley see how much he cared for her. Loved her.

His actions five years ago had not only broken her heart but her trust as well. He'd known it then. He knew it now. It was a risk he'd taken at the time and lived to regret. More than anything in the world, he'd wanted Riley to come home to Palm Harbor. To come home to him. And then she'd walked into the restaurant as if he'd somehow conjured her.

And he couldn't risk it. Could not risk her giving up her dreams for him, just like he couldn't risk it at eighteen. She knew what she wanted from the time she was old enough to verbalize the idea. Riley wanted to be a doctor. And five years ago, she had been well on her way to realizing that dream. He knew her goals before she came in that day. He and Griff had remained friends. He saw her parents almost weekly in the restaurant. He'd just listened to her mother go on about 'match day' the week before and how excited and nervous Mrs. Layne had been.

Of course, Riley had no way of knowing any of it. Just like she had no way of knowing he stood on the lawn at Dartmouth a few months later and watched her graduate from medical school.

"Here you go, Luca," Stella said, placing his first round on the table before him. "I know you're surrounded by food all day, but I also know it's possible you didn't eat. Can I get you anything?"

"No thanks, Stella." He grabbed the shot and threw it back, wincing slightly at the burn. "You're too sweet. Dusty is a lucky man."

The waitress laughed. "Sweet is not the usual word used to describe me." She leaned in closer to whisper in his ear. "I have a reputation to protect. Keep it to yourself, huh?"

He barked out a laugh of his own. "Understood. Another round when you have a chance and keep them coming." He grabbed his beer and downed half of it before coming up for air.

Stella sighed. "Okay, what did you do? You may as well tell me now. They always do."

"Why are you so sure I did something wrong? How do you know it wasn't Riley? Maybe she wronged me," he stated.

Stella cocked one hip, fisting her hand against it. "Did she?"

He stared her down, or tried to, but Stella handled drunks for a living. Luca knew he was hopelessly outmatched. With a sigh, he broke eye contact first.

"I wouldn't know where to start. Let's just say, I hope I'm hurting more than she is."

"Good answer. Let me get your next round." She turned and left before he could respond.

He grabbed the other shot she'd left, downing it as quickly as the first. Then he reached for the beer, nursing it a bit as he waited for the alcohol to do its trick. Nothing would get solved tonight, but he'd settle for numb.

Because he apparently had become a masochist, he wondered where she was. What she was up to. Was she working? Studying? On a date?

Wait, what? Where had that come from?

Luca shook his head and tried to rein in his wild thoughts. Riley, as she had always been, would be laser-focused on her board exam. It's how she went through life. He should know, since he was her oldest friend. Okay, so he had a little time to work with. She wouldn't go running out to meet anyone new until after her exam. Good. He had time. Now, all he needed was a plan.

"Ah, so this is where the desperate come to drown their sorrows," Owen said by way of greeting before dropping into the booth across from him. He took a sip of the draft beer he brought with him then slid a shot toward Luca. "Here you go. On me. It doesn't help, you only think it will. I know."

"Thanks. I think." Luca downed the shot, noticing it didn't burn anymore. He wasn't sure if that was a good thing or not. "So, what do you know about drowning sorrows?"

Owen laughed. "Oh, I know all about it. Stella was kind enough to throw up the bat signal, as she did for me when I was in your position, not all that long ago. You remember when I was stupid enough to almost let Harper get away."

"Ah, it makes sense now. Stella asked me what I did wrong when I started ordering rounds of alcohol," he admitted.

"Do yourself a favor," Owen advised. "Smarten up and fix whatever you did quicker than I did. My liver is still recovering."

"He's not wrong, although my bank account isn't complaining," Stella joked before dropping off another round of alcohol for Luca and a plate of loaded potato skins. "I've been thinking of renaming these. Maybe something to do with heartache?" she joked before turning away.

"I didn't order those," Luca pointed out.

"Never question Stella," Owen advised. "Besides, you'll thank her later when your stomach has something to soak up the alcohol."

"Am I going to need my shovel?" Griff asked before joining Owen on his side of the booth. He stared at Luca for a long, uncomfortable moment.

"That won't be necessary," Luca muttered. "I'm going to fix this."

"Okay then. Ooh, skins!" Griff said before grabbing one.

"Hey, save me some," Jack protested as he slid in next to Luca. Turning to him, he grinned. "Your turn, huh?"

"Turn?" Luca asked.

"To be an idiot. We've all been there. But look at us now.

Griff is happily married with an incredible baby girl. I'm engaged to the most beautiful woman in the world."

"Still trying to figure out that one," Owen joked.

"She obviously has great taste," Jack said. "And even Owen has talked a woman into living with him. So, it's your turn to mess up and then fix it. So, what did you do?"

Luca felt his ears grow warm as three sets of eyes focused on him. "I am so not drunk enough for this conversation."

Chapter Thirty

"Sometimes when you're overwhelmed by a situation — when you're in the darkest of the darkness — that's when your priorities are reordered."
-Phoebe Snow

Tossing the covers off, Riley gave up on the idea of sleep. It hadn't been her friend in quite some time. What was one more night? She swung her legs off the bed and staggered from her bedroom. Taking the motion as playtime, Lucy pounced on her toes, razor-sharp claws finding purchase in Riley's delicate flesh.

"Ouch, stop it," she cried, leaning down to scoop the mischievous kitten from the floor. She cuddled the black kitten to her chest as she continued to the living room and sank into the couch cushions. Her body ached from lack of sleep. All of it, from the roots of her hair to her toenails. *Could your eyelashes hurt*, she wondered? If so, then hers did. She needed sleep, something more than an hour at a time, uninterrupted by dreams of Luca.

Really more like nightmares. She hadn't seen him in over a week and had no idea what to do about it. She missed him, missed *them*, to the depths of her weary soul. He'd always been her person. Her rock. When they were kids, some unspoken bond existed between them. A bond she never believed could be severed. Then they grew up. Became adults. Grew apart. And she'd missed him more than anyone or anything from

Palm Harbor, in all the years she was away. When she returned, and they'd grown close again, closer than ever before, she once again believed their bond would stand the test of time.

Except for the tiny seeds of doubt in the darkest reaches of her heart. The ones Luca planted five years ago, the day he broke her heart. She didn't have to close her eyes to see the utter lack of emotion on his face that day when he informed her she needn't have bothered coming home to share her good news. Sitting there in the dark, she recalled the contempt dripping from his tone. Even his date had the decency to wince.

But not Luca.

She'd stood there, staring for the longest moment, trying so hard to make sense of his words. But nothing about *those* words from *his* mouth made any sense. Nor did the blank look in his eyes.

Numb after his verbal lashing, she'd merely nodded, spun on her heel, and left the restaurant. She didn't cry for two whole blocks. No way would she give him the satisfaction. But his words had hit their mark. Left their damage behind. And even now, as she'd let him back into her life, she couldn't help holding back a piece of herself, a piece of her heart, to protect herself from him.

Something she'd never done before.

"Meow," Lucy protested, making her realize she hugged the kitten a little too closely to her chest. She loosened her grip a bit.

"Sorry, Lucy. Mommy's sad, not mean," she apologized.

Gabriel, seemingly not wanting to be left out, jumped onto the couch and settled into her lap. The loud rumble of his purr soothed Riley's ragged soul. She stroked his fluffy, white head with one hand. She sank further into the couch, yawning.

"It's okay, I can be a cat mom. I'll pass my boards, take care of other people's kids and be the best aunt ever." She sniffed and didn't bother to wipe the tears slipping down her cheeks. "It'll be enough, won't it, guys?"

Being cats, they didn't answer.

*****

Hours later, Riley awoke. She rubbed her eyes, which felt like they held five pounds of sand each.

"Mreoooowwwww," Lucy cried from the floor next to her.

She turned her head to look down, groaning as she did.

"Note to self, Mommy is too old for sleeping on the couch. Good morning, are you hungry?"

Gabriel shot out from under the coffee table and sat next to his sister. He blinked his large, blue eyes at Riley as if answering.

"Okay, then, time for kitten chow," Riley announced before dragging her tired, sore body from the couch.

She glanced at the microwave clock. Ten in the morning. At least she had managed a few hours. Still, she was way behind on sleep. She almost wished she had to work today. A shift in the ER would keep her mind off her board exam.

And Luca.

She was no closer to figuring out either.

Her stomach rumbled as she fixed breakfast for her kittens. Thinking back, Riley couldn't remember the last time she'd eaten. *Probably not a good sign.* Then her phone dinged, announcing an incoming text. Her stomach dipped. She both hoped for and dreaded one from Luca. She walked back to the couch to look at her phone and burst out laughing when she read the missive from Sam.

"Lunch at La Hacienda. High noon. Don't even think about not coming. We know where you live."

They did, and she knew Sam well enough to not consider blowing off the invite. The other woman would only hunt her down. Knowing she had an hour before she'd have to jump in the shower, Riley grabbed her first cup of the day and headed into her home office to study for a little while before meeting her.

*****

Luca lost himself prepping for the lunch rush. He wouldn't think about Riley. Didn't have time. At least that's what he tried to tell himself. Then images of her, wearing nothing but moonlight, flitted through his brain. And he was lost. He continued slicing and dicing, luckily the rhythm as second nature as breathing to him.

Until something whacked him across the back of his head.

"Ow, watch it!" he cried, turning to look at his mother standing there, hand raised as if ready to smack him again. "Are you crazy? Never hit a man wielding a knife." He motioned with the knife in question, pointed down at the chopping board.

"Pfft, the worse you would get is a flesh wound. You've had them before." She raised her arm to display the scar that ran along her thumb. "Wouldn't be the first time a Rinaldi bled for the cause."

Luca gritted his teeth and resumed chopping peppers. There was a peace he found in it lacking in this conversation. The headache that started above his left eye told him it wasn't over yet.

"Where is my Riley? Why don't I see her anymore? What did you do to her?" Mama demanded, hands on very full hips. "Do not make me get the spoon," she threatened. "You're never too old for it."

Matteo, who had just entered the kitchen, did an abrupt one eighty at the word 'spoon.' Nico, never as smart as his cousins, snickered from his corner of the room.

Mama raised one perfectly plucked and penciled brow. Nico, not *that* dumb, shrank a bit right in front of Luca's eyes.

Without taking her eyes from his cousin, she demanded, "Well? Are you going to answer me?"

Luca tossed aside the knife. He'd grown attached to his fingers. All of them. "I'm not the only one to blame in this, if you really want to know," he told her.

A hush fell over the normally bustling kitchen. For a long, pregnant moment, the prep crew froze in place. He could see the indecision in their expressions. Stay to hear the juicy details? Leave before the wrath of Mama Rinaldi unleashed in the small space that housed many sharp instruments? As one, they filed out without so much as a peep. Even Nico.

"Excuse me?" she asked in a voice barely above a whisper which sent a chill down his spine. She might be famous for her yelling, but when his mother was truly angry, like baseball-through-the-kitchen-window angry, she grew oh, so quiet.

Like now.

He wiped his hands on the apron tied at his waist before dragging one through his hair. "There cannot be any more talk of weddings and grandbabies, Ma," he started, only to have her flush an alarming red and open her mouth. He held up a hand. "I'm serious. Riley and I have some things to discuss, fix really, before that ever happens. And right now, all she can think about is her board exam at the end of next week."

"What things?" Mama all but spit. "What could be more important than love and family?" She made the sign of the cross then stared at him. "Please, tell me of these issues that are so important."

He closed his eyes. "I broke her heart, Ma. Five years ago, I broke her heart, and I'm not sure she's forgiven me. Or even if she ever will." The last words came out raw, as if he hadn't spoken in days.

He felt the slightest touch of her hand on his cheek. Luca opened his eyes.

"Oh, my dearest Luca, my little one will forgive you. She has to." Mama's dark eyes shone with unshed tears. "Nothing else in the universe makes any sense. You two are anime gemelli, soul mates, meant to be together. Surely, there was a misunderstanding. You can make her see?"

Luca shook his head, his own eyes burning, he suspected not from the onions in the kitchen. "I don't know, Mama, I don't know."

She placed her hands on his cheeks and stared into his eyes. "Riley was put on this earth for you, Luca. I believe this to my very soul. Just as your father was made for me and me for him. You need to find your way back to her. Make it right. She will not always be waiting for you," she advised before turning and leaving the kitchen.

Luca closed his eyes again. His mother had just voiced his worst fear.

Chapter Thirty-One

"If you want something said, ask a man; if you want something done, ask a woman."
-Margaret Thatcher

With one minute to spare, Riley slipped inside La Hacienda. She slid her shades up onto the top of her head and glanced around, letting her eyes adjust to the dim interior after the blazing sunshine outside. She spied Sadie, Sam and Jamie, seated in a large, round booth near the back, so she headed their way. Harper, coming from the restrooms, met her there.

"I see the gang's all here," she joked, though she didn't feel it.

"Don't you mean coven?" Sam queried.

Jamie winced. "Leave it to my jackass husband to come up with such a name."

"I rather like it," Harper added. "Witches have power and are to be respected."

"Agreed," Sam said around a mouthful of chips and salsa. She finished chewing and swallowing. "I'd apologize but why bother? This is how it's going to be for the next however many months I have left."

"You have nothing to apologize for. You're growing a human," Sadie said in Sam's defense.

Sam graced Sadie with a huge smile. "Yeah, what she said," she chortled before grabbing another chip and dunking it in a bowl of queso. "Mmmm," she groaned.

"Where is my precious niece?" Riley asked, hoping to buy herself a little time.

"She's with your parents," Jamie answered, narrowing her eyes. "Nice try, by the way. You're not getting off so easily."

"Nope," Sam seconded.

Harper just grinned and dunked a chip in the salsa. "Not pregnant but want to get my fill before Sam eats it all."

"Hey, uncalled for!" Sam started then grinned. "Nah, not worth it. Go ahead. I'll tell Javier to bring more." She glanced at Riley. "Okay, no more stalling. Spill it."

And to her horror, she did. Riley broke down crying. Large, ugly-cry sobs tore from her, taking her—and everyone else judging from the looks on their faces—by surprise.

"Oh my gosh, you broke her!" Harper gasped.

Riley waved a hand before grabbing her napkin and dabbing at the tears. "I'm not broken," she protested. "Just sleep-deprived." She sighed, knowing she was amongst friends and needed them. Needed to unload. "And sad. I'm very sad and stressed." Then she sobbed louder. "I'm a freaking train wreck," she wailed.

"Well, it is your turn," Sam offered before grabbing more chips, earning glares from Jamie and Harper but for different reasons. Sadie glanced around the table, one blonde brow raised.

"Wh-wh-what does that even mean?" Riley wailed.

Jamie soothed a hand over Riley's shoulder-length hair. "Nothing for you to worry about. Sam only means we've been there and not very long ago."

Riley sniffed back the few remaining tears. "You can't possibly have been such a hot mess," she protested.

The other women started to laugh as Javier approached their table with more salsa and chips. He lowered the bowls before backing away from the table. His movements made the women howl even more.

"Oh, come on now, Javier," Sam protested, even as she gasped for breath. "Surely, you're not scared of us?"

"I wouldn't say scared. Maybe healthy respect are the

words I'd use," he added. "Look, no offense, Sam. You know you're a favorite of mine. But you were a little scary even before." He waved his hands around, gesturing to her still flat belly.

All five women fell silent. Sam's eyes grew impossibly large. Riley held her breath, awaiting the other woman's reaction. She didn't know her well but well enough to know this would be interesting.

"Miss Harriett doesn't even know yet, and that woman knows *everything!*" She narrowed her bright, green eyes at him. "Tell me your source. Did Jack put you up to this? Ooh, when I get ahold of him," she muttered, before grabbing another handful of chips.

"No, of course not. Jack would never reveal such a thing to me before you were ready to tell people," the owner assured her. He came closer to the table. "I have four children of my own. I know how a pregnant woman eats. And I know how you *normally* eat." He pointed to the chips clutched in her fist.

Before Sam could respond, Jamie pumped a fist in the air. "Yes!" she exclaimed. Then she glanced around blushing. "Sorry, not sorry." She grinned at her best friend. "Just remembering all the times you picked on me for 'eating for two.'"

Sam shrugged her slim shoulders. "I now know the error of my ways. Growing a human takes a lot of calories." She nodded at Sadie before scooping a load of queso onto a chip and popping it in her mouth, groaning.

"Then what's my excuse?" Harper asked as she dipped into the fresh bowl of salsa.

Javier smiled. "Don't worry, Sam, your secret is safe with me," he assured her.

Sam shook her head. "I'm not worried about you. Now, Jack, that's another story altogether. I'm more than a little shocked he hasn't let it slip already. And goodness knows the second he does, Miss Harriett will have it everywhere." The soft smile on her face made Riley think Sam didn't really mind so much.

Javier pulled a small pad from his back pocket. "Now, what may I bring for my favorite customers?"

Riley enjoyed a momentary reprieve while the other women ordered, debating lunch entrees versus splitting appetizers for the table. But because she wasn't stupid, she knew it wouldn't last longer than it took everyone to order. And once Javier promised speedy service and walked away, all eyes returned to her.

She held up both hands in surrender. "I get it. My turn to spill my guts."

"You're not wrong," Jamie declared. "But what we started to say before we all lost it earlier is everyone at this table was in your position. And not long ago." Then she turned to Sadie. "Oops, sorry. Shouldn't assume."

The blonde waved a hand. "No worries. Been there, done that, have the T-shirt to prove it. Mine was just a decade ago or so."

Riley felt her own eyes widen as she watched the other women nod.

Harper winced. "Mine is the most recent, freshest. I had to let go of a lifetime of not trusting, of only depending on myself." She let out a deep breath. "I had to learn to hold on to Owen, to let him in. To trust him. None of it was easy, Riley, but oh so worth it.," she ended with a huge smile on her beautiful face.

"Pfft!" Sam snorted. "You want to talk about trust issues? Try having parents who've turned marriage into an Olympic sport. They'd both wear gold medals if you won by the number of 'I dos' they'd racked up. Of course, longevity can't be a factor." She waved a hand. "Be that as it may, I had to make a decision, a choice. I chose Jack. I chose to trust in him. In us." She laid a gentle hand across her belly. "I chose well. But it was the hardest thing I have ever done, giving up a lifetime of mistrust and lessons learned at my parents' knees."

"We all have our own stories, different yet the same, me included," Jamie confessed. "I set out to win the attention of a ghost from my past, very nearly missing the best thing that ever happened to me, right under my very nose." She wiped a tear from her eye. "And now, I'm married with a baby I love more than I ever thought possible." She leaned in. "I would literally kill for my little girl."

"She's not kidding," Sam joked.

"Wait, your turn is coming," Jamie warned. "Soon, you'll know what I mean," she pronounced, wagging a finger at Sam.

"I'm beginning to understand it," Sam whispered, hands cradling her stomach.

"If it helps, Riley, I too understand," Sadie added. She glanced at the other women seated at the table. "Each of us has a different story to tell. Mine is all about loss and poor choices. But in the end, it's about coming out the other side a better, stronger person."

Jamie clasped Riley's hand, giving it a squeeze. "The point is we've all been where you are now. I mean I don't know exactly where you are right now because I don't know what the lug head did. But we've all been in the cry-for-days-sun-is-never-gonna-shine-again spot. It gets better. But here's the tough part. You have to make it better. You have a choice to make. What do *you* want, Riley?"

Riley collapsed back into her chair, absorbing all the women had said. It was a lot to think about. *What did she want? Could she ever really trust him again? Could she imagine a life with Luca? Could she imagine one without him?*

She shook her head, brain smarting with the overload of information.

"I love him," she whispered. "He was my best friend and having him back has been the best. But…"

"But maybe you're not sure you can trust him?" Sam guessed.

Tears burned her eyes. She let them fall, uncaring. She nodded. "He broke my heart a few years ago. The details don't matter. We've never talked about it. Well, until now, but still haven't dealt with it. How do I know he won't hurt me again?"

Harper shrugged. "Maybe, you don't."

"What? That's it? I'm supposed to trust he doesn't break my heart again?" She shuddered, more tears falling. "Not sure I can do it."

"What's the alternative?" Jamie asked, laying one of her hands over Riley's.

"Not trying to be a bitch, but you look terrible," Sam added. "I can tell you haven't slept."

"And none of this is helping the fact your board exam is next week," Harper said. "Don't you think things would be easier for you if you cleared the air with Luca?"

Riley looked at the three women, really looked at them. All three from different places with different stories. All ended up here in Palm Harbor, happy and fulfilled.

What if that could be you?

"I want this for myself."

"Then you'll have to trust him again," Sam advised.

Riley startled, not realizing she'd spoken the last bit aloud. "Oh!" She dashed a hand at the tears on her face. "But is it really so easy? I just trust him? Put my heart in his hands? Again? Didn't end so well for me last time."

Sam leaned in and gave her a one-armed hug. "Of course, it's not that easy. Nothing worth having is, silly. But then neither is the alternative. Because from where I sit, it's not working so well for you, either."

Riley looked at the other women again, and for the first time today, in days really, something warm stirred in her chest. Hope? Maybe.

She leaned in, a grin starting to spread on her face. "Tell me more."

*****

In the wee hours of the early morning, Luca lay in his bed not sleeping. Again. Nothing new for him these days. He missed her. Missed her warmth next to him. Missed the soothing sound of her breathing. Missed waking up next to her in the morning.

His mother, as usual, was right. Riley wasn't the kind of woman who would remain single forever. The fact she still was bordered on the miraculous. What's his name was all wrong for her. Anyone could see that. Proposing to her in a huge crowd! Rookie mistake. But the next person might not be so stupid. The next guy might take the time to get to know her, really know her.

He sat bolt upright in bed. *No one knew Riley like he did! No one...*

So, what did it mean? What could he do? How could he convince her to trust him again? To win her back. To make her see he would cut off his own arm before harm a hair on her head. Surely, she must know he would never, ever break her heart again.

He pushed a few pillows behind him and slumped against them. Think! How to make her see he did what he did for her own good? How to make her understand he would never hurt her again? Now that they were back in Palm Harbor, together, there was no longer a need to 'protect' her as he thought he was doing all those years ago.

He yawned and rubbed his burning eyes as fatigue took over him. He needed sleep. And a plan. He thought maybe the first would help him with the other as he drifted on thoughts of a life with her.

Chapter Thirty-Two

"It's all about quality of life and finding a happy balance between work and friends and family."
-Thomas Merton

"Do not judge me," Riley scolded the kittens who sat on her bed doing just that. Or at least that's how it felt. Two sets of eyes, one blue, one green, stared back at her unblinking. "I can feel your derision," she informed the kittens. Then she shook her head and wanted to cry.

Great! Now I'm talking to myself or to cats. Which is worse?

She stood there, wrapped in a towel, debating the meager offerings in her closet. She'd already reached for and discarded everything that wasn't scrubs. Some things twice. Sighing—it wasn't as if something would magically appear in her closet— she grabbed a pair of linen, navy capris and a lemon and navy shirt she'd bought at Sadie's shop. Putting them on, she walked into the bathroom to deal with her hair.

Grimacing into the mirror, she settled for fingering the damp waves into submission with a bit of product and leaving before cutting it all off. Her hair was in the wonderful in between place where it was either too short or too long to do anything with. On a daily basis she struggled with the urge to shave her head.

"Goodbye, my loves, make good choices," she called to Lucy and Gabriel before tossing a salmon treat to each and leaving.

Riley made it all the way to her car before debating staying home. A win for her. With her board exam mere days away, she really should stay and review. But she feared Sam just a little, and the text had a bit of command feel to it. 'Just a few friends' she'd assured her were gathering at Owen and Harper's home for dinner. Nothing formal. No need to bring anything. She glanced at the bottle of wine and flowers on her passenger seat. As if she hadn't been raised better than that!

Riley started her car and drove out of her driveway, knowing Sam was right. She needed a break. She was getting to the point in her review where the men with nets would be coming for her soon. She'd confided in Brody she feared she might start forgetting stuff soon. Maybe tonight would be good for her. She could chat with friends, eat too much, maybe have a drink or two.

And she could leave whenever she wanted…

Feeling better about her decision to go, she lowered her windows, letting the ocean-infused breeze play with her hair as she sang along with the radio. In less than ten minutes, she pulled up to the house, having to park down the block a bit in order to find a space. *She must be the last one here*, she mused. Grabbing her purse and keys and the things she brought, Riley headed out of her car and around the side of the house where the sound of happy people grew louder as she approached.

"Riley!" Brody called out in his booming voice as she rounded the corner of the patio.

She held back a wince. So much for sneaking in quietly. She waved the hand clenching the bottle of wine at him and headed for where Harper stood with Sadie and Jamie.

"Hey, everyone," she called out and thrust the wine and flowers at Harper. "Didn't know what everyone liked, so I went with a white."

Harper grinned. "Well, I don't drink, but you can never go wrong with flowers." She leaned down to kiss Riley's cheek. "Thank you so much. You know you didn't have to bring anything."

"As if!" Riley protested. "Have you met my mother?

She'd find out, somehow, and I'd never hear the end of it. Anyway, sorry I'm late. I struggled with what to wear, which is really code for tried to talk myself into staying home to study."

"Well, glad you decided to come. Saved Sam from going to fetch you," Harper scolded. "She would have, as I believe she made clear."

"I'm so glad you did, too, Riley! It looks phenomenal on you. Have you ever considered modeling?" Sadie gushed.

"Uh, no." She fingered the clothing. "Feel free to dress me every day. Your clothing is gorgeous!"

"Ooh, is this from your place?" Harper asked. "I have to stop by."

"It is, and you do. I was serious about the modeling, Riley. I have a fall show coming up in a few weeks. I always recruit local women to model the clothing. Gives it a real feel if you know what I mean. You should consider it." She grinned at Harper. "Both of you. Well, all of you, really. And there's a discount for anything you buy that day."

"Now she's not playing fair," Harper complained. "I will if Riley will," she announced with a gleam in her eye.

Riley felt her mouth drop open. She stared at her friend for a long moment. Then before she could even think about what she was doing, she nodded. "Fine. I need something in my closet that isn't scrubs or jeans anyway."

"Oh, yay," Sadie yelled, clapping her hands.

Several people turned to look. Sam and Jamie darted over to them.

"What did we miss?" Sam asked. Her gaze darted around the small gathering. "You know how much I hate to miss anything."

"Riley just agreed to model at my fall fashion show," Sadie crowed.

Riley, who could feel heat building in her cheeks, and wished the earth would open up and swallow her, threw up her hands. "It's the new me. No more shy girl hiding in the bleachers."

"I hope there's a little of her left. I was always a huge fan of the shy girl in the bleachers," Luca murmured before coming to stand next to Riley. He tucked a chunk of her wayward hair behind her ear, setting off a different kind of heat. "But then, she was my number one fan."

Riley looked up into his face and longed to see what the shades hid in his dark eyes.

"That was all a very long time ago. That girl grew up. Learned a thing or two."

Her heart clenched when his smile dimmed.

"Maybe so, but I'm hoping there's still some of her in there," he said in a low tone only for her.

"Luca, we need you on the grill!" Jack called.

He waved a hand in their general direction, never taking his eyes from hers. "This conversation isn't over."

Riley watched him walk away, her heart thudding in her ears.

"Wow!" Sadie cried. "What I wouldn't give for someone to look at me like that."

"I have someone who looks at me like that, and I still need a cold shower," Harper agreed with a laugh.

Riley waved a hand in the air. "He was, uh, just being Luca," she muttered, unable to come up with a better explanation.

"Sure, he was," Harper agreed, tongue firmly in cheek. "I've never seen Luca talk to another woman quite that way before. But if that's what you have to tell yourself..."

"I need a drink," Riley claimed, excusing herself and heading inside the house.

She kept going until she found a powder room and locked herself inside. After splashing cool water on her overheated face, she stepped back to stare at her reflection in the mirror. *Could that really be her with the overly bright eyes and pink cheeks?* She gripped the edges of the counter to ground herself. She could do this. She could handle seeing Luca again. Small town necessitated it, after all. After drying her hands, Riley got it together and left the sanctuary of the bathroom.

She grabbed a bottled water—didn't trust herself with

anything harder — and left the house again. Brody grabbed her by the elbow as soon as she stepped out on the patio.

"There you are. Come sit with me and enjoy some dinner," he commanded.

Easier than making any decisions on her own, she let him lead her to the other end of the table, away from Luca. After handing her into a seat, Brody loped off to grab some food for both of them, promising to be right back. Ignoring the full weight of Luca's stare, Riley turned away to speak to Sadie at her side.

"He seems like a good guy," the other woman mentioned, nodding toward her coworker's retreating back.

Riley smiled. "Brody's the best. Not sure how I would get through this ridiculous board exam without him to keep me sane." She waved a hand in the air, gesturing around them. "Reminding me to eat even." She took a sip from her water bottle. "He's gone so far as to ensure our schedules line up at work so he can be there to lend moral support, quiz me, and talk me off the ledge."

Sadie raised one blonde brow. "Are you sure he's just being a good friend? Seems like an awful lot of trouble for someone he's only met a few months ago." She held up both hands. "No offense. Sorry, I tend to blurt before I think."

Riley grinned. "Understood. I have a similar diagnosis. If it were anyone else, I might share your suspicions, but he's simply a nice guy. You'll have to take my word for it." She glanced across the patio to where the man in question stood in line at the grill for their dinner. She felt the smile dim on her face. "Besides, I'm not the woman for Brody. He's already made his choice."

"Oh, I didn't realize he was in a relationship. I've never seen him with anyone around here," Sadie said.

"Not my story to tell," Riley offered by way of explanation. Before she could say anything else, he rejoined them.

"I wasn't sure what you wanted, but since you're about to waste away to nothing, I got a little of everything. And Sadie,

I brought extra for you as well."

Riley jumped up from the table when she saw him standing there with several dangerously overloaded plates of food.

"Goodness, Brody, are you expecting to feed an army?" she exclaimed, taking two of the plates from his hands. He set the third down on the table himself.

"I like to eat," he said, shrugging. Then he turned to her. "And you have more than a few missed meals to make up for, missy," he said in a mock, severe tone.

"Yes, Dad," she returned, grinning.

He slumped into the chair next to her, clutching his chest. "Dad? I'm not that much older than you!" he protested. Then he cocked his head and grimaced. "Ugh, technically, I might be. What a terrible thought."

"Well, at least she's already through medical school, so you're off the hook for the bill," Sadie offered.

Brody sat up straighter. "Ah ha! A silver lining at last. Have we formally met? I'm Brody Matthews." He leaned around Riley and offered a hand. "I have the mixed bag of emotions of working with this one."

Sadie reached forward, shaking his hand. "I'm sure I've seen you around. I'm Sadie Benson. I own a boutique in town, Threads & Things."

Riley bit back a smirk at the electricity that crackled between the two of them. *Hmmm…*

"I was telling Sadie about your misguided attempts to save me from myself while you were off fetching food," Riley explained. She grabbed an empty plate and chose some things from the food he'd brought.

"Not sure how misguided they are. Everyone needs saving sometimes, Riley," he said, his voice a much more somber pitch than she was used to hearing from her perpetually jovial coworker.

Both she and Sadie stared at him.

Brody glanced up from the corn cob he held in both hands, half-way to his mouth. He lowered it to his plate, untouched. He turned to face Sadie.

"All I meant was everyone has times in their life when they need a little help. If you know Riley at all, then you know she's struggling right now with her upcoming board exams and finding a work/life balance. My job, as self-appointed life coach and all-around nice guy, is to make sure she finds it. If it means ensuring she eats, doesn't stress out too much, and backs away from the parking garage ledge, then my work here is done." He grinned at both women, his customary smirk and twinkle in his blue eyes back in place.

"He's not wrong," Riley declared. She laid her head on his shoulder, closing her eyes, and sighed. "There was that one time when I couldn't even remember the rule of nines. I did think about heading to the parking deck," she joked.

"Rule of nines?" Sadie asked, a question in her voice.

Riley sat back up, opening her eyes. "It's something we use to calculate the percentage of burns suffered in patients. Nothing a normal person like yourself would ever have to know. My point was, it's fairly basic and learned early on in training. One day, after hours of quizzing me in between patients, Brody asked me about it..."

"And she pretty much forgot it," Brody finished for her.

"And off I headed to the parking deck. Well, more like the coffee cart," Riley amended.

"After all her years of training, this one decided she would try a career as a barista," Brody joked. "Like I said, my job is to keep her head on straight for the next little while, offer support, keep her sane." He leaned in and patted her head, much in the way Griff had done since she was single digits.

"As long as that's all you're doing with her," Luca stated in the deathly calm voice he reserved for special occasions. Usually when someone had picked on her. "I'd hate to think you were taking advantage of the situation. I was just starting to like you, Brody."

Riley stood so fast her chair flew backwards, toppling over. "Luca! Stop! What's gotten into you? What are you doing?"

Brody rose from his own chair at a more leisurely pace. "Luca, nice to see you again."

She watched as the two men stared each other down for a few moments longer before coming to one of those weird, male bonding agreements no woman had ever understood. After a subtle nod she would have missed if not staring at both of them, Luca turned to face her.

"Something I should have done a long time ago. I need to borrow you, please." He held out one hand, slightly shaking, toward her. She didn't even think before placing hers in it. He glanced at the people seated around them. "Enjoy your dinner."

Then he tugged on her hand and walked off the patio into the shaded recesses of the backyard. He only stopped when they were far enough away from everyone else to assure privacy. Then he turned back to her. His dark eyes had grown almost black. Her stomach somersaulted as she waited for him to say something, anything.

"We need to talk," he croaked in a roughened tone.

Chapter Thirty-Three

"When you forgive, you in no way change the past — but you sure do change the future."
-Bernard Meltzer

His breath froze in his chest while Luca searched for the right words to make her understand what he'd done and why five years ago. To make her see he'd never meant to hurt her. To see how, in his own twisted, ridiculous way, he only meant to protect her. But what mere words could say all that? He dropped his hands to his sides and hung his head.

And felt her small hand caress his jaw.

"Look at me, please," she whispered.

He raised his face to look into her eyes, terrified of what he might see there.

"Say whatever it is you wanted to say, Luca." She let out a shaky breath. "I'm ready to hear it."

He placed his hand over hers still framing his jawline. He entwined her fingers with his, pulling her farther into dusk-coated yard to a small, wooden bench.

"Please, have a seat. This may take a while," he joked. Then he sat and waited for her to do so also. When she did, he continued. "There's so much, I hardly know where to start." He glanced down at their still joined hands. "Before anything else, please tell me you know I love you."

"Of course," she cried. "Luca, I have never doubted that. In one way or another, we have always loved each other." She dropped her gaze. "Loving you was never the issue," she whispered.

"No, it never was. Trusting me with your heart is another story, though, isn't it?" he asked in a flat tone.

She jerked her head up. "I want to, more than anything in the world, I want to trust you with my heart, with everything I am." She squeezed her eyes closed. "I cannot get your words out of my head. I hear them in my sleep, Luca, telling me to go away. To not come back." She opened her eyes again, tears now slipping out of them. "Coming back here was one of the hardest things I've ever done. I wanted my best friend back, but I didn't know…"

He reached out one finger to wipe the tears from under her eye. "You didn't know how I would react," he finished for her in a ragged tone. "Isn't that what you meant to say?"

She nodded.

"Who could blame you? Oh, Riley, there aren't enough ways to say I'm sorry to make up for that one day. I wish I could take it all back, go back in time and never say those words in the first place." He bit out a harsh, humorless laugh. "The worst part is I never even meant them."

Her eyes widened, dashing back and forth, searching his as if for the truth. "What? Then why? I don't understand," she sobbed.

He shook his head. "I don't really know. For a million reasons that don't matter now. You came in, like a bolt from the past. I couldn't believe it was really you standing there in front of me. My heart felt like it had stopped. And then I remembered I was with another woman." He shook his head. "First time seeing you up close in years, and I'm with another woman."

"Not gonna lie, it hurt," she grumbled. "Not that I expected you to be a monk. I didn't consider it in my mad dash home."

"She meant nothing to me. Another place holder while I waited for you. Nobody meant a thing to me. They were a way to pass the time. I didn't get close to anyone, nor did I allow them to get close to me."

"Oh," she said.

"And I was so ridiculously happy for and proud of you when you shared your news, but all I could think, all I could feel deep down in my soul, was this was taking you away from me again. So, I lashed out. I know it's not a good reason. I know it's immature, but it's also the truth. And on some level, I had to be sure you left. I had to be sure you didn't have some misguided notion of throwing it all away to stay. Not then. Not when your future was calling. Not when you'd worked so hard."

She sat there, staring, in the gathering darkness, while fat tears rolled down her face unchecked. "Oh, Luca, we could have talked about it."

He shook his head. "If we had talked, even for a moment, I would have thrown everything I owned in a bag and gone back to Dartmouth with you." He smiled then, wiping her tears. "See, I knew you weren't in Boston. In fact, I was there when you graduated."

"What?" she asked, her trembling hands flew to her mouth. "What do you mean you were there?"

"On a hot Sunday in June, without a single cloud in the blue sky, I watched you walk across the stage. I watched you become Dr. Riley Layne. I've never been prouder of someone in my life."

"I don't understand. You were so cold to me. Now you're telling me you came to graduation? And you would have left with me that awful day? You would have done that for me?" she breathed.

"I wanted to more than anything. But it wasn't just about *me*. My family, my father's legacy, depended on me, on all of us. We were turning a corner, really doing better then. I couldn't leave, and you couldn't stay. It was what it was. You had to go, and I wanted to make it easier on you. Not make you feel like you were choosing."

"I thought you didn't care," she whispered in a broken voice that shredded his heart to ribbons.

"Oh, Riley, no. Not caring was never the issue. I cared

too much. I loved you so much, always had. I can't even say when I first fell in love with you. It's always been there, these feelings for you. They've always been in my heart, waiting to come out. Waiting for me to put a voice to them."

"Dancing with you," she murmured and placed her hands in his. "That's when I knew. Do you remember?"

He grinned. "I do. Those awful dance lessons we took. The ballroom was about a hundred degrees. You were so nervous."

She ducked her head. "Oh, my goodness, that first day, I thought I might die. Mom made me go. 'Every proper, young Southern lady knows how to dance, Riley Jane.' She wasn't letting me out of it. I swear I thought I would drop over on the spot. Then I saw you in there."

"And you knew you were saved," he joked.

She whacked his chest. "More like I knew you'd make it bearable and most likely you'd do something to draw attention to yourself and away from me." She glanced up into his eyes. "But then, you took me in your arms, and even though we'd touched each other a million times, somehow this felt different." She sighed. "It felt as though a thousand tiny jolts of electricity coursed through my body wherever you touched me. I'd never felt anything like it."

He smiled down at her, warmth coursing through him from her confession. "For me, it was the way we fit. You stepped into my arms as though you belonged, as though we'd done it a million times before. It felt like coming home. And even though I was a stupid, teenaged boy, I knew."

"Knew what?" she asked, eyes huge in her face.

"Knew I wanted to only dance with you," he said.

The End

Acknowledgments

Okay, so this will sound odd, but thank you to Niall Horan for his amazing song, "This Town." The entire inspiration for *Dancing with You* comes from it. Thing 1 will tell you…I was OBSESSED with this song when it came out. She groaned and/or rolled her eyes every time she heard me play it on repeat, but my love for this song knows no bounds. Even now, years after its release, I find the lyrics haunting, and the idea for Riley and Luca was born. You know a song is successful when its words move the listener. Now, every time I listen to this song, I picture Luca watching Thomas propose to Riley in the opening scene…

For my amazing writer friends, Katherine L.E. White, Ester Lopez, Maria Elena Alonso-Sierra, and Victoria Saccenti, with whom I spent a few lovely days at the A Weekend with the Authors signing in Nashville this past May. I wrote, or tried to anyway, the last chunk of this book there. But more than anything, you ladies offered up sage advice, humor and good, old-fashioned friendship. I thank you for that and wish for more.

Thank you to Jeni Burns, my intrepid editor, as always. I sent her this manuscript…then worried. After Harper and Owen's story, I didn't know what to expect. Theirs had almost been *too* easy. But she loved *Dancing with You* and pushed me to make it even better. Thank you for that!

Thank you to Rebecca Pau of The Final Wrap for this amazing cover. Again! Her talent knows no bounds and always astounds me. This time, the word was 'boardwalk.' And here we are…

Thank you to Chelly Hoyle Peeler, my proofer and formatter, for your continued support and seemingly endless supply of patience. I'd like to say I'll get easier to work with, but we both know that isn't in the cards.

What's Next?

Not gonna lie, this one kicked my butt a little, as I predicted. It didn't come as easily or seamlessly as the one before it. Let's hope Brody & Sadie's story flows a little easier.

As soon as Brody popped up, now two books ago, I knew I had to tell his story! Here is a sneak peek into Brody & Sadie's story!

Chapter One

"Even between the best of friends, mistakes and misunderstandings can happen."
-Avigdor Lieberman

The bells hanging over her shop's door tinkled, announcing a customer. Sadie Benson chose to remain perched on top of the ladder, feather duster clenched in her hand. While cleaning was far from the top of her list of favorite things, it was long overdue. She leaned as far as she dared to peek around the corner but being 'horizontally challenged' as her brother Gage liked to remind her, she couldn't glimpse the newcomer. She swiped once more at a light fixture and sighed. "Be right there," she called out before climbing down from her perch.

"Take your time," a low, deliciously male voice responded, sending off a wave of something low in her belly. "I'll just, uh, look around."

She chuckled at the note of desperation she detected. *He must be on his own.* In her experience, single males, at least the straight ones, viewed clothing shopping on par with root canal. Without anesthesia. In other words, avoid it at all costs. Feeling sympathy for the as yet unknown guy, she rounded the corner, smile in place.

"Afternoon and welcome to Threads & Things. I'm…"

She didn't get any further when she saw exactly *who* stood in her shop.

"Sadie!" the man finished for her. He grinned and walked toward her. "Wow am I happy to see you. Both Riley and Harper swore you'd keep me safe in here." He glanced around him, almost as if expecting something, or maybe someone, to jump out from the racks of clothing at him.

She bit back a laugh. "Ah, thank you, I guess. How may I help you, Brody?"

His blue eyes, the color of the Carolina sky in summer, lit up at the mention of his name. "You remembered!"

"We just had dinner at Harper and Owen's house a few weeks ago. How could I forget? Besides, that night was memorable," she said with a smile.

He took a few steps closer to her, closing the gap between them. "Because you met a dashing ER doctor, of course." He wiggled his brows and grinned at her.

She slowly shook her head, despite the herd of Antelope performing Swan Lake in her belly. "I see confidence is not an issue for you. What I meant was it happened to be the night Riley and Luca finally got their shit together."

"Sure, that too," he allowed, waving a hand. He stepped closer, closing the distance between them and reached toward her.

She held her breath. *Was it hot in here?* Sadie resisted the urge to fan herself.

"You have something," he murmured. His fingers weaved into her hair, sending shockwaves down the length of her. "Go it!" he announced, pulling back. He held up a rather large dust mote.

She could have wept. Whether in disappointment or embarrassment she wasn't quite sure.

Grasping it from his hand—while most definitely ignoring the zings racing up her arm when their fingers met—she marched behind the counter to toss the offending bit of dust into the trashcan.

"Normal people have dust bunnies. I seem to have acquired a dust rhinoceros," she muttered. She attempted to ignore the heat blooming in her cheeks.

Brody stared at her for the length of several heartbeats before throwing back his head and roaring with laughter.

She glanced around the store to ensure they were still alone. "I'm not that funny," she grumbled. "At least not on purpose."

Her words only set him off again. Sadie walked out from behind the counter to stand next to him, arms folded across her chest, one foot tapping.

"Was there something I could help you with? Did you come here for some reason other than to laugh at me?" She winced at her tone, knowing she'd landed somewhere between bitch and fishwife just now.

Either her tone or words sobered him. "Sorry," he said, both his tone and expression backing up the word. He scrubbed a hand down his face. "I need you, so probably best to not tick you off first thing." He leaned toward her, blue eyes crinkling at the corners. "Please say you'll help me."

She stared into those incredible eyes a full moment longer than she should have, trying to not drown, before she forced herself to look away. "Guess that depends on what you need," she murmured. "Tell me."

"What I need is the perfect gift, and I need it like yesterday," he pled.

"Okay, this is a good start. Since you came here to Threads & Things, I'm assuming this gift is for a woman."

"Yes," he answered, grinning. "The most special woman in my life."

She sucked in a quick breath at the sharp dart of disappointment striking her in the chest. But then all the good men were taken. She suddenly flashed back to the dinner at

Owen and Harper's. Hadn't Riley mentioned him not being single at the party at Harper and Owen's house? Best to remember those little details.

He placed a hand on her arm. "Are you okay?" he asked, concern laced in his voice.

Sadie smiled and stepped back, causing his hand to drop away. *Better this way*, she tried to tell herself. "Oh, sure, I'm fine. Tell me more about this woman and what type of present you'd like. Were you thinking clothing or maybe jewelry? If you're leaning toward clothing, do you know her sizes?"

She stifled a smirk at the panicked look on his face.

"Oh, well, I'd say she's maybe an inch or two taller than you." He held his hands as though measuring Sadie. "Maybe not quite as slender. Her hips might be a bit, I don't know, broader?" He swiped the back of his hand across his forehead.

"Are you sweating?" Sadie asked, finally letting out the laughter she'd held back.

"What? No, of course not. Well, maybe a little. It's hot in here," he muttered. "Now, who's laughing?"

Sorry," she exclaimed, though her tone said otherwise. She snickered again when he glared at her. "You men are all the same. You come in here, completely unprepared then spout off vague things like height as if it'll help." A soft snort escaped her, and Sadie threw her hand over her mouth.

"Did you snort at me?" he accused, blue eyes now dancing with merriment.

She crossed the fingers of one hand, held behind her back. "I have no idea what you're talking about."

"Really?" he challenged. He took a step closer until barely any space separated them. "And if I were to look behind your back? Would that hand have its fingers crossed by chance?"

"Maybe…"

He tilted his head as if trying to figure her out.

Then she remembered he was flirting with her. And married. The smile slid from her face. "Seriously, you men come in here expecting me to be some sort of wizard. 'She's this tall and this wide' as if that translates to a size somehow." She stomped her foot for good measure then regretted it. No need to act like a toddler.

He laughed again, not looking in the least bit put off. "First, your foot is the size of a child's so not impressed, and I thought you were a witch, not a wizard. Don't they come with some sort of magical powers?"

"Sorry, did you just call me a witch?" she asked in a very calm voice. The type of calm that had been known to make grown men tremble for centuries.

The grin slipped a bit from his face. His clear blue eyes darkened. "Oh, uh, I was referring to The Coven. You know, your friends." He held up both hands as if he expected her to attack him. Or maybe fly on her broom at him. "In my defense, I didn't make up the name. I told Griff it was a ridiculous one," he muttered mostly to himself.

She bit the inside of her cheek so hard, she had to concentrate to keep from wincing. She shook her head instead. "Which is it? Either I'm a witch or I'm not."

"Not sure I know you well enough to judge yet," he answered. Then he leaned in a bit closer. "But I'd like to. You're feisty. I like that in a woman. Besides, if you are a witch, you could make me disappear about now, stop me from saying anything else stupid."

He'd leaned in close enough for Sadie to smell him. Salt air, spice, and a hint of clean male. And she'd taken a whiff to be sure. Then she remembered. He had a woman, was here to buy her a present, and now was flirting with *her!* Nope! What was it about him making her lose her mind? She'd already read this book and knew how it ended. She straightened up, moved a safe distance away and put on her 'professional' face she saved for the people she waited on, didn't mind taking their money, but didn't particularly care for.

"So, you said something about needing a gift? And since sizes are a wash, let's stick with something other than clothing." She pointed to the opposite side of the store where several displays held accessories including jewelry. "I have many things that don't include you having the appropriate knowledge base. Shall we?" she invited and took off at a brisk pace without waiting for him.

*****

Brody shook his head and followed in the wake of the petite blonde. *What just happened?* He thought they were having a good time, joking a bit, flirting a bit. It seemed as though she even leaned in to sniff him. He figured it was a good sign. Then in the blink of an eye, the temperature in the store dropped a good forty degrees. He shrugged and lengthened his stride to keep up with the little dynamo. What she might lack in height, she certainly made up for in attitude.

"Maybe something like these," Sadie suggested, pointing to a rack of silk scarves in an array of watercolors.

"Not a bad jumping off point," he said with a smirk. He refused to make this easy for her. Nor was he leaving before he figured out what had gone wrong between them. Sure he was out of practice with women, putting it very mildly, but this felt different.

He fingered one of the scarves. The swirling hues of blues and greens screamed his sister to him. Sheila was a graphic designer who lived near the beach in Alabama. She'd actually love this. "Maybe," he said in a non-committal tone. "What else do you have?" He bit back a laugh when Sadie gritted her teeth.

"It might help if you told me something about, uh, the recipient," she griped.

"You mean other than how tall and wide she is?" he joked. He knew he shouldn't poke the bear, so to speak, but how could he not? Her flushed cheeks caught his eye.

She stared at him for so long he couldn't be sure if she counted to ten in her head or plotted his death. Her dark blue eyes blazed at him, causing a riot of things he hadn't felt in, well, forever.

"I meant something like does she wear earrings and if so

does she have pierced ears. You know, normal things one asks when helping to pick a gift." She gritted out from between her clenched jaws.

"Oh, makes sense. Whew! For a moment, I feared you might ask her zodiac sign. I would have been at a loss," he said with a grin. "Although her birthday is November sixteenth, if that helps."

"Why would it help? And why would you expect me to ask such a question?" she asked. She plucked at her skirt with one hand. "Just because I dress this way doesn't make me a gypsy," she informed him. "I wear what I like and what I'm comfortable in," she told him. "Or are we back to your tired witch joke?"

His took a step back even as he raised both hands. "I, uh, didn't mean it as a slight, just joking." He blew out a breath. "Look, I'm totally out of my depth here, as if you couldn't tell. Sheila means a lot to me. I want to get her something nice. Can you help me?"

Sadie stared him down for a moment. The kind of stare that stopped grown men in their tracks and made them rethink their actions. Then she too let out a sigh.

"Without thinking about it, tell me three things about her," she commanded.

"She loves the ocean. She's an artist. Dawn is her favorite time of the day," he said then blinked. "Wow, you're good."

"I know," she said without a trace of humility. "This is what I do for a living." She tapped a finger against her chin. "Give me a moment," she declared before turning away and roaming through her store.

Because the store was small and had an open floor plan, he never lost sight of her as she apparently wandered for a few moments. But even though he wasn't quite sure what she was up to, he sensed purpose in her movement. Brody watched as she stopped at various shelves and displays, touching items, choosing and discarding. He smiled as he watched, imagining her touching him, running her hands over his skin. He shook his head.

Where had that thought come from?

He waited for the customary flood of guilt, but nothing other than a slight pressure in his chest followed. The fact he had a harder time these days recalling Nora's features is what awoke him in a cold sweat. It's been four years. Maybe time to cut himself some slack.

It's only been four years...

He started at the soft hand on his forearm.

"You looked a thousand miles away just now," Sadie said. "Didn't mean to scare you."

"Not a thousand but then not sure I can measure them." He straightened and shook himself a bit. "What did you find?"

"Well, given your complete lack of help, I think I've done pretty well, actually." She nodded to the counter. "Come see for yourself," she invited before turning away.

He caught a whiff of her subtle scent, something citrusy and reminiscent of summer even as winter bore down on Palm Harbor. Not that this part of the world had much of a winter.

"I'd follow you anywhere," he joked, earning himself a narrowed glance from her.

Again, he wondered what had changed between them then shook his head. He'd made it to the wrong side of forty-five without ever understanding women. Why did he think he would start now?

"Ta da!" she cried, waving an arm over several items laying on the counter. "Now, I stuck with a color scheme that said ocean to me, since you mentioned she loves it." She picked up a matching necklace and earrings in a light green color. "Sea glass is always a good choice for fans of the ocean."

Brody took a few steps forward, crowding her a bit against the counter. He felt her sharp intake of breath and hid a smile.

"She would certainly love these," he commented. "Do they come in other colors?"

"They do. These are made locally. A friend of mine has a small studio, and I carry some of her work here." She turned and pointed across the room. "You can see I have a small area dedicated to Melinda's work," she informed him. She gasped as she turned back to face him. He'd taken the moment to further encroach into her space. "Uh, feel free to take a look for yourself. I'm sure you can find something interesting," she suggested.

The wobble in her voice gave him hope. "Oh, I'm pretty sure I already have," he replied, looking at her and ignoring the other items she'd laid out for his perusal.

He stared into her eyes, the swirling emotion in them drawing him in further. In the years since losing Sheila, no other woman had grabbed his attention like this. He shook his head, breaking the contact.

Did he want this? Was he ready for this? Would he ever be?

"Then you'll take the green set?" she asked.

Before he could answer, the bells over the door tinkled, announcing another customer.

"Excuse me while I see to this customer. I'm sure you'll have made an excellent choice by the time I come back."

"Welcome to Threads & Things, how may I help you," she enthused to a trio of older women browsing just inside the door.

"I may have already," he assured her as she walked away.

About the Author

Kimberley O'Malley is a transplant to Charlotte, North Carolina from the frozen North. She is learning to say y'all but draws the line at sweet tea. Sarcasm is an art form in her world. She writes small town Contemporary romances and hilarious Cozy Mysteries. When not writing, she is a full-time nurse and part-time soccer Mom, but not necessarily in that order. She shares her life with an amazing husband of more than 25 years, two teenagers, and two sweet but mischievous Shetland Sheepdogs, Molly & Callie.

To ensure you're up to date with all the shenanigans and news, click the link to follow along with my monthly newsletter: http://eepurl.com/dgonEX

Are you following the Author?

Facebook - https://www.facebook.com/KOMalley67/
Instagram -
    https://www.instagram.com/kimberleyomalley67/
Twitter - https://twitter.com/K_OMalley67
Website - www.kimberleyomalley.com
Amazon Author Bio -
    www.amazon.com/author/kimberleyomalley
Good Reads Profile - http://bit.ly/grKOM
Book Bub Profile - http://bit.ly/bookbubKOM

Made in the USA
Columbia, SC
14 September 2022

66940272R00165